The Price of Innocence

by
James P. Kass

Sterling House
Pittsburgh, PA

The Price of Innocence

ISBN 1-56315-128-6

Paperback Fiction
© Copyright 1999 James P. Kass
All rights reserved
First Printing—1999
Library of Congress #98-88533

Request for information should be addressed to:

SterlingHouse Publisher, Inc.
The Sterling Building
440 Friday Road
Pittsburgh, PA 15209
www.SterlingHousePublisher.com

Cover design: Michelle Vennare - SterlingHouse Publisher, Inc.
Typesetting: Drawing Board Studios

This publication includes images from Corel Draw 8 which are protected by the Copyright laws of the US, Canada and elsewhere.

All rights reserved. No part of this publication may be reproduced, stored in a retrieval system, or transmitted in any form or by any means—electronic, mechanical, photocopy, recording or any other, except for brief quotations in printed reviews —without prior permission of the publisher.

This is a work of fiction. Names, characters, places, and incidents either are the product of the author's imagination or are used fictitiously. Any resemblance to actual events or persons, living or dead is entirely coincidental.

Printed in Canada

CHAPTER ONE

The day had begun no different than any other: He awoke after three or four hours sleep to an outburst of screaming obscenities from his wife, directed toward Ron and the girls. He argued with her many times and one of her favorite reasons was: "If you would help me with them and spend more time with them, maybe I wouldn't get so angry like I do."

For some time they had been fighting over the kids. He told her that he wished he could be with them every day, but it was impossible. Someone had to work and pay the bills and that was his job. They had determined that it would be her job to stay at home with the kids. He tried to impress upon her that being a stay-at-home mother meant that she couldn't just walk away whenever she wanted. That was not the way that he wanted it to be. He had grown up in a two-parent home, with two brothers and four sisters. It was not easy being raised in a big family, but his parents loved him and them.

This was the way he wanted it for his kids: to be there, whenever they needed him.

Well, the day went on as usual. He woke up tired. He was always tired. It seemed like he never got enough sleep.

Naomie attended school in Cantonville. She started at eight thirty every morning. Ron's bus also came at eight thirty every morning, so one of them had to put Ron on the bus while the other one took Naomie to school.

He chose to take Naomie to school, just like he did most of the other mornings. With him working the many hours that he did, it was a special time that they had to spend together, even if it was just the time they spent riding to school. In addition Kristy came with them bringing along her own little book bag. She liked pretending that she was going to school just like her big sister.

Until just recently, he had been working two jobs, delivering pizza for Five Flag Pizza in Warrington during the day and for Five Flag Pizza during the nights in Cantonville. There had been weeks that he was putting in as many as seventy hours or more.

For some time Kate had been complaining that he was never home and he was never spending any time with the kids. She was right. When you work seventy hours a week, it doesn't leave much time for anything else.

It was not always like that. Three years back, he had a job as general foreman for one of the largest telephone construction companies in the world. They were living in Massachusetts then and everything was wonderful.

The strike came and after it was over things began to get worse. He had twelve crews working for him. As the work load began to decline, one by one he had to tell the guys that they were laid off. Finally, one day he was called into the office to face what he had known was going to happen to him. After eighteen years in the profession and at what seemed to be the height of his career he was told that he, too, was going to have to stand in the unemployment line.

He was driving a new pickup while working for the telephone construction company, living off credit cards and company expenses and making almost $40,000 a year. Now, here he was making barely $12,000 a year and trying to raise three kids on a wage that was below poverty level.

That morning had began with an argument about Ron.

"I am probably going to be over at Mom's later today," she told him as they were getting the kids ready. "Ron's caseworker is coming by the school to pick him up at one o'clock. This is his weekend for respite, so you won't see him again until Sunday evening."

"Damn it Kate—I don't know why you agreed to this respite shit. I told you I don't like it and I still don't think it is right that you are having him dumped off in some foster home just so you can have a break from him. He is our son and I don't care what kind of problems he has—he is still our responsibility and not some stranger's."

"Jim, I don't want to argue with you," she answered. "You know what the doctors said."

"I don't care what the doctors said!" he replied. "I thought that when I quit working at the Warrington store we were going to have more time to spend together with the kids. Instead, you put Jon in a foster home every other weekend and run off to bingo with your Mom."

Respite was just another term for placing Ron in a foster home. This was all arranged through Warrington County Mental Health and Ron's caseworker. To him, all it proved was their own inability to cope with another situation that was so vital in teaching their children how to love and respect each other.

He got angry every time they talked about it and he was almost glad that their lack of time prevented their argument from going any further.

From the very beginning, Jim hated CYS'S intrusion into their lives. He had tried to intervene on more than one occasion, but it was pointed out to him that in cases where they deemed it necessary, only the signature of one of the parents was required. He had argued, and many times pleaded, with Kate to stop all of this so they could get on with their lives. It was no use though: Kate was convinced that the system was helping them. She was caught up in what he felt was a web of deceit, with little hope of escape.

Their first involvement with social services began three years ago when he had lost his job in Massachusetts. They had moved back to Pennsylvania to be near her family. Having signed up for employment and not receiving a check for almost six weeks, their bank account was almost depleted. All his life had never taken money from anyone. His situation was getting desperate though, and he had his wife, their son Ron, daughter Naomie, and their unborn baby to think of.

They applied for assistance and what was to become only the beginning. Soon, Kate discovered, there was a whole network of services that were available to the needy. Their son Ron was an exceptionally hyperactive child and at some times could be very difficult to handle. She was referred to the Warrington County Metal Health Clinic for help. Ron was soon accepted as a patient and diagnosed as A.D.H.D. (Attention Deficit with Hyperactive Disorder).

Jim, foreseeing what could happen from experiences in his own past, cautioned her about becoming too involved with these agencies. Her mother and other friends and family members also warned her about the danger of letting the system interfere with their lives.

It began with just a diagnosis, but soon it escalated into something that neither one of them could have imagined. First, it was the two weeks Ron spent in a foster home, so they could have a break from him and what the system deemed his uncontrollable behavior. Then there was the four months in another foster home. They never knew where he was or whom he was with. The system only told them: "that he was well taken care of and provided for."

He had signed the papers along with Kate when they placed him in the foster homes, and every day he hated himself for what he had done. He had made a promise then, swearing that he would never again do such a thing.

After his arrival home, Ron's time with his family was again cut short by the system. Ron, who by then was determined to have serious behavior problems, was referred to ICM (Intensive Case Management). He was assigned a caseworker by the name of Devlin, who had immediately begun preparations to have Ron admitted to a psychiatric hospital for evaluation and treatment.

This was the first of Ron's three stays in the hospital, ranging from the first of four weeks to the last stay of three months. They monitored his actions closely and prescribed his medicine accordingly. Each time he returned, it was because the medicine wasn't doing the job.

Due to the visiting hours and the fact that they were fifty miles from the hospital, they were only able to visit him on weekends. Every time they went in to see him, Jim felt like the situation had become worse. The doctors had managed to control his behavior problem by giving him medicine, or drugs as he preferred to call it, but it seemed like Ron was being drawn further and further away from them. The first time he was admitted and they came to visit him he was overjoyed at their visits. He expressed the feeling that he didn't want to be there. He talked to his mom and dad about wanting to go home and play with his sisters.

Later, when their time was up and they had to leave, there was an emotional scene that took place. They both hugged Ron and kissed him as he cried and begged them not to leave him. There was panic in his eyes as he looked at his mom and his dad and pleaded between sobs for the answer he wanted to hear. "Please, Mom, Dad—I am better now and I want to go home with you!" he said as he grabbed his mother's hand and tried to make his way closer to the door.

Kate was not a strong person when it came to hiding her emotions and she did not want to lose it and break down in front of Ron.

"Please, Jim," she said as she knelt down, hugged Ron, and then got up and opened the door.

Jim looked at her as she prepared to step out in the hallway. She didn't have to say anymore; he knew what she was feeling.

"I will be out in just a minute," he said, understanding her urgency to leave as she did.

He turned to Ron and his legs began to tremble as he knelt down. His gut felt like it was tied in knots and he started to sweat as he resisted the almost overwhelming urge to scoop him up in his arms and take him out of this place. He had a lump in his throat and his words came out in a dry raspy voice as he tried to explain to Ron why he had to stay in the hospital.

"Ron, you are here so these people can help you," he said, cupping his little hands in his own as he tried to think of the right words to say. "You have some problems that other kids don't have, and all the kids in here are just like you. These people are nurses and doctors who know all about these things and they are here to help you."

He didn't know if Ron understood everything he said. He knew he had to stay in the hospital, but Jim couldn't help thinking as he wiped the tears off his little cheeks, that in Ron's mind and heart he felt like he did something very wrong and he was being punished by being locked up in there.

The first visits were like that, but his last stay was a lot different. He was excited when they first came, but it soon wore off and after a while he almost seemed to ignore their presence.

Upon his release from the hospital, the doctors explained to them, his behavior was a reaction to the drugs they had prescribed for him.

"Kate," he said as he sat beside her waiting for two of the psychiatrist's to give them the diagnosis. "I know you believe in what they are doing and feel that everything is helping to alleviate Ron's problem, but I still don't like it. There has got to be another way. Somehow, I find it hard to believe that keeping him sedated with drugs is the only answer."

"Boy, you are hard headed," she answered, sounding a little bit disturbed that he didn't go along with everything that the doctors were suggesting as she had. "How much is it going to take to convince you that Jon is not a normal child and needs special attention?"

He glanced toward the doctors, trying to keep his voice down as to avoid attracting any attention. "I am not arguing that fact. It is just that I don't like the idea of giving him some kind of medicine so we can keep him under control."

The doctors were finished with their discussion and they turned to him and Kate. Among other things, they were also told that his mental condition bordered on being handicapped and were given special instructions on how to deal with his abnormal behavioral patterns.

Ron finally got to come home and everything seemed to be normal. As it was explained to them, Ron did need special care and a lot of attention. It was difficult to comply with his special needs and again things got out of hand, with Kate feeling that she could do nothing with him.

Without Jim's knowledge she contacted CYS, who upon receiving her call immediately made preparations to place him in another foster home. Jim was furious when he found out what she had done and refused to sign any papers.

The following evening when he came home, he discovered what little significance CYS considered his role as a father to be.

"Where is Ron?" he asked, sensing something out of place as soon as he walked in the door.

"Hi, Dad," said Naomie, looking up from her toys next to the Christmas tree where she sat playing with Kristy. "He is gone. Some people come and took him."

"Kate!" he shouted, hearing sounds coming from the kitchen. "What the hell is going on? Who came and took him? I thought we talked about this and I told you that I didn't want him sent off to some foster home."

"They told me that it would be for his own good. I am sorry Jim, but there was nothing else that I could do."

"Christ, Kate—It's Christmas! Couldn't this all have waited until later? I at least would have liked to talk to him before he left."

"It was their idea to come when you weren't home," she said. "They thought it would be best if you weren't here when they came for him so there wouldn't be any confrontation."

He sat on the sofa with one of his girls on each knee staring at the Christmas tree. It was beyond his control. His family was being torn apart and there was nothing he could do about it. Ron was gone. With his permission or not, they had done what they said they would do and again took him from his home.

It was the day after Christmas when he left, with all his presents still under the tree. It was in May, over four months later, when he came home. Still it was not over, because after that came the respite.

In the past three years, Ron had spent almost half of that time in either the hospital or foster homes. CYS had controlled his life: everything he did and everywhere he went was only what they felt was best for him. Little by little Ron was being taken from him, and it was becoming more and more apparent that he was to have no say in the matters of his own son. He had protested at Ron's respite placement but, as before, his efforts were useless.

CHAPTER TWO

Kate had applied for S.S.I. for their son Ron, when he was diagnosed as A.D.H.D. She applied on the recommendation from mental health in hopes that this might relieve some of their financial burden engendered — through Ron's problem.

Upon receiving this good news about the four hundred and sixty two dollars of added income, Kate suggested that he quit the Warrington store. With the extra income they were getting for Ron, she felt that she could use some of the money to help out with the bills and he would have a lot more time to spend with the kids.

What she meant was that he had a lot more time to stay with the kids so that she could have more time to do all the things that the kids hindered her from doing, such as going to bingo. In other words, his extra time off wasn't their quality family time, but rather her time to get away from him and the kids.

After eating breakfast with the girls and hurrying to get them ready, he took them off to school. An hour or so later when he returned with Kristy, he was greeted with an unexpected surprise from Kate.

"I got a call from CYS while you were gone," she said. "It was from a caseworker by the name of Mariane Mayer. She said that I was to pick Ron up at school and bring him down to her office."

He asked her what it was all about. " The caseworker," she explained, " just told her that it had something to do with Ron's last weekend at respite and she would tell her all about it at their meeting," which she had scheduled for one o'clock that afternoon.

Kate seemed worried: if this meeting was about something pertaining to Ron, why weren't the both of them asked to attend and not just her?

Jim tried to reassure her, telling her not to worry but he was worried too. He thought about the last three years and all the things that had transpired with Ron and the CYS. He didn't trust anyone at CYS and he felt that he had every reason not to. This latest upcoming incident was one more example of the deceit he felt CYS was capable of.

"Call me as soon as you get out of that meeting," he told her. "I want to know what is going on and why they felt it wasn't necessary to even talk to me."

"Jim, I am scared. Why do they just want to see me, and why won't they tell me anything?" she asked, as she sat there on the sofa next to him, rubbing her hands and turning her wedding ring on her finger like she did when she was nervous.

"Kate, relax," he said, grabbing her hands and gently holding them in his, trying to ease her tension a little. "It can't be too serious or they would have wanted to see the both of us. You are just going to have to go in there and talk to this woman and find out what this is all about."

He thought about going with her, but it was almost time to go to work. It was too late to call in and try to get someone to replace him. The way things were now, and money being as short as it was, losing his job was the last thing he could afford to do.

He kissed Kate, gave her a hug and then Kristy, as she squeezed herself between them with that 'me too' look on her face and headed off to work. Several times he had asked Mark, the store manager, if his wife had called but each time his answer was the same. He called his house, and as the phone began ringing he remembered what she said about dropping the girls off at her mother's while she went up to see the caseworker. There was no answer, which was not surprising, because with Ron gone to respite for the weekend, she did not have to be back to meet him when he got out of school. He looked at the clock: it is after three—she must be out of the meeting by now. Why hadn't she called him and let him know what was going on?

He picked up the phone and started to dial his mother-in-law's number when two other phones started ringing almost simultaneously. It was getting busy again; his call would have to wait till later.

It was after five when he got his next chance. He had still heard nothing from her. He had just came in and there were no orders up for immediate delivery. There were also two other drivers on duty now, giving him ample time to call and find out what was going on.

Her cousin Donnie answered the phone and he could tell from the sound of his voice that something was wrong.

"Let me talk to Kate," he asked Donnie, hearing Naomie and Kristy talking in the background and assuming that Kate was also there.

"She's not here, Jim; she is with Mom and Norma," he said. "I am baby-sitting the girls."

Norma was her sister-in-law and another devoted bingo fan. As soon as Donnie mentioned Norma's name, it was pretty evident to him where she had gone.

"Thanks Donnie. If I get off early, I might stop by," he said and hung up.

There was no need for Donnie to tell him; he knew where she was. They had argued about it that morning. He thought he had gotten through to her, but apparently he hadn't. He was not only puzzled now, but also angry. Not only hadn't she called him and told him what happened at the meeting, but also, against his wishes she had gone to bingo. She knew how tight their money situation was and that meant one more bill they would have to put off till later.

How could she, he thought, *and what about the meeting? Why hadn't she called and told him what had happened?*

It was after ten when he got off, and he decided to stop by her mother's. Being as it was Friday, the girls would not have any school tomorrow and Kate would probably want to hang around for a while.

Her mother and stepfather lived in the country about five miles from Warrington. Their large, spacious, five bedroom home was situated on five acres of mostly wooded land. Over the years, Harley, Kate's stepfather, having been retired from a permanent disability, had cleared some of the land and planted fruit trees and flowers. Now with the help of his sons and nephews where there was once woods strewn with fallen trees and overgrown with dense briars, there was instead, a big yard where the grandkids could play in the summer.

There were a half a dozen cars in the driveway, when he pulled in. It was not unusual since Kate came from a big family consisting of eight brothers and sisters. It was the weekend and this was the norm and not the exception.

He pulled along the side of the driveway, making sure he wasn't blocking anyone in. Just as he got out of his car and started toward the house, Kate's cousin Donnie pulled up behind him and he had Naomie and Kristy with him. As Donnie went around the other side to help them, they spotted him. Hurrying to get out of the car, they came running up the driveway to meet him. There was no yard light but it was a clear night with the sky illuminated by a full moon, making them easy to see as they ran, stumbling on the coarse gravel. Their coats were open, flapping, and their long hair blew in the nippy breeze as they raced each other.

Naomie reached him first, snuggling under his outstretched arms as he stooped down and grabbed her. "Hi dad, we have been bumming," she said, using a term she had adopted.

"Yeah," said Kristy, as he reached out and grabbed her next, only a step behind Naomie and tucked her under his other arm. "We went with Donnie to the store."

They both began to shiver from the cold, huddling closer to him. He hugged them close, giving each of them a kiss on the cheek and then stood up taking each one by the hand. "Come on, you guys," he said. "Let's get in the house where it is warm."

Donnie had not yet gone in the house and was standing a few feet away, leaning on one of the cars as if he was waiting to talk to him about something. When Jim headed for the door, instead of following him, he called him asking him to wait for a minute, stating that there was something he had to tell him.

"Go on, girls," Jim told them, letting go of their hands. "I will be in there in a minute."

He turned to Donnie after he watched the girls disappeared through the basement entrance. "All right; what's up, Donnie? Just what the hell is going on?"

It had to be something besides her just going to bingo he thought, as Donnie began to shuffle his feet and look at the ground, ostensibly reluctant to tell him what he had to say.

"She is really pissed at you about something," Donnie said, avoiding any eye contact as he spoke. "I guess when she came back this afternoon, she was hollering and screaming and calling you all kind of names."

"Donnie, what the hell has she got to be mad about?" he said, letting his anger show at her defiance to his wishes. "She is the one that went to bingo after I told her not to."

"Look, Jim," he said, trying to hurry and end the conversation as soon as possible, since as he didn't have a coat on and it was almost freezing outside. "I don't know anything. I was out helping Uncle Harley all afternoon and I wasn't here when she got back. When we did get home, she was getting ready to leave for bingo. She was cussing and swearing about something and Uncle Harley got mad. He told her that he did not want to hear any cussing and swearing in his house and if she wanted to do that to do it someplace else."

Jim knew what he was getting at now and why he had stopped him from going in the house.

"Well," Donnie continued, "Kate and Aunt Jane are back from bingo and you know how Kate is when she gets mad. Uncle Harley doesn't want any fighting and arguing in his house and being as there are a lot of people here especially, he thought it would be best if maybe you didn't come in."

So this is what it came down to, he thought: now he was barred from his in-law's house. He was mad now and Harley was right: if he went in there, there would be a fight.

"All right," he told Donnie. "I will respect Harley's wishes. I won't come in. But you tell Kate to get her ass home, because I want to know what is going on and what this is all about."

There was uncanny silence as he came into the basement entrance and headed up the stairs into the kitchen. It had been quite a while since he had come home to an empty house. The absence of all the normal sounds seemed almost depressing and yet, in a way a welcome relief to what he was used to.

He poured a cup of cold coffee and slipping it in the microwave went in and turned on the TV. Finding a movie that looked to be interesting, he sat back and relaxed, enjoying the peace and quite. He had planned on staying up and waiting for Kate, but after dozing off a couple of times and glancing at the clock discovering it was after one o'clock, he decided to go to bed.

He guessed what she was doing: she had laid the girls down and was playing cards. It was not unusual for her family to sometimes stay up until four in the morning on the weekends.

It made him all the angrier when he thought about it. He knew that Donnie had told her what he said and she was deliberately staying late and playing cards.

CHAPTER THREE

He awoke startled, as if out of a frightening dream. It was after ten o'clock and quiet, just like last night when he came home, only this time it seemed different. The stillness seemed to be overwhelming and he suddenly had a nauseating feeling. Something was wrong. She had not come home last night. If she had, he would never have slept this long. The girls wouldn't have let him.

Kate tried to let him sleep in on Saturdays and Sundays when he didn't have to get up and take Naomie to school. It only seemed appropriate, though, for the kids to want their dad to get up and eat breakfast with them just like on any other day.

Her not coming home was not unusual—it had happened before. He knew that she would have laid the girls down. If she had stayed up until three or four, like he guessed she did, then she would not have wakened them and would have went in and lain down herself before coming home.

After last night, it was obvious that Kate was mad at him for something he did, but he just wasn't sure what it was. Sooner or later she would be home and there was no sense calling her knowing how she was. Her not coming home last night was evidence to how angry she was about the incident and until she was ready to talk about it, it would be useless to try to adjudicate the obscure reasons for her actions.

Later that day, when she still had not come home, he called her mother's to talk to Kate. At first, Kate didn't want to get on the phone and when she did, what she had to say still didn't make any sense to him.

"Kate?" he asked her. "What are you trying to do? Why didn't you come home last night?"

"You know why," she said. "It's obvious, isn't it? I told you that I was going to leave you and I wanted a divorce."

He heard what she said, but he still didn't believe her. There had to be more to it than that. Yesterday morning, everything was fine. Then she had the meeting with CYS and all of a sudden she decided it was time to walk out on him without any warning and take the kids with her.

He tried again to get a reasonable explanation. "Kate, what about the meeting? What did they want to see you about?"

"Oh, it was nothing," she said. "It was something that Ron was supposed to have done in the last foster home he was in, but they said that it was nothing to worry about."

"Well, what was it?" he asked her. It had to be something serious enough to ask her to come down there and talk to them about. After all, he was still his father and if it was something pertaining to Ron, then he did have a right to know what it was.

"I told you that it was nothing," she said, suddenly becoming angry.

"Kate, look," he said. "Will you please come over here so we can talk about this? Whatever it is that you are mad about I am sure we can work it out, if you will just come over here so we can sit down and talk about it."

She raised her voice, almost screaming at him over the phone. "I don't want to talk to you and I am not coming over there so you can try to change my mind. I have said everything that I have to say to you. I am leaving you and that is it. I am staying over here at Mom's until I can find a place. And," she added, "Mom and dad don't want you coming over here and arguing with me trying to change my mind either." Then she hung up.

The days passed and he tried to talk to her several times. However, it was always the same thing: whenever he tried to find out what was going on, she just would get mad and hang up. He missed the kids and wanted to see them, but didn't want to cause any trouble at her mother's. With Thanksgiving coming up Thursday, he had hoped that she would have come to her senses and they could settle their differences, whatever they were, and spend the day together as a family again.

The last three years they had spent Thanksgiving at her parent's house. It was like the traditional Thanksgivings he remembered having with his parents when they were alive years ago. Everyone chipped in and brought something to add to the feast of turkey and ham that her Mom prepared. It was not only for family, but friends and neighbors as well were invited to share in the abundance of food that good fortune had provided for them.

Each time he called her since she had left, he had begged her to reconsider what she had done. Nothing he said did any good and needless to say, this year he was not invited to his in-laws for Thanksgiving.

He watched television most of the day, trying to keep his mind occupied. He missed her and the kids and several times he called her mother's, but she refused to talk to him.

Somehow he made it through that day and the next. It was like being in a trance. He went to work as usual but everything that happened during the day seemed to be nothing but a blur, and most of the time he was hardly conscious of what he was doing. All he had on his mind was Kate and the kids. He knew that they could come to a solution to their problem, if they would just get together and work things out. Nevertheless, for some reason that he failed to understand, she would not discuss anything about the nature of the problem.

He went to work at eleven Saturday morning. He was on a split shift and drove during the lunch rush, then he came in again at eight o'clock and worked till two, which was their closing time.

It was around one in the afternoon when he got off and headed home. As he turned off the main road and started up the driveway that led to his house, a warm feeling of joy and anticipation began to creep through his body: her car was parked next to the house.

She is back, he thought. She finally came to her senses and came back home. He wasn't angry with her anymore; whatever it was that caused her to leave him didn't matter. All he cared about was that she came back.

The curtains parted and he could see Kate standing by the kitchen window as he headed for the door. He didn't see the girls, who he knew would be at the window waving at him as soon as he pulled up. He assumed that she had left them at her mother's, so the two of them could be alone to talk.

His feeling of joy and anticipation became short-lived when he stepped through the door adjoining the kitchen into the living room. It was the first time they had talked to each other face to face since she left over a week ago.

Her face was contorted with an angry frown and she snapped at him in a tone of voice that almost frightened him.

"What the hell are you doing home?" she said. From the bitterness in her voice, he was convinced that she had not come back to talk to him and settle their differences.

"I had to work the lunch rush. I have to go back in at eight and work till close," he said as he pulled out a chair and sat down at the table. Their kitchen was too small for their table, so they ate in the living room which adjoined their kitchen.

"Now," he continued, "will you please sit down and tell me what is going on?"

He felt a little ray of hope when Kate put her hands on the back of a chair, as if she were about to pull it out and sit down. She stood there a minute gazing out the window on the other side of the table, as if she were contemplating following his request and then turned and walked across the living room toward the hallway.

"I told you—there is nothing going on," she said in a raised tone of voice that seemed to be filled with anger. "I found a apartment for me and the kids and I just stopped by to get a few things. I thought you were at work. If I had known you were home I would not have come."

He got up and followed her down the hall at the end of the living room, sensing by her attitude that it would be useless to wait for her to come and sit down and talk to him. She picked up a cardboard box and he watched as she stepped into the bathroom and began to fill it with her and the kids personal items off the shelves. He stood in the doorway, unintentionally blocking her exit as he again tried to appeal to her common sense and asked her what had happened at the meeting with CYS last week that had made her change so abruptly. Kate stopped what she was doing and turned to stare at him. There was something so evil and threatening about her look it sent a cold chill through his body. She broke her gaze for a minute and looked around at the small-enclosed bathroom like a trapped animal. She turned back to him and exploded in an unexpected rage.

"Are you trying to stop me?" she screamed in a voice that was almost unrecognizable. "You are in my way. If you don't get out of my way, I swear I will make you pay for this."

Jim backed out of the doorway, letting her know that he had no intentions of stopping her. Her face was beet-red and she was trembling as she stood there staring, holding the box in her arms and waiting for him to move. Caught off guard, he was momentarily frightened by her sudden rage. Like any other average couple they had their arguments, but he had never seen her so angry and hostile before. Although he was alarmed by Kate's actions, he sensed that she was terrified even more. She seemed scared of something and he was certain that her frightening burst of emotions were brought on by her sudden run-in with CYS and stirred by the meeting last Friday. After cooling down from her sudden rage, he helped her take some boxes down to the car. The back door was open on the station wagon and it was now completely filled.

When she first left all she had taken was a few clothes for her and the kids because she had been staying at her mother's. She explained that with having an apartment now, she had room for a lot more things. She told him she was coming back with her cousin Donnie and her step-dad's pick-up and take some of the furniture.

He followed Kate back into the house and watched her as she went about from room to room, checking to make sure she hadn't forgotten anything she needed right away. She wanted the sleeper sofa and coffee and end tables, which he promptly say no to. He agreed to let her have the home entertainment center, which she said he bought for her, but drew the line when it came to the television and VCR.

When the old television went bad last year they had no money in the bank. It was not because he wasn't making enough money; rather, with her going to bingo almost every night of the week she was spending it as fast as he was making it. Unbeknownst to her he had been saving money for some time and had enough to go out and buy a new one.

Although he had bought the new television out of his own savings, she became angry with him because he was hiding his money and not sharing it with her. He just didn't think that she deserved the television and VCR.

He was sure that there would be no reconciliation here today as he watched her. The feeling he had when he first pulled in the driveway and seen her car was gone now; instead it had become replaced with anger and resentment for what she was doing to him.

How much was he supposed to take? Here was this woman, his wife of almost seven years, who left him for no apparent reason a week ago, walking around telling him the things she felt he owed her. She left without a word or explanation of any kind, and worst of all, she took his three kids.

"Kate," he told her, "what in the hell do you think gives you the right to walk in here and tell me what you are entitled to? You walked into my life with nothing but a suitcase and a promise of love and companionship, and I believed you. Because of that we had three beautiful children. Now, without even giving me a reason, you have decided to leave and take even that from me."

Everything they had he either had when they met or had earned through hard work over the years. All he had ever cared about was his family's needs. The sorry part about it was that it seemed like she had been fighting him every step of the way. Sometimes she acted like she never cared about anyone but herself. Many of the arguments they had stemmed from money. Whenever they faced a financial crisis, it was because she spent everything they had, not on them but on herself.

Ten years ago when they first met, things were different. He had a good job and lived in a nice affordable seven-room house in the country. He had a dependable car and a motorcycle. He wasn't rich, but he had excellent credit.

Boredom was not a problem for him, because in his back yard he had a big garden and he always had plenty to do. However, he had a void in his life: he was lonely. Now, as he thought about what had happened the last week and he watched what he felt was the reason for his entire existence being destroyed, he wondered if the enormous cost of filling that void had been worth it, and if he wouldn't have been better off to coping with the loneliness.

After all these years, he was twenty thousand dollars in debt and owed every major credit card to the maximum. He came back to Pennsylvania to be near her family, giving up his career in telephone line construction and any chance of a pension.

He had tried to remain calm in hopes that they could still work things out, but her steadfast defense to her actions had made him become furious. She stood there facing him with her hands on her hips and a defiant smirk on her face. It almost looked like she was daring him to try to stop her.

He felt like he just wanted to reach out, slap the smirk off her face, and knock some sense into her head. He knew he couldn't do it, though. Never in his life had he ever hit a woman, and he was not about to start now.

He slammed the cup he was holding in his hand on the hardwood coffee table and looked at it, wondering why it hadn't shattered. In spite of his principles, still fighting the urge to just reach out and smack her, he screamed at her as he lost his temper.

"Who in the hell do you think that you are?" he shouted, fighting to control the deep seated anger buried inside of him since the breakup of his first marriage. "How can you stand there telling me what I owe you?"

He was almost in tears now as he felt a repeat of his first divorce close at hand. "Better yet," he murmured, turning away from her to avoid her piercing stare, "Why don't we just wait until we go to court and see what they decide?"

She was fuming at his determination of how they should settle the distribution of their possessions, and he expected her to burst out with a stream of obscenities any moment. Her face again turned beat red and she shook with intense anger as she blurted out her stuttered reply,

"We—we shall see," she said, as if struggling for the right words to say. "Just, just you wait. Then, then you will see who gets what."

"Just you wait? Wait for what? Just what the hell is that supposed to mean?" he asked her.

She didn't answer. She turned her back as if she hadn't heard him and took a couple of steps toward the living room door. There was a front entrance to their house which entered from the front porch to their living room. They seldom used it because of the carpet, but she seemed to be in a big hurry to leave.

"I have got to go," she said.

God, he hated when she did that. It was always one of his pet peeves. Whenever they would get into an argument and he would ask her something that she did not want to answer, she would just ignore him like she didn't even hear him and walk away. He followed her out on the front porch, still thinking about what she said and trying to make some sense out of it. Stopping at the porch rail, he watched her go down the steps to the car and open the door.

"I will be back later with Donnie to get more things," she said as she got into the car.

His anger having subsided, his thoughts suddenly turned to the kids and he hurried down the steps in a last attempt to reason with her before she left.

"Kate," he said, reaching the car just as she started it. "I am going to be off tomorrow. Why don't you bring the kids over? I want to see them and I am sure they would be glad to see me. Look," he said, grabbing the door as if clinging to his last ray of hope for some kind of reconciliation. "I know we have had our problems, but there is no reason why they should be made to suffer."

"I will be busy tomorrow and I won't have time," she snapped in a tone of voice that had not wavered from the moment she had first spoken to him that day.

"Kate, if not tomorrow—then when?" he asked, as she shifted the car into drive, holding her foot on the brake.

"I don't know when. Now I have to go," she replied in a cold callous voice as she released the brake and started to coast down the driveway.

"I will call you," he said, taking a few steps and then finally letting go of the door as she picked up speed.

He stood there and watched as she turned on to the main road and soon disappeared out of sight. He started to shiver and zipped up his jacket. It wasn't the weather, though: it was from the cold emptiness he felt when he watched her drive down the road.

In his mind, he hoped that they could someday be together as a family again but he had to face the dismal painful facts: Kate was gone and she had taken the kids. He was alone whether he liked it or not, and for the time being, it was the way it was going to be.

The thing that bothered him the most now was the way that Kate was acting. It seemed like she was being driven to her actions. The way she spoke to him was not natural and it seemed as if some coercing force was controlling her, threatening her with retaliation if she didn't make the proper moves and say the right things. Of course, that was his own opinion and he could be wrong. What he did know for sure was that ever since the meeting last Friday Kate was a different person.

His blood began to boil when he thought about CYS. At first it seemed like they were trying to help them with their children, and CYS was concerned about their well-being. Soon that turned into a nightmare and now he had been almost completely denied all his rights as a father to his son Ron.

What happened at the meeting, he thought. *Why did they want just Kate, and what did they say to her? Most of all*, he wondered, *why wouldn't she tell him what it was all about? Did it have something to do with all of this?*

Thinking about the possibility of CYS interfering in their personal life made him all the more angry and he began to swear to himself. Those bastards! If they are responsible for all of this, there will be hell to pay. He didn't know when or how, but he swore, they would pay.

He called her mother's on Sunday. Her cousin Donnie answered the phone and said that she was at her new apartment and wouldn't be home all day. The rest of the following week was pretty much the same. Every time he called, the answer was the same: he was told that she wasn't there.

It was Friday again before he saw her. Having to work the night shift, he was home all day. It was around one o'clock in the afternoon when he got up from the sofa where he had been sitting watching television and glanced out the window. Kate was sitting at the end of the driveway, waiting for the mail.

Slipping on his shoes and grabbing his coat, he hurried out the door so he could talk to her before the mailman came. There was something he had to tell her that she was not going to like. He had thought about it, and made up his mind: he wanted the car back. It was in his name and he was paying the insurance on it. If she was going to walk out on him with out any explanation, then she was not going to leave driving his car.

She was furious when he told her. "But you can't take the car," she said, imploring him to reconsider. "How will I get the kids to school and to the doctor's?"

"You should have thought of that before you left," he said. "Now, will you stop all this nonsense and tell me what is really going on? Kate, you and the kids are my life. I don't want a divorce and I can't let you do this."

He had thought that threatening to take the car might force her to reconsider her decision and at least tell him what this was all about. Instead, it just made her all the more angry, and that fiery look in her eyes convinced him that she wasn't ready to tell him anything he wanted to hear.

"You bastard!" she said. "I will see to it that you *never* get our kids! I guarantee it—I will do *anything* that is necessary to stop you."

He was sure that she meant every word she said. He didn't know how, but from her tone of voice and the ominous unyielding look on her face he felt that she was prepared to carry out her threat.

The mailman finally came and she got out of her car and crossed the road to the mailbox. Opening it, she took out a letter and brought it back, concealing it as if she was afraid if he might see whom it was from. "I will bring your damn car back tonight," she said as she slammed the door and drove off.

It was not a real busy night for a Friday and he managed to get out of the store fairly early. He must have gotten home around twelve. He was surprised to see the station wagon in the driveway when he pulled up, even though she said she would bring it back.

Used to being up late, he wasn't tired and didn't feel like watching TV, so he decided to go out for a cup of coffee. It was not just for coffee; he had to get out for a while and talk to someone.

He hadn't driven the wagon in a while, so he took it instead of his Dodge. He went down to Denny's in Warrington. At this time of the night, it was just about the only thing open, and of course he could always find someone in there to talk to.

A man was sitting at the counter when he walked in and he sat in the empty chair next to him. He appeared to be in his mid-fifties, of medium build, with thinning gray hair. Jim, noticing a little excess around the mans waist, thought about himself and the extra pounds he had put on since he quit smoking a few months ago. The man's worn brown work jacket hung open at the waist, revealing a red flannel shirt with faded blue jeans and exposing his midriff bulge. It wasn't long before they struck up a conversation, and in the next hour they talked about everything from politics to religion. Somewhere along the line they discussed women and their relationships, discovering that they equally shared the same problems. He too had been married and divorced and was now struggling to get by.

After an hour or so, Jim decided to leave. He got into his car, only to discover that he had another problem: it wouldn't start. He tried several times but all he was doing was running the battery down. His other car was at home and he had no way of getting there, so he went back into Denny's, sat down and ordered another cup of coffee while he decided what to do next.

The gentleman he was talking to earlier noticed that he had come back in again and asked me if he was having trouble. After Jim explained to him what was going on, the stranger told him that he was about to leave anyway, and offered to drop him off.

You know Jim thought as he followed the stranger to his car, *Life can sure be strange. Sometimes, when you are convinced that nobody in the world gives a damn about anyone but themselves, you run across someone like this.* He did not even know his name or where he was from— he just volunteered to help.

They got into his old car and he proceeded to give him directions to his house. He had gone out of his way to drop him off, so Jim offered him five dollars for taking him home. The man seemed insulted.

"Look, mister," he said, "I can't take any money from you for just doing a favor. I could see that you were in kind of a bind and I was just glad that I was able to help."

"Thanks," Jim said, as he shook his hand and wished him good luck.

"You, too," he said. "And I hope that everything turns out all right for you."

Jim closed the car door and watched him drive off.

When he got in the house, he called a twenty four -hour wrecker service and made arrangements to have his car towed to the Sunoco station, where on rare occasions he had mechanical work done. They told him that he could pick it up after work the next night.

The last few weeks had taken its toll—it was getting harder and harder each night for him to come home to an empty house.

Kate had come by some time that week and had taken some more things. He didn't even know when she came. All he remembered was coming home one night and noticing that the TV and VCR were sitting on the floor. He had thought it strange, though, that she had left the kids playschool table and chairs. Not only that, the girls' book bags were still lying over in the corner of the living room where they had been since the first day she left. The kid's beds were gone but the girls bedroom was strewn with clothes and stuffed animals, including Naomie's lion and Kristy's seal that they used to tuck under their arms every night when they went to sleep. Ron's room was the same. She had even left his collection of Hot Wheels cars that Jim knew were his favorite toys.

He sat there at the kitchen table with his forehead resting on his clenched hands, trying to fight back the tears that were beginning to form.

God, he was so lonely. He wished he could just hear the kids' laughter and giggles that he missed so much.

In spite of what had happened, he still missed Kate. He knew she was not the cruel heartless person that she had portrayed the last few weeks. There was a gentle side to her. She could be kind and considerate. Something or someone had changed her and it just didn't make sense. Nothing seemed to make sense to him anymore.

He knew he could not go on like this. Each day was getting harder to cope with and he knew that he had to do something.

He had even thought about going to the mental health clinic at Warrington to see a therapist, but he had been there before with Kate and heard what these people had to say.

Because of their low income, Kate had discovered that they were eligible for many different services and therapy at mental health was just one more of them. She had been to them several times, and one day she convinced him to go with her.

He was against it from the very beginning. With Ron being bounced around from foster home to foster home and them being kept in the dark about his whereabouts or anything at all that pertained to his well being, he didn't trust them. They were all part of the same organization and he felt that he had every right to feel the way he did.

It was only an hour session, so he agreed to go one morning before work. After signing in, they barely had time to sit down before they were escorted into a small office. A woman sitting at the desk rose to greet them and introduced herself to him as Didi Hargrove. She was in her early thirties, of average height, with long auburn hair. It was evident, from her ghost-like-appearance, that she was not the outdoors type of person and was much better suited to her desk job. She was a little on the heavy side, but her loose-fitting blouse and ankle-length full skirt did a superb job of hiding her chubby figure. There was a stack of papers on her desk in a exceptionally neat order and a briefcase sitting on the floor, which gave her the appearance of the very business type woman.

Kate had been there and talked to her before, so she asked him to begin and tell her about what he felt were some of the problems they were confronting in their marriage.

He began by making her aware of his two jobs and all the hours he worked just to make ends meet. He told her about Kate's problem with money and her gambling habits, putting emphasis on lotto tickets and bingo. He went through the whole bit about life: he talked about sex and the raising and disciplining of the kids and all those things that are inherent in a marriage.

Of course, Kate did her best to downplay the amount of money he accused her of spending on eating out, lottos, and bingo. She made it look so good to the therapist, almost as if he was trying to deprive her of her one night a week out when she would get to spend a few hours by herself away from the kids.

As he listened to Kate, he had the feeling that this therapist had heard all this before. Judging from her reaction, it had become evident to him that she wasn't going to be any help at all.

She sat stern-faced, leaning back in her swivel chair showing no signs of detectable emotion that would indicate her concern. When Kate had finished, she sat forward in her chair.

"What about that, Mr. Hess? Don't you think that she deserves a night out?"

He tried to appeal to this woman's common sense.

"Ma'am look—most of the time I work seven days a week and that doesn't leave much time to be with her and the kids. However, once in a while, I do get a night off. When I do, I don't want to go out with the boys and have a good time and party or whatever it is that they do; I want to go out with my wife or just spend an evening with my family. I don't want to sit home and baby-sit while she goes out and spends my hard-earned money on bingo.

"If I wanted to go out by myself or with the guys, I would have stayed single. But, I am not single—I have a wife and kids and I want to spend my time with them."

From her pokerfaced expression, he got the distinct impression that his appeal had not been the least bit touching. Oh, she had some great advice for them, too.

"Why don't you two just separate and get a divorce?"

He wondered if she any children. Was she married? Did she know what it was like to have her own family? Did she know what it felt like to have someone tell you to just give up what you have worked for for eight years? If she had no kids, how could she know what it felt like to be with them from the day they are were born and then have someone tell you to just give them up? To be told you could still be their parent, but couldn't be part of their life anymore? Would it have been so easy for her to take the advice that she was so willing to give?

Well, he knew what it was like. He had been through all of this before over twenty years ago, and he knew how much it hurt. It still hurt. She had sat there telling him that, in her opinion, it would be best if they decided to just go through it all again.

He had agreed to come to this therapist in hopes that she could help them with some of the problems in their marriage. Instead, it seemed that what she had managed to do so far was to help influence Kate into believing that what she had been doing for the last seven years of their marriage was the perfectly normal and right thing to do.

The last thing he wanted in his life was another divorce. He loved his family and would do anything to help keep them together. If a divorce were what he wanted, he would have gone to see an attorney.

He raised his head and rubbed his eyes, smearing the few tears that had run down his cheeks. As he looked at the smiling faces on his kids' pictures hanging on the wall, he felt a warm glowing feeling. They were his pride and joy and, along with their mother, he was their inspiration and role model. They had always looked up to him and he couldn't let them down.

He slept as long as he could the next day. As there just seemed to be no purpose in getting up. He had no initiative to do anything except what was absolutely necessary. Even cooking was something he seldom did anymore. Pizza and subs were his main diet because he brought a lot of returned orders home from the pizza shop at night instead of throwing them out. Warming up some pizza, he lay on the sofa and watched TV until it was time to go to work.

On Sundays the shop closed at midnight and by twelve thirty he was home. He did not look forward to the next two days. He was not on the schedule to work. Trying to change the manager's mind did no good and he even tried to switch with someone else. Going to work and being around people made it much easier to cope with his present situation but now with two days off, he didn't know what he was going to do.

He needed to talk to someone, either a good friend or close relative. Someone that he could trust and confide in. The only people he knew that were near were her friends and relatives and though he still considered them his friends, he just didn't feel right going to them for any kind of support at a time like this. There was only one person that he could consider a good friend.

Denny, his wife Connetta, their son, daughter, and three grandchildren lived in a little house in Montgomery, Pennsylvania, a little town north of Harrisburg. He owned a little piece of land along the Susquehanna River valley. Jim had been to visit him at his home on several occasions. Looking out the windows facing the river, he had seen the boats dotting the river that flowed through his backyard as the fisherman tried their luck. It was a quiet peaceful place without any close neighbors and away from the wild and furious pace of the big cities that they worked in.

Denny was a supervisor for Henkle & McCoy then and he, as a general foreman, had worked under him. Denny wasn't just his boss, though: over the years that they worked together, he became far more than that.

When he first went to work for the company, Denny, needing a general foreman, had recommended him to the division manager for the job. He was given the position, along with a new pickup and expenses that went with it.

Denny was a special kind of a guy. Jim had not been given the promotion because he was a good friend. When he started it was as a line foreman and they had never met before. "It was your ability and qualifications," Denny told him. "I have your resume and I have watched you work. I needed a good man and I felt that you would be the best man for the job."

He did his best to live up to his expectations and through the close contact that was required through their work, they had become the best of friends.

His courage and ability to confront any situation head on, was the thing that he admired about Denny the most. When a serious tragedy involving the accidental drowning of his daughter and two of his granddaughters touched their lives, he and his wife had managed to overcome their overwhelming grief and go on to raise their surviving infant granddaughter.

They had promised each other that they would keep in touch when he came back to Pennsylvania, but it had been several years since he had talked to him.

It was about a four hour ride to where he lived, he thought, as he dug through his junk drawer looking for his address book, *but he had the next two days off and it would do him good to just get away.* Besides, Denny was the one person that he needed to talk to right then.

He found his number and gave him a call. After a couple of rings he got his answering machine, so he left a message.

CHAPTER FOUR

He had just gotten up the next morning and had been sitting at the kitchen table debating with himself about going for a ride when the phone rang.

"What are you doing home today? Aren't you working?" Kate asked him when he picked up the phone. He had thought it might be Denny returning his call and she was the last person that had expected to hear on the phone. For some reason she had seemed startled when he answered.

"What happened to the car?" she asked in a surprising, almost pleasant tone of voice.

"How did you know about the car?" he asked her, assuming that it was the station wagon that she was talking about.

"Well, when I came by the other night, both cars were gone."

"I had trouble with it again and I had to take it to John's Sunoco to get it fixed," he told her. "Kate—why did you call me?"

"I just wondered what happened to the car when I didn't see it in the driveway," she continued in what he felt was just her little charade.

He knew that was just an excuse when she said it.

"Look, you didn't call me just to tell me that—now, what the hell is going on?"

Her voice changed sharply, sending a cold chill through his spine.

"There is nothing going on. I don't have time to talk right now. I will call you back later," she said, and hung up.

He was more confused now than ever as he sat back on the sofa and pushed the button on the remote, turning on the television. Why had she seemed surprised when he answered the phone? It was almost as if she hadn't expected him to be home.

His attention turned to the television as a Pearl Harbor anniversary special came on. He was still unsure about his plans for the day and after a few minutes he became interested in the old movie. Besides, she had said that she would call back later and he was curious as to what she wanted to talk about.

It was after one when he heard the car pull up in the driveway. The movie was over and he was waiting to see what was coming on next. Kate still hadn't called back yet and he was still anxious to hear what she had to say.

He got up to see who it was and almost wished he hadn't. There was a Chantilly Hunston Police car in his driveway. Two cops, one of whom he recognized as a officer that he had the previous encounter with, were coming up the steps onto the front porch.

The first thing that came to his mind was Jean, his neighbor, and landlord's mother. She must have called them again. They had to be here to serve him some kind of an eviction notice.

The whole problem began shortly after they moved there back in May of last year. Jean's son, Will, owned the house that Jim was renting. He also owned the house that his mother lived in, which was located on the adjoined property.

In the back of his house was a huge hole that had been excavated for an addition to be added on. It had left a ten-foot drop to the ground and a potentially hazardous situation if one of the kids managed to get the back door open. However, owing to money problems, it had never been finished. Will had promised to build a porch, making the back entrance accessible. The summer had passed, and still lacking the money, he had made no attempt to do as he had promised.

Due to their involvement with CYS and the mental health, James Ramour, a caseworker, frequently visited them for CYS, and Devlin who was Ron's ICM caseworker.

Kate told James and Devlin that on several occasions she had complained to Will about the problem. Opening the door and looking at the ground below, she showed them how much good it did.

Following the suggestion of CYS'S caseworkers, she decided to write Will a letter threatening to hold back the following two months rent unless he did something about the back entrance.

Jim had warned her about sending such a letter: they were already living in a hostile environment and something like this could only make matters worse. Against his wishes, Kate had sent Will the letter anyway.

Jean had a boarder, Karen, that shared her house with her. For some reason that he never did quite understand, they never got along. They had tried to be neighborly, but all their attempts failed and she continued to constantly harass them. Most of the complaints had been trivial, but after a time, became quite aggravating. They complained about where Jim and Kate parked their cars, using the excuse that it made it difficult to get in and out of their garage, which was right across from Jim's house. Neither one of them hardly used the garage and parked next to their house instead.

There were other things that Jim thought were unnecessary harassment, Such as moving the entire swing set every time she cut the grass. The legs were anchored but she removed them, making it very dangerous if the kids happened to use the swing set before he got a chance to put them back.

Several days after the suggestion from CYS about writing a letter, Kate got a phone call from Jean. Overhearing the heated conversation that she was engaged in, it didn't take long to figure out what it was all about. Soon after she hung up, Karen came across the front yard toward the house, stopping about fifty feet away.

Jean had become so angry she could not even continue her conversation with Kate and it seemed like Karen had taken over as her spokesperson. She was standing on the front lawn screaming at them and threatening to call the police and have them removed from the premises. Meanwhile, Jean had called her daughter, Kathy, telling her to come over also.

Kate stayed in the house with the kids, arguing through the open window, while Jim went outside and tried to deal with what he felt was becoming a winless situation. He went out and confronted her, soon becoming angry at her intrusion into something that he felt was none of her business.

As their argument continued, consisting of little more than screaming obscenities at each other, Kathy, not living far away, arrived and pulled up toward the house blocking the driveway. She got out of the car and came over to join in the argument.

Kate, sensing that the situation had become out of control, called the township police. She was informed, to her surprise, that they had already been notified and were on their way.

When the police arrived, he had expected some assistance in helping to resolve his situation. What he got, though, was far from what he had expected. The officers, one who he later identified as Detective Kotter, were met by Jean, who had come out of the house and joined Karen and Kathy.

He started toward the car but was stopped by the other officer and told to get back on the porch. He stood there and angrily listened, as the three of them continued to vomit forth a stream of lies and accusations.

Becoming frustrated at not being able to speak his peace, he tried to intervene and tell them his side. He was told by Officer Kotter that if he tried to interfere again, he would be arrested.

Karen pointed to the open garage that Will told him he could use and all the things that he had stored in there and exclaimed that they owned it. Since the rent wasn't paid, they were entitled to keep everything in it.

After listening to Jean, Karen and Kathy blurting out their wild stories, Detective Kotter came over to him impatiently waiting on the front steps of the porch. Jim could sense by the unwavering tone of his voice and the emotionless expression on his face that he had already made up his mind. He had the feeling that nothing he had to say was about to make any difference.

"Mr. Hess," he said before Jim had a chance to speak. "It seems that your not having paid your rent has caused these people to become very upset. And," he continued, in a very professional tone of voice, "in order to avoid any further trouble, I would suggest that you remove your things from the garage."

Jim, after being threatened with arrest, had become very indignant toward this officer's biased decision. He tried to explain to him that Jean and Karen were renters, just like him, and Kathy, Jean's daughter, didn't even live there and had nothing to do with this situation. "Will, Jean's son" he explained, "owned the property and he was the one that they had to answer to."

Nothing Jim had to say had any effect and he wasn't surprised. He had watched and listened and from the way they talked, it appeared that they were well acquainted with each other. It was not unexpected that Officer Kotter would acknowledge their accusations as the truth.

There was one more thing Officer Kotter added when they prepared to leave.

"Mr. Hess," he said, in a threatening tone of voice. "Because of your actions, you have cause a disturbance here today. If this happens again and we are called, you will be arrested."

Now if that isn't a hell of a note, he thought. In the first place, it was the suggestion from CYS that prompted his wife to write the letter that started all of this—now, the township police threatened to arrest him.

Blaming CYS for giving her the suggestion, he went to them informing them he would hold them responsible for any repercussions that might occur. He was amazed at how quickly they attended to the matter. They took all the information and gave it to a law firm where Devlin's brother practiced and told Jim and Kate it would be taken care of and they had nothing to worry about.

He got up and slipped on his pants as they came up to the front door. They were here for something and he was about to find out what it was. He was sure the last matter had been settled, but since Kate had left there was always the chance that Jean and Karen had found some other reason to cause trouble.

He opened the door and glanced at Officer Kotter, still feeling a certain amount of contempt for the way he had threatened him the last time he was here. He had always been taught to respect the law and feeling he had nothing to fear, he tried to be polite by inviting them in.

"Look, if it is about the eviction notice and the past rent, that matter has been all settled and you can tell her that I will move just as soon as I can find another place to live," he said, assuming that this was the reason for their presence.

"That is not why we are here," said Officer Kotter, in a characteristic tone of voice, sounding like something right out of the TV show "COPS". "We have a warrant for your arrest and we are here to take you in."

He stood there for a few seconds in shock. It was almost as if what he had heard had come from the television and not from the man in uniform standing in front of him.

"There is got to be some mistake," he said, trying to retain his composure. "What the hell could they possibly charge me with?"

"It was not your neighbors." Kotter said, replying in his cold callous voice of authority. "You have been charged with molesting your daughter." He removed some papers from an envelope and handed them to him, still folded.

Jim took them. Finding it hard to believe that this was all happening he almost dropped them from his shaking hands as he opened them up. His knees began to quiver as he read the charges. He had been accused him of sexually assaulting Naomie.

He felt nauseated as an overwhelming fear started to overcome him. Every nerve in his body began to tingle, causing him to sweat and tremble violently as he stared at the papers in his hands.

He had been hungry and he had almost frozen on one occasion. He had faced the fear of death more than once, but none of them could compare to what he felt then.

Why? What could have happened to warrant such extreme measures? Kate had swore last Friday that she would guarantee he would never get custody if they went to court, but he could never believe that she would resort to something this low. He had to talk to her; He had to stop this before it went too far. Somehow, he had to find out what was going on that could have caused all of this.

He got up slowly, stunned and fighting the unsettled feeling that accompanied his intense fear. If he went to jail he would be helpless. There was no one he could call.

"I have got to call Kate," he said, making a move toward the phone a few steps away. "She will straighten this whole thing out."

The other officer reached him before he could get to the phone and took him by the arm. "Come on and get dressed," he said, indicating an immediate response to his request by picking up his shirt and handing it to him. "It won't do any good to call your wife," he said, almost sympathetically. "She was the one who came down to the station and made the charges against you."

Taking the shirt from the officer, he put it on. His hands trembled as he sat down and pulled on his socks and slipped on his shoes. Fumbling with the buttons on his shirt as he stood up, he looked around the room. He tried to think about what he was going to do, but he felt like he was in a trance. Everything seemed to be moving in slow motion and although the officers appeared to be speaking to him, there was no sound. This whole ordeal felt like a nightmare in a dream and any minute he expected to wake up.

Feeling something touch his arm, he turned to face the officer that had handed him his shirt. "Come on," he said, "get your jacket— we have to get going."

He knew it was no dream now—this nightmare was for real. He tried to clear his thoughts, but everything was going around in his head so fast that he couldn't seem to make sense out of anything that was happening. He knew that he was going to jail and there was nothing that he could do. He was helpless. The system had taken his son and he was convinced they were responsible for his wife leaving him. Now, they were here to take him to jail for something he didn't do. He would be behind bars and at their mercy, making it impossible for him to find out the reason for what was happening.

He had to think. Never before in his life had he ever been in such a situation and he just didn't have any idea how to deal with something like this.

They were ready to put the handcuffs on when he thought about the money he had saved and hidden downstairs. Over the course of the summer when he was working long hours he had managed to save fifteen hundred dollars. Kate knew he had money saved, but didn't know where it was or how much. The minute she found out they took him to jail she would be tearing the house apart trying to find it.

He had to get his money. At least he could hire an attorney, or maybe post bail, if it wasn't too much. Following his innate instinct to retrieve his money from it's hiding place, he headed for the kitchen and the basement stairs. Still not fully conscious of the gravity of his situation, he was surprised at the manner in which the officer reacted.

With a handcuff on one wrist, the officer was in the process of putting them on when Jim headed for the kitchen. Sensing the attempt to elude him, he grabbed his wrist with both hands and twisted his arm behind his back, subduing him in an effective but painful hold. Jim tried to pull away, but the pain was excruciating and brought instant tears to his eyes.

He started to panic as he visualized Kate finding the money he had hidden in the books over his work- bench. Struggling to get loose, he suddenly realized that he was responsible for this officer's aggressive actions.

"Please," he said, as he stopped struggling. "I have to go down in the basement and get my money."

"What money?" asked Detective Kotter as he came over to assist the other officer, in what they both must have seemed to think was a attempt to escape.

"I have some money put away in the basement," he said, in an effort to convince them of his real intentions. "I had to hide it from my wife to keep her from spending it. She knows I have some saved and if I don't take it with me, she is going to come back and find it."

"All right," said Detective Kotter, "but we will all go down together."

They followed him through the kitchen and down the steps into the basement. He went over to the workbench and took down a book from one of the shelves overhead. Opening it, he took out the neat stack of money that was compressed in the middle and counted out fifteen one hundred dollar bills.

"Shit, he wasn't lying," said the officer who had first halted his mistaken escape attempt. "I have never had that much money in my pocket at one time."

"All right," said Kotter, motioning for the other officer to put the handcuffs on. "Now lets get going."

Jim put the wad of bills in his wallet and stuffed it into his back pocket. He felt a little better now. What he had wasn't much, but it could be crucial in the situation he was facing. With it he stood a chance of coming back home, instead of spending who knows how long in jail.

He put his hands behind his back, making it easy for them to put the handcuffs on and they led him out the basement door to the police car. He slid into the back seat, flinching as the handcuffs dug into his wrists. The back seat of the police car was narrow and with his hands behind his back, it was almost impossible to sit in any kind of a comfortable position. He turned sideways as they rolled down the driveway and stared out the back window.

A great fear of hopelessness overcame him as they turned onto the main road and his house disappeared from his view. *Would he ever see it again? In addition, if he came back, would things ever be the same again?*

He turned away from the window and laid his head against the back of the seat. They had been through a lot, him and Kate. Together they had found the strength to confront any situation and survive, but she had left him and he was alone now. He loved her more than anything else in the whole world. Her and the kids had been his whole life and now they were gone.

All kinds of crazy thoughts were going through his head when they pulled up in front of the magistrate's office. Without her and the kids, he had nothing to live for. He knew that he couldn't face what lay ahead alone. Maybe everyone would be much better off if he were dead.

They opened the back door and helped him out. With his hands still cuffed behind him, he was escorted up the steps into the old wood frame building. The office was quite small, with a few chairs and a desk that filled just about the whole room. With the rows of law books on the shelves and on the desk, he was inclined to believe that this was Magistrate Molly Hill's private office. Officer Kotter left the room and he sat down with the other officer to wait. In a few minutes, he came back accompanied by a women dressed in a black robe. She pulled out the chair and sat behind her desk. Officer Kotter said a few words and laid some papers in front of her.

As he sat there and watched her, he felt like he was in a drunken stupor. It took every bit of effort he could muster to concentrate on his surroundings. She reminded him of a nun who taught in a catholic school that he had gone to. She sentenced him to pull weeds in the convent's garden an hour every night for a week, just because she caught him chewing gum in class. Well, he wasn't in that much of a stupor not to realize that this wasn't a classroom, and what she was planning for him was going to be considerably more demeaning.

"Mr. Hess," she said, looking up from the papers in front of her with an expression that warned him to expect the worst. "These are very serious charges, and I am setting your bail at ten thousand dollars."

His hopes of getting back home again soon diminished as he though of the fifteen hundred dollars in his bulging wallet. It seemed so trivial when he envisioned the remainder of the ten thousand dollars that he knew would be impossible to raise.

Sensing that the formalities were over from the gesture by the officer that had remained in the room with him, he stood up and headed for the door. One of the officers opened the back door of the police car and he slid in, repeating the procedure of attempting to get comfortable in a space that did not allow for it.

It was a short ride to the police station. He hardly had a chance to get in a position that would somehow relieve the discomfort of having his wrists handcuffed behind his back when they had stopped and he was being helped out of the back seat again.

Guided by the first officer with the other one a few steps behind, he stepped through a side door into the main hall. After pausing for a few minutes while someone removed his handcuffs, he was directed toward the end of a hallway to be fingerprinted.

He rubbed his wrists as he slowly walked by the two holding cells meant to temporally detain prisoners until they could be taken to the county jail. Breaking into a cold sweat, he suddenly lapsed into his last memory of the small steel cages.

CHAPTER FIVE

It was Tuesday evening, September 14. He was sitting on the bunk behind the bars, trying to get some feeling back into his hands that were left numb by the handcuffs officer Clancy had so forcibly applied. There were deep impressions on his wrists and his hands were almost black and blue from the lack of circulation.

Kate, her mother and the kids were in a room down the hall. Someone had opened a door and their voices seemed to reverberate through the hallway. He had pleaded with anyone that seemed to be in authority to please let them come in and talk to him. Nevertheless, his pleas were ignored, and instead he was visited by a caseworker from CYS.

She came over to his cell and standing next to the bars as he stood up to greet her, she introduced herself, explaining the reason for her presence. Her appearance was expected, considering the number of times he had asked someone to notify CYS so they could straighten this whole mess out. She seemed quite pleasant, accounting for the fact that she probably been called from home to come down there. However, there was a puzzled look on her face as she revealed what she had learned so far.

"I have read the charges Mr. Hess, and I have talked to the officer in charge. I have also talked to your wife and mother-in-law," she said, nodding toward the closed door at the end of the hall, indicating their presence in the other room. "After examining Ron, I am a little bit confused, though," she pronounced, indicating the reason for the troubled look on her face. "There doesn't appear to be any evidence that such a event that has been described took place. Would you like to explain to me just what exactly happened?"

Finally, he thought, as he sat down on the bunk and rubbed his wrists, trying to stop the tingling sensation that accompanied the return of the circulation. Someone wants to hear what I have to say.

It was around seven thirty that evening, he began, and one of the rare occasions that he had a night off. Kate had gone to bingo with her mother and he was home baby-sitting. It was a warm evening and the kids were outside playing while he attempted to take advantage of one of his rare nights off. Since he had been working two jobs it was hard to fine the time to get anything done.

He was cleaning out the garage, and although being out of view of the kids as they played on the swing set in the front yard, he could still hear them and would check every so often to make sure that they were all right.

"Everything seemed to be fine" he told her, "until halfway through the evening." Hearing a peculiar commotion, he came around the corner of the house to discover all three of them jumping on their plastic swimming pool. Just the sight of their dad catching them in the act of doing something they weren't supposed to be doing was enough to make then stop. Except Ron, that is: he was in one of his feisty moods and he continued to tease the girls.

Jim picked up the pool and headed across the yard to the side of the house to put it out of the way. Ron had ignored his request to stop picking on his sisters, so he stopped and picked up one of the plastic toy bats and tapped him on the backside, indicating what might follow if he didn't do what he was told.

Jim looked at her, and noticed a frown appear on her face as he mentioned tapping him on the butt with the plastic bat. He knew how CYS felt about child abuse, but he didn't feel that what he had done was child abuse. There was a fine line between discipline and child abuse, and all he felt he had done was indicate to his son who was the boss.

After turning the pool over and beating the dents out of it, causing an incredible racket that made them all laugh, they went over to the garage with him to help.

In a short while, in which they seemed to have a great time assisting him in removing some things from the garage, they finished. They were just about to go into the house and have the treat he had promised them, when a police car pulled up the driveway.

"Officer Clancy got out," he said, looking toward the cop sitting over at a desk across the room at a typewriter, indicating that he was the one he was speaking about. "He came over to me and the kids and said 'that he was called by the neighbors to investigate a very serious incident of child abuse!'"

While Officer Crane stayed with him, Ron and the girls, Clancy went down to talk to the neighbors who had been drawn together by the excitement.

Jim recognized Officer Crane as one who he spoke to occasionally, meeting him at the gas station where he always stopped after work. Finding him quite friendly, he struck up a conversation with him as the officer gave Ron and Naomie a grand tour of the police car that was sitting in the drive-way. Kristy, not being at all partial to strangers, stood close to him hanging on to his leg, as he tried to find out from officer Crane what was going on.

Officer Crane was just as much in the dark as he was about the whole situation. Having the short time to spend with the kids, it seemed like he had made his own summation of the alleged child abuse, and was just as anxious to find out what this was all about.

He could only hear bits and pieces as the neighbors shouted at Officer Clancy, pointing to the swing set and the pool over at the side of the house. There seemed to be a dozen people that had gathered trying to tell their story all at once and although they were within earshot it was almost impossible to make out what they were saying.

What amazed Jim the most as he looked at the crowd that had assembled in the front *yard*, was that earlier when the kids had been playing there was not a person in sight. Now, all of a sudden they seemed to appear out of nowhere, anxious to give their description of the scene that they had witnessed.

He had wanted to go down and confront these people face to face, but he was advised by Officer Crane that it would be best if he would just wait until officer Clancy came up to tell his side of the story.

Almost an hour had passed before Clancy finished with the neighbors and headed back up toward his house. Stopping on the way, he bent over to pick up one of the plastic bats lying in the yard.

"I didn't have a chance to say anything," he told her. "He just came over and told me that he had a signed statement from a dozen witnesses, testifying that they had observed me beating Ron in the head with a baseball bat."

Jim was outraged at their accusations, pointing out that it would be impossible to do such a thing without leaving some kind of marks on Ron. Officer Clancy referred to a slight discoloration under Ron's eye, indicating that this is where he felt that Ron had been hit, and announced that, he, was arresting him for assault and intent to commit bodily harm.

"I am aware of the mark under Ron's eye," the caseworker cut in, clarifying something that had been a mystery to Jim since it had first been mentioned. "Your wife has told me all about it. She said that Ron had accidentally been hit with a hair- brush while she was brushing one of the girl's hair. It happened over a week ago and since she had never told you, she was sure that you weren't even aware of it."

"Look, that is about it," he told her. "They arrested me and brought me down here. My wife was notified and you were notified and you probably know more about what happened after that then I do."

Hearing everything he had to say that seemed important, the caseworker left without saying a word and went into the other room, leaving him to contemplate what was to come next.

Since everything had been clarified about the mark under Ron's eye it became quite obvious that their was no other indication of abuse. He was now certain it had to come to someone's attention that nothing had ever happened and he would be let out of here.

As he sat there thinking, a door opened and an officer came out commenting on Ron's erratic behavior. "Boy, that Ron sure is an active kid," he said, making it obvious to Jim that this was not his normal behavior for this time of the evening. "I just wish I had half of his energy."

He should be asleep now, or at least sitting on his mothers lap fighting to stay awake, he thought. On the other hand, he would be—if someone had given him his medicine like he had asked them to.

It was after nine when they brought him to jail. He had told them more than once before they left that Ron was on a prescribed drug and it was imperative that he have his medicine at a certain time. He had asked them to let him give it to him. However, his pleas were denied, and he was told that it would be taken care of. It seems that they had been so intent on arresting him for alleged child abuse that they neglected to attend to Ron's immediate needs and give him his medicine. One of the officers came over to the cell and unlocked the door. He had thought that they were going to release him, but instead they took him back into a small room that reminded him of a photo shop to be fingerprinted. They were not going to release him: they were going to take him to the County Jail.

Someone took him by the wrist and placed his thumb on a pad of black ink, rolling it back and forth. He started to pull away and suddenly stopped, letting the officer continue, as a sudden fear of realization engulfed his senses.

This was no dream. It was happening all over again. Only this time it was different. Kate and her mother were not in the other room. There was no one out there to help him. He was all alone.

When they finished and came out, he turned toward the cell, assuming that he would be detained there until they were ready to take him to jail as before. Instead, he was ushered toward a door at the end of the hall and told to go in.

Opening it, he stepped into a spacious office with tiled floors and a drop ceiling. The police station was housed in the new township building, and it seemed like they had spared no expense in providing ample room for Detective Kotter's few furnishings. Aside from his desk, several chairs, imitation leather sofa, and an end table with a lamp and several magazines on it, there was not much else in the room.

He stood there for a few seconds surveying his surroundings! Detective Kotter motioned him to sit down opposite him.

Now comes the part when they interrogate him and try to get him to confess to the allegations, he thought. He was sure of it. Why else would he be here? He had seen it many times on TV and in the movies.

He sat there staring at the windowsill and a tropical plant in a huge flowerpot absorbing the bright sunlight that lit up the room. "You have the right to remain silent. Anything you say can be used against you," he heard him say as he read him his rights.

"Do you have an attorney Mr. Hess?" said the officer as he finished. "Is there someone I can call for you?" he said a little louder this time, sensing that Jim had not heard him.

Startled by the abrupt interruption of his thoughts, Jim was momentarily at a loss for words. "No," he said after a few seconds, not being able to think of anyone.

"If you can't afford a attorney, Mr. Hess, would you like the court to appoint one for you?" he said as he continued.

"No, wait," said Jim suddenly, almost as if he were afraid it would be too late to change his mind. "There is someone, but I can't remember his name. He is the same one that I had last time," he said referring to the incident regarding the allegations concerning his son.

Remembering that Officer Kotter had been present at the hearing, he presumed that he would remember who the attorney was that represented him.

"You mean Franco Rambsy?" he replied without hesitation, knowing just who he was referring to. "Is he the one you want to represent you?"

He didn't know why, but somehow he sensed the officer's doubt to his choice of attorneys. "I don't know if he will take my case," Jim said, "but he is the only one that I can think of."

As he sat back in his chair waiting while the officer dialed the number, he tried to remember what he knew about Frank Rambsy.

He had only met him twice. The first time was when Devlin, Ron's caseworker, introduced them. Devlin's brother and Franco were partners in the same law firm. There was something about his nature that made him feel uneasy, but he was assured by Devlin at the time that Frank was a very competent attorney and he had no reason to doubt his word.

The second time was at the hearing. Although he had gotten the charges dismissed, he was still not all that impressed about his performance. He had done nothing more than establish to the court, what seemed to be obvious to everyone else that was aware of his situation. Especially after Officer Clancy was left sitting on the stand, giving a verbal account of the accusations, that there was no one there to testify to.

Officer Clancy was angry. Moreover, he could understand why. Clancy had been made a fool of. "At least a dozen witnesses had testified to his beating Ron," he said, "and they had all signed a statement." Now he was sitting there with a statement that was worthless, because not a single one had showed up to testify.

Well, Jim was angry too. Moreover, he had every right to be: he had told Officer Clancy that they were all lying, and nothing had ever happened. However, he did not want to listen to him, and proceeded on the grounds that everything they said was the truth.

Jim was certain also that none of them would show up to testify. They weren't all complete fools, either. They knew that he had never beaten Ron, as they claimed he did, and weren't about to sit on a witness stand and perjure themselves. There was no need to, because they had already accomplished what they had set out to do. It was just one more sick perverted attempt to discourage him and Kate from living where they were not wanted.

He remembered asking Franco something after the hearing. He did not feel that the officer had acted in accordance with his duty. He felt, that prompted by a surge of emotion projected by the wild and frenzied actions of the neighbors, Officer Clancy had disregarded all proper procedure and imposed a cruel and brutal force upon him that was unnecessary and uncalled for.

"All he wanted," he told Franco, "was for someone to apologize for the way that he had been treated." It had cost him over eight hundred dollars to be cleared of this incident, not counting the humiliation of being arrested and spending the night in jail. Now that it was proven in court that he did nothing wrong, all he wanted was for someone to admit that they had made a mistake and say that they were sorry.

"It is out of the question," said Franco, blank-faced and showing no remorse for the ordeal he had just gone through. "I already mentioned it to him. He is not about to apologize for anything. He says, 'he still thinks that you are guilty as hell, and everything he did when he arrested you was in the line of duty.' I think that it would be best if you didn't pursue this matter any further and just forgot the whole thing."

Well, he had not forgotten about it and he had even tried to pursue the matter, to no avail. No one seemed to want anything to do with accusing a police officer of using unnecessary force. The incident was over, but he didn't think that it should be right for the officer's actions to be overlooked the way they had, and he still felt contempt every time he seen him.

His memories of Lieutenant Kotter at the hearing were kind of vague. The only thing he recalled, was that his white shirt seemed to stand out from the standard gray uniform that the other officer wore and the silver bars on his collar designating his rank. He assumed that he was Officer Clancy's superior, and had been there to advise and assist if necessary.

He even looks like an officer, he thought as he glanced at Kotter leaning back in his swivel chair. His shirt was starched and tailored to fit so snug that it failed to show any creases. Being a former Army sergeant himself, he noticed that his silver bars were well polished and even his shirt pockets were buttoned.

Finishing his conversation, it just dawned on Jim as Kotter replaced the receiver that he had not looked up Franco's number. This left Jim inclined to believe that he must have known Franco quite well, or at least had a number of dealings with his law firm before. He was beginning to have some doubt as to his choice of attorney now, as he became suspicious of what kind of a relationship there might be between Lieutenant Kotter and Franco.

"He was not in, but I left a message with his secretary. She said 'that he will get back to you as soon as possible," he said, as he turned facing him and explaining what their conversation had been about. "Would you like to tell me what happened?" said Kotter, startling him for a second. Kotter sat forward and put his elbows on the desk, as if anxious to get on with his interrogation.

Jim's mind was still in a fog, and the officer's words jolted his senses back to reality. His palms began to sweat and a nauseating feeling began to creep through him, as he thought about what was imminent. He avoided looking at Kotter, trying to focus his attention on a row of law books held up straight by a heavy set of bookends on the windowsill behind him.

The officer seemed disturbed by his reluctance to respond and sensing his unwillingness to cooperate, he tried another tactic in an attempt to get Jim to answer his questions.

"Look, Mr. Hess—your wife has come down here and made some very severe allegations. If convicted, you could be looking at some serious jail time. All I want you to do is tell me in your own words what you feel could have caused her to make such accusations."

A chill went through his body, causing him to tremble as he envisioned the gut-wrenching terror of spending time in prison. "Look, Lieutenant," he said, calling him by his official rank for the first time and pausing for a second, not sure why. "I told you, nothing ever happened. I don't know what this is all about, or why I am even here."

His thoughts again returned to a couple of weeks back, and the meeting Kate had with CYS at their office on that Friday afternoon. Although he knew that it had something to do with Ron, she never told him what it was about. He had hugged her and assured her that everything would be all right when he left for work that day. Now, two weeks later he was sitting in the police station, facing charges of sexual abuse to their daughter Naomie.

"We had a argument a couple of weeks ago," Jim said, thinking about their little confrontation down at the mail-box. "She told me that she was leaving me and getting a divorce. I was very upset at the time at her decision and told her that I was going to go to court to fight for custody of our kids. She became furious and threatened to do anything it took to stop me. This whole thing is preposterous," Jim said, trying to appeal to the officer's common sense. "Can't you see what is going on? She is only doing this to guarantee what she has promised she would do, and that is to make it impossible for me to get custody of my kids."

"In her statement, she claims it happened one night back in October while you were baby-sitting," Lieutenant Kotter continued, almost as if he hadn't heard a single word he said. "She had gone to bingo with her mom and when she came home, she witnessed you molesting your daughter Naomie."

"This is crazy," he said, trying to think of the night in October when he had been home baby-sitting. "This is all a lie. She made the whole thing up. I told you why she is doing it."

"I have her signed statement, accusing you of such acts, Mr. Hess, and that is plenty of reason to suspect that you are guilty of molesting your daughter."

He started to feel warm all over, as if he were running a high fever. His sweaty palms began to itch and he found difficulty breathing, almost as if there was a noose around his neck and it was slowly being tightened. The word "guilty" when spoken by the Lieutenant made him feel like he had already tried and convicted him.

"Why don't you tell me what happened, Mr. Hess? Maybe when I have heard both sides of the story, I will be able to better understand just what this is all about."

Now comes the time when they try to trick you into saying something that can be used against you, he thought as he remembered his rights being read to him. However, this wasn't the way he had seen it on TV. There were always two officers in the room, and a tape recorder or notepad or something that his statement could be taken down on. Besides, what could he possibly say that could be used against him? Nothing had happened and Kate knew that nothing had ever happened, so what harm could it do to tell this officer what he remembered about the night in question and what he felt had brought this all about?

"Well," Kotter said, folding his arms and sitting back in his chair as if he was satisfied that he had coerced Jim into telling him his side of the story. "Would you like to explain everything that happened in your own words, so I can better comprehend what this is all about?"

He still had doubts about telling him anything without an attorney present as he tried to clear his mind and remember everything he could. He was sure that after the officer heard about the supposed incident that night, he would have to agree that Kate had made this all up.

It was a rare occasion when he had worked days and business being slow, he had come at around three in the afternoon. It was Tuesday, he remembered, because Kate had gone to the American Legion to play bingo that night. She had left before five to go over and pick up her mother, leaving him to make dinner for himself and the kids.

He didn't mind making dinner for them. Working as he did didn't allow the time to be with them like he wanted to be, so every bit of time that they spent together was precious to him.

It was a warm evening for the third week in October, and after eating they all went outside to play. The next couple of hours were spent involved in a very torrid game of baseball. After expending most of their energy running around the yard having a good time, they retired to the swing set where the kids could show off the new things that they learned. As always when you are having a good time, it had to come to an end. It soon became dark, leaving him no choice but to take the kids into the house and get them cleaned up and ready for bed.

After filling the tub and getting the girls undressed, he let them play in the water a while before attempting the difficult task of washing their hair. Naomie, his four year old, and Kristy, his two year old, were like any normal kids when it came to getting their hair washed and by the time he finished he was just about as wet as they were.

It was Ron's turn next. The girls were reluctant to get out of the tub, seeming to be having a good time splashing water and getting everything in the bathroom wet. He managed to coax them with a promise of a little snack when they got done, and it wasn't long before he had them dried off and sitting in front of the TV with their nightgowns on ready for bed.

Ron, being six and a half, was big enough to wash himself, but he still had to check on him now and then because of his hyperactive condition to make sure that he didn't get into any trouble. Sometimes he failed to get himself clean in all the right places, like his knees and elbows. Jim had come in to check on Ron when he exclaimed that he was all done and ready to get out of the tub, and discover that he had somehow managed to forget to wash his face.

The girls were all settled down on their pillows in front of the TV watching one of their Barney tapes and it wasn't long before Ron had finished his bath, dried off, put his pajamas on and came out to join them.

Getting their snack like he had promised them, he brought them each a bowl of ice cream and a glass of pop. Ignoring their tape for a few minutes as they sat down at the coffee table trying hard not to get too messy, he praised them for being well-mannered as they had for him that evening.

It was after eight when they finished and getting well past their bedtime. Ron, having been given his medicine with his snack, was not a problem. Within a few minutes after eating, he became drowsy and laid his head on one of the pillows. Jim, helping him to his feet before sleep completely overtook him, guided him to his bed. After tucking him in and giving him a kiss, he went back out into the living room to turn his attention toward the girls, who seemed reluctant to follow in their brother's footsteps.

It was not often that their dad was home to watch them instead of their mother. Working the hours that he did, it was rare that they even had a chance to see him in the evenings. So, when on rare occasions like this one, that he was home to watch them, they figured that it seemed only natural, that he should make an exception and let them stay up later than usual.

Jim could understand their motives, but he knew that if their mother was home that she would not see it their way. Bedtime was bedtime and as far as she was concerned, there were no exceptions. She had put them to bed as early as seven o'clock, which he thought was ridiculous. Naomie and Kristy were both talkers and sometimes they would lie in their beds for hours and jabber to each other to stay awake.

He preferred to use what he called reverse psychology: he would let them stay up, thinking that they were getting the best of him. They would both sit beside him on the sofa, huddling as close to him as they could. Within a short time, Kristy, getting tired of competing with her big sister every time she had something to say, would retire to the floor in front of the TV to watch her Barney tape. Soon, as Naomie continued to ramble on about all the things that she had to tell him, Kristy had lain her head down on a pillow and fallen fast asleep.

Naomie, seeing too that Kristy had fallen asleep and sensing the opportunity to take advantage of the situation, decided to get cozy and curl up next to her dad on the sofa.

"Can I lay down by you, dad?" she said, the slow drawn-out words revealing her own drowsiness.

"Sure, honey," he said, as she lay on her side cuddled up to his chest and he put his arms around her, drawing her even closer, adding to her comfort and security.

He knew that she would be asleep soon, and then he would take the both of them and put them in their beds.

He must have dozed off himself and Kate's voice startled him when she spoke.

"Jim, what the hell are the girls doing up? Why aren't they in bed?"

He looked down at Naomie snuggled under his arm. He sensed by her calm undisturbed breathing that she must have fallen asleep. Sitting up gingerly on the edge of the sofa, being careful not to wake Naomie, he rubbed the sleep out of his eyes as he looked at the clock on the wall in front of him. It was a little after ten.

"Look, Kate," he said, trying to justify his decision to let them stay up later then normal. "They don't get a chance to be with me that often. I couldn't see any harm in letting them stay up for a little while. Besides," he said, bringing to her attention that they were both sleeping "if I hadn't dozed off myself I would have put them to bed already."

Naomie's eyes half opened and a little smile emerged from her lips, as he lifted her in his arms and prepared to carry her into her bed. After taking her in and laying her down, he came back out and picked up Kristy. She was in a deep sleep and she felt like a rag doll in his arms as he carried her in to her bedroom. After tucking them both in and giving them a good night kiss, he came back out and lay on the sofa.

Not finding the coffee she found in the pot when she came home to her liking, Kate made a new pot and she was sitting at the kitchen table, leaning back in her chair facing him and sipping a fresh cup when he came back in. He could see from the frown on her face that she was still upset about coming home and finding the kids laying down out in the living room. Not wanting to argue with her, he asked how she had done at bingo.

He sensed her unwillingness to drop the subject and was not surprised when she answered his question, but then went back to the matter of the kids being in the living room when she came home.

"I won one game," she said, "but I had to share it with someone else. Jim, why do you do that?" she said, in what seemed like an attempt to start an argument that he was trying to avoid. "You know that I hate it when you do that. I don't want the kids to get into the habit of falling asleep out here."

"Kate will you just forget about it? It doesn't even happen once a month. I assure you that they are not going to get in the habit of doing it. Did anyone else win anything?" he said, changing the subject again and trying to make it clear to her that the discussion was over and he did not want to talk about it any more.

"Mom won a hundred dollars again," she said, indicating that it was not her first time that she had been so lucky. "But you know how she is. It seems like every time she goes, she wins something."

Kate had been lucky once, he remembered. She had won a jackpot worth almost one thousand dollars. However, that was two years ago and since then he would not be exaggerating to say that she had spent at least five times that much trying to do it again.

His neck was twisted at an uncomfortable angle as he looked at her. He lay back on the pillow and rubbed it trying to relieve some of the soreness, as he listened to her talk about her evening. She went on to tell him about all the times that she had come close, and how frustrated she was when she didn't get the right number.

That's funny, he thought as he listened to her. She went out to relax and have a good time, and now she is telling him how frustrated she has been all evening.

After a while her speech became slow and she started to mumble, making it impossible to hear what she was saying.

Still not wide awake himself and realizing that she had stopped talking, he raised his head up thinking that he had dozed off, to look at her. She was leaning back in her chair with her head resting on her shoulder, fast asleep.

He laid his head back down fighting his own drowsiness and wondered how she could do it. No matter how tired he got, he still didn't think that he could sleep sitting up in a chair. There might have been times when he had been so exhausted that he would have dozed for a few seconds. There were occasions when he had witnessed her sleeping that way for at least several hours.

His own eyelids became heavy and he had just about drifted off to sleep in a much more comfortable position, when he detected a faint thumping noise. It was almost like a dream as he heard it get closer and closer. His eyelids felt like they weighed a ton as he fought to open them and see what this strange sound was that he had heard.

Standing in front of him, a few feet away, was Naomie. A smile spread across her lips as he opened his eyes all the way and she grinned at him.

"Can I lie down by you dad" she said. "You can go back to sleep. I won't bother you. I just want to lay down by you." That soft warm voice of his child pleading for the closeness that only her parents could give, was something that he could never say "no" to.

"Come on," he said, looking over his shoulder at Kate still sleeping, as he rolled over on his side to make more room. He knew from the sound of her voice and the way she rubbed her eyes, that it would only be a matter of minutes before she would be asleep again. He would just have to carry her back into her bed. Helping her up as she snuggled up close to him, he put his arm around her giving her as much room as he could so she wouldn't roll off the sofa if she stirred in her sleep.

"Goodnight, dad I will see you in the morning," she said, copying what both he and her mom always told them when they put them to bed.

He bent over, kissed her on the cheek and whispered in her ear, "Goodnight honey, I will see you in the morning."

Meaning to stay awake, he had not even realized that he had dozed off until he heard a voice that sounded like it was way off in the distance calling him. Opening his heavy eyelids, he discovered that Naomie must have stirred and rolled over. Only his arm around her legs had prevented her from slipping on to the floor. Sliding back a little to give her more room, he eased her back onto the sofa and looked over his shoulder to find Kate staring at him.

Her eyes were glazed over and she looked like she was terrified of someone or something. "Jim", she said, in a deep loathsome voice that made him shudder. "What the hell are you doing? I thought you put them to bed. What is Naomie doing out here?"

"Kate," he said, trying to understand the reason for the look on her face and her tone of voice. "She was sleeping but she must have had a bad dream or something. All I know is I had dozed off and woke up to fine her standing here wanting to lie down by me. What is wrong with you anyway? You look like you have seen a ghost."

"I don't know, Jim. I thought I seen something. I woke up and when

I saw you lying there with Naomie I thought I saw you with your hand in her underpants."

"Kate, are you nuts? I have lain down with these kids hundreds of times. You know I wouldn't do anything like that. You know I couldn't do anything like that."

"Jim, I am sorry. It was just that when I woke and saw you, it was like a dream. I felt like something had happened. I don't know where or even when, but I felt like something had happened."

Their conversation had awakened Naomie, and she was sitting up on the edge of the sofa rubbing her eyes. "Hi, mom" she said with a wily little grin.

"Hi, Naomie," she answered her. "What are you doing up so late?"

"I woke up and I just wanted to lay down by dad," she said, still grinning like she had gotten away with something.

Kate came over and after giving Naomie a hug and a kiss she stood up and turned to Jim with a different kind of a look on her face.

"Jim, I am sorry. After what I have accused you of I wouldn't blame you for being angry at me. I almost hate to ask you this, but would you please take Naomie in on our bed and lay down with her and see if you can get her to go back to sleep?"

"Kate, I am not angry with you—I am just confused," he said as he took Naomie by the hand. "It just bewilders me why you would think that I could do such a thing to our kids."

Within a few minutes after laying down with her, Naomie went back to sleep and he picked her up and carried her into her own bed. Kate was sitting in a chair staring off into deep space when he came back into the living room. It appeared as if she was traumatized and her mind and body were in a different time and place. She wasn't even aware of his presence when he knelt down beside her until he spoke, startling her back to consciousness.

"Kate, are you okay?" he said, reaching out to take her hand in his. What is the matter? What is happening with you?"

"I don't know Jim," she said, taking his hand with her own trembling fingers. "I feel like there is something that happened a long time ago, but it frightens me, and whenever I try to think about it my mind just goes completely blank. Come on," she said, getting up, still holding his hand and kissing him on the lips. "The kids are all sleeping. I am tired and you are tired, so let's go to bed."

The lieutenant had been leaning back in his chair with his arms crossed as Jim unraveled what he thought was the solution to this bewildered situation. Sensing that Jim was just about through, he sat forward resting his arms on the desk as if he were about to say something.

Jim couldn't help thinking as he waited for the officer to speak about CYS and the meeting that Kate had a couple of weeks ago with them. He knew that it had to do something with this. He was sure that something they done or said had triggered a regression deep into her past where something traumatic had happened. Her fear of recalling the incident was evidence to the serious nature of what must have transpired.

"Is that everything, Mr. Hess?" he said, as if he wanted to make sure that he was finished before he commented on what he had just heard. "You understand, Mr. Hess, that these are very serious charges and you could be looking at some lengthy jail time. But being as this is your first offense, I am sure that the judge will probably be quite lenient and be persuaded to let you off with several years probation with the required counseling."

Jim sat in awe as he listened to the officer construe the penalties befitting the charges against him. From his manner of speech, he seemed to be making it quite clear that he had not taken anything Jim had said into consideration. It appeared to Jim that in the eyes and the mind of this officer, he was already tried and convicted, and all that remained was the matter of sentencing.

Recovering from the officer's sudden interpretation of the law, he became angry at his assumption of his predetermined guilt and began to lash out at him.

"Lieutenant, haven't you heard anything that I have said? I told you everything that happened. It has got to be obvious that this whole thing is a big mistake."

Officer Kotter sat up and slid his chair back, getting up he walked around the back of his chair to the window sill and pointed to a row of books that Jim had noticed earlier. "You see these, Mr. Hess? These are only some of the books that contain the laws on rape, molestation and abuse. Many of their interpretations are unclear and in some cases something as simple as a slight touch can be consider a form of child molestation or abuse."

What bothered Jim was the way he said it: he made it sound like something as simple as changing a baby's diaper could be considered abuse, if for whatever reason it was interpreted in the wrong way. All it would take is someone's sick distorted mind and a few choice words to use the system against some despised individual to destroy their lives forever.

Jim shuddered as he looked at the books and thought about the atrocities committed by mankind that these symbolized.

Kotter turned away from the books and returned to his chair behind the desk. After pausing a few seconds, as if he was thinking about what he was going to say, he began again.

"Mr. Hess, have you ever had any problems with your sex life? Do you and your wife enjoy a normal relationship or is she unwilling, leaving you frustrated most of the time?"

Taken aback by the lieutenant's frank line of questioning about something that he felt was quite personal and none of his business, it didn't take long for him to realize just what he was getting at. All of a sudden, he felt like he was on a witness stand and this line of questioning was meant to suggest to a jury that he had an unhappy and deprived sex life and his frustrations led him to sexually molest his kids.

"Look, lieutenant" he said, becoming irritated by his persistent insinuation of his guilt. "We have been enjoying a perfectly normal sex life, I am not constantly frustrated, and I didn't molest my little girl. Everything had been normal in our life up until a few weeks ago when this all started with a meeting Kate had with CYS. We have even been looking for a place to move after that incident with the neighbors a few months ago and have checked on several places since then."

He assumed that Kotter remembered the incident and knew what he was referring to.

There was a knock on the door, and after acknowledging officer Kotter's approval to come in, another officer entered and came over to speak to the lieutenant.

Jim sat in his chair meditating about the explanation that he had given to the officer for why he felt this had all occurred. He still felt that nothing he said had done him any harm and he had hoped that by enlightening him on the whole situation, it might do him some good. It began to seem pretty obvious by then though, that when he was arrested his destiny had already been predetermined and it was only a matter of time before they would take him to jail.

As he sat there, vaguely overhearing the two officers' conversation, it came to his sudden attention that they were talking about him. After making a phone call, which Jim assumed that was to the county jail when he mentioned bringing a prisoner in, Kotter turned to the other officer and instructed him to put the handcuffs on the prisoner.

Getting up and putting his hands out in front of him as the officer directed, he began to tremble as the officer stepped toward him. His knees felt so weak that he was almost certain that his legs were going to buckle under him. Up until then, in spite of all the events that had taken place, every new development just seemed like another part of some delirious dream. When the officer snapped the handcuffs on his wrists he knew that the inevitable was about to happen, and the sudden awareness of the reality of his situation evoked an incomprehensible terror that began to spread through every nerve in his body.

They escorted him out the police car, and as he slid into the back seat his mind began to race with all the horrors he heard existed within the walls of the jail he was about to be incarcerated in. He had read in the local newspaper on several occasions about the rapes and beatings that went on in there, and in one case even a hanging. He knew what he was accused of was a serious crime, and looked down upon by other prisoners. As they headed toward Warrington, he shivered violently as he envisioned what revulsion might be awaiting him within the confines of those concrete walls.

CHAPTER SIX

It was a short ride to downtown Warrington, and within fifteen minutes they had pulled into the private parking lot in back of the courthouse. The jail was located behind the County Courthouse, just off Main Street in the center of town.

Many times he had driven by this lusterless old gray building, constructed from concrete and stone with the bars encased in what he felt were its few insufficient windows. He had delivered pizza to the courthouse, to several office buildings that surrounded the jail, and every time we walked by it gave him a cold chill when he looked at the steel bars in the windows.

A cold chill again began to creep through his bones now as he stepped out of the back seat of the police car and looked up at the old gray building that always reminded him of a medieval castle. In spite of the cold chill, he began to break into a sweat as they approached the steel doors that separated whatever was contained within these walls from the outside world. Never had he ever envisioned that one day he would step through these doors to experience first hand the horrors that had only existed in newspapers and movies before.

After ringing a buzzer and the two officers escorting him being recognized through a view slit, the door opened and they stepped into a small hallway. They paused for a few seconds as Kotter and the other officer removed their guns and handed them through a window to a man dressed in dark brown trousers and a light tan shirt with patches on the shoulders, that identified him as a County Sheriff's Deputy. Jim knew from the many movies and TV shows he had seen that it was a precautionary measure and that no one wore any weapons inside the jail, where they could be easy accessible to any of the prisoners.

He jumped as the heavy steel door slammed shut behind them. A feeling of despair overcame him as he turned and looked at the locked exit, cutting him off from the outside world and leaving him like a trapped animal.

Another deputy from the other side unlocked another steel door, this one with bars on it. They entered, finding themselves in what appeared to be the main hallway on the first floor of the jail. There were several rows of picnic tables in the center of the expansive floor space, which suggested that this might serve as the dining room.

He took in the repugnant surroundings of what he had the distinct feeling would be his new home for a while as he waited for someone to find the keys to his handcuffs. He felt like he was in a dungeon, as the rank musty odor entered his nostrils making him feel almost sick to the stomach.

There was faint odor of bleach coming from a mop bucket as one of the trustee inmates came out of a room and made an effort to clean the dull gray concrete floor. It was hard to see if he was making any progress as he sloshed the mop back and forth. The walls and ceilings were painted with the same flat gray paint, which was peeling in many places, showing years of neglect and adding even more to the dreary nature of his surroundings.

As he looked around at the doors that seemed to exit from all corners of the room, he couldn't help but become aware of the loud and irritating banging and voices that emitted from them and echoed throughout the building. Judging from what he had already become aware of, it appeared hopeless to think that the intolerable racket wouldn't go on all night, and he wondered how he was going to manage to get any sleep.

Lieutenant Kotter and the other officer, who seemed to be in question as to who had the keys to the handcuffs they had put on him, managed to resolve the issue and after removing the handcuffs, he was directed around the corner to his left into a small office.

Jim emptied his pockets and after finding a clear spot, lay everything on the desk in front of him. He looked around the cramped little room as a burly sergeant sitting behind the desk opened his bulging wallet and began to count his money. Every bit of available space seemed to be taken up with a filing cabinet of some kind. The desk in front of the only chair in the room other than the one that the sergeant was sitting on and the one he had decided to occupy since it was empty, was cluttered with books and stacks of papers. Over in one corner back against the wall stood a huge safe that he imagined must have weighed at least several tons. The top of it was piled high with junk as were all the filing cabinets and any other surface that was flat, giving this overcrowded little office the appearance of being in total disarray.

He wondered, oddly enough, considering what unknown destiny awaited him as the sergeant put his now empty wallet and other items that he had removed from his pocket into an envelope and dropped them into a drawer in one of the filing cabinets, if he would ever be able to find them again.

The sergeant, who he assumed to be the one in charge, slid his money and a receipt across to him and asked him to count it and verify that it was the correct amount on the receipt. After counting and finding his figures to be correct, it was explained to Jim as the sergeant put the money in the safe that it would be put in his account and be available to him if he wished to purchase anything from the jail's commissary.

Noticing that one of the several sheriff's deputies also occupying the room, making it seem all the more overcrowded, appeared to be in wonderment as he noted the amount of cash Jim had been carrying, he decided to satisfy his curiosity.

"It is my life savings," he said, looking at him and all of a sudden wondering in his chaotic state of mind why he had felt it necessary to explain to this officer, or any one else for that matter, how he had accumulated such a amount of money.

A young baby-faced officer, looking like he could still pass for a high school student, came in and led him into another room to be photographed and fingerprinted. His already humiliating feeling sunk to a new low as the officer snapped his picture and he envisioned the long number across his chest that distinguished him as criminal.

After being directed to another room and submitting to a strip search, he was instructed to get dressed and wait out in the hall while the young officer checked to see what cells they had available.

A man dressed in a light blue uniform identifying him as another prisoner came in and handed him a pillow and a blanket as he stood there waiting for the guard to return. He looked around the room, again becoming annoyed by the intense racket that seemed to echo throughout the building and tried to identify its source. It seemed to be coming from everywhere, and the only thing that he was becoming certain of was that it never seemed to stop.

He turned as he noticed out of the corner of his eye the baby-faced officer approach him to the right. The young deputy looked at the blanket and pillow in his arms and a slight smile came across his face, signifying his gratitude of someone having already taken care of that chore for him.

"We have a cell ready for you on the third floor," he said, motioning for Jim to follow him. "I will show you where to go."

Jim suddenly felt giddy as they walked toward a door at the far end of the room. His complete hopelessness of his situation had caused his thoughts to be ridiculously irrational.

Right this way, he thought, just like he was in some boarding house. *Your room is ready. Just follow me.*

They stepped through the doorway and he found himself in a corridor adjacent to a cell-block.

"Just follow those up to the third floor," the officer said, pointing to the stairs at the end of the corridor. "There will be someone up there to take care of you."

His eyes were affixed on the stairs that the officer had pointed to and he wasn't even aware as he slowly walked toward the staircase that it was the women's cell block he was partially passing through, until he heard someone shout. He instinctively turned and looked to his left, searching for the source of the woman's voice that had momentarily startled him. Several women inmates had become aware of his presence and had stood up peering through the bars of their cells to get a good look at the new prisoner that they had brought in. Even as he turned away from them, he could still feel their eyes follow him as he covered the short distance to the stairs.

"Hey, baby," he heard the same voice say, as he started up the steps. "What did they put you in here for?"

He didn't look back or answer her; he had enough problems of his own to contend with, as his feet and even his legs felt like they were filled with lead every time he tried to raise them the few inches to take another step.

Each step was agonizing. His head began to reel and he began to stagger as he realized that each step brought all of his submerged fears closer and closer to reality. He looked behind him and in spite of being terrified with each step, he started to feel giddy again as he discovered that he had been climbing a spiral staircase, just like he imagined would be in an old castle.

After stumbling several times, he made it to the third floor and stepped through the open doorway. The room was similar to downstairs, although somewhat smaller, with tables and benches. To his right and left were steel doors with a view slit in them, like the one downstairs that shut them off from the outside world. They stood open, and looking beyond them he could see the cells that housed the prisoners, the major source of the now almost unbearable noise.

A guard had been sitting at one of the tables reading a book when he came in and he stood up and motioned for him to come over to the side of the room where he was sitting. Taking the ring of keys from his belt, he moved toward the door on his right as Jim approached him. Pausing a moment after stepping through the open doorway into the cell block while he unlocked the door, to what he could only describe as a steel cage, he surveyed his temporary home.

They were in a room, with the only exit being the doorway that they just entered. Surrounding the steel cage that he was about to be enclosed in was about a three foot- space on all sides. There were two windows on each of the three outside walls, but with the distance separating them, it made it next to impossible to distinguish anything on the outside other than the difference between night and day.

He looked inside the cage and at the three inmates whose attention he had attracted by his presence. There were five separate cells with two bunks in them. Another cell on his left contained a shower with a ragged and torn mildew plastic shower curtain hanging over the door.

Each cell was separated by a concrete wall, but both ends contained steel bars, leaving them exposed so they could be easily observed by the guards as the made their rounds.

The guard having unlocked the door swung it open and he stepped inside. There was the loud banging of metal against metal that seemed to be to be consistent with some of the various noises that echoed throughout the building, as the guard slammed the door shut behind him. He shivered, standing there behind the locked door of the steel cage, feeling like a animal in a zoo, with the only thing to look forward to being the next feeding time.

Waiting in silence as the three occupants of the cell-block looked at him and sized up the new prisoner they had brought in, he looked more closely now at his temporary accommodations.

In front of him were a table and benches, like the one outside in the hall. Over in the corner, to his left by the shower, stood a mop bucket. Overhead, in front of him mounted in the corner of the cell, was a TV.

He had thought that the loud voices he heard thundering within the confines of the building had belonged to the inmates, but he discovered that it was not the case. Blasting from a channel, signifying the presence of cable at what sounded like the maximum volume, was the source of the inconceivable uproar. Combined with the fact that every cellblock in jail probably contained a TV that was presumably controlled in the same manner, it was not a wonder that the sound reverberated within these walls as it did.

The man nearest him had been sitting when he entered and after observing Jim for a few seconds standing there with the blanket and pillow in his arms, he stood up. "We got two available," he said in a loud voice, turning to his side indicating the empty cell next to him, and then pointing to the cell next to where Jim stood.

Jim looked at the man that had just spoke and the cell next to him and then the cell next to himself, indicating that he had heard him.

He was about Jim's height, of five foot ten and maybe a little lighter then his weight of one ninety. He looked to be around thirty, with neatly cut and combed jet-black hair and a cleanly shaven face. In spite of the current conditions, he appeared to adhere to them quite well by keeping himself clean and well kept.

Choosing the cell next to him, being a few more feet away from the TV, he hoped that the wall to his back might help to muffle some of the sound. Even with being the middle of the afternoon as it was, the light was very dim. Feeling around he found the bunks, but not before bumping his head on the top one as he sat on it waiting for his eyes to adjust. After a few seconds, with the help of the light coming through the window from the outside, he could make out a sink attached to the bars at the other end of his cell and a stool next to it. Beneath him, was a hard thin mattress separating him from a steel bed frame that was attached to the wall by chains.

Laying his blanket and pillow at the head of the bunk, he decided that it was time to go out and introduce himself to the other hapless inmates of this deplorable institution.

As he stepped out of his cell and he attracted the gaze of the three men who seemed to be patiently waiting at the table; Jim glanced up at the single naked light bulb suspended from the ceiling. No wonder the whole cellblock appeared to be so tenebrous—the single bulb hanging from the ceiling was their only source of light.

CHAPTER SEVEN

Under normal circumstances, Jim was an easy person to get along with. He liked people and he made friends easily. However, these weren't normal circumstances and from the looks of his surroundings, it was unmistakably clear that these weren't normal people.

As he sat down at the table, something inside warned him to be cautious and think very carefully about what he was going to say. In spite of their friendly appearance, he could not erase from his mind everything he had heard about what the other inmates did to child molesters and he knew that the only thing that these individuals in here knew about him, what he himself revealed to them.

"I'm Bill," said the clean-cut man who had invited him to take his pick of the cells when he came in, standing up and holding out his hand in a surprising gesture. "I see that you made yourself at home."

"Yeah, but it's sure not much, is it?" Jim commented on the crudeness of diminutive cell.

"Well," said Bill with a grin, "this isn't the Conrad Hilton and it's not exactly known for it's luxurious accommodations. That's Tom, over there" he said, speaking for one of the two black men sitting across the table from them. "And that's Henry," he nodded toward the other one.

Tom was light-skinned and around the same size as Bill, and he guessed him to be about five or six years younger.

Henry was much darker than Tom and several inches shorter. He was also quite heavier than any of them, weighing somewhere around two forty and exhibiting excess flab from his head to his feet.

Tom was the one that started asking the questions that Jim knew was going to be asked sooner or later.

"What have they got you in here for?" he asked, seeking to satisfy, his, as well as the other two inmates' curiosity.

Hesitating a moment, not sure if he should say anything at all, he decided that if he was careful to explain his story piece by piece it might be more easily accepted by them.

"Well," he said. "They arrested me for aggravated assault, with intent to commit bodily harm," purposely omitting the word indecent.

"What did you do—beat the hell out of someone?" asked Tom, urging Jim to fill in all the details.

"No, it was nothing like that," Jim said, meaning to play down the allegations a little, not wanting them to get the impression that he was some kind of a hardened criminal. "The whole thing is kind of complicated and it is a long story."

He had hoped that by making his charges seem less important and telling them it was a long story would have discouraged them. However, as he could see from their reaction, all he had managed to do was make it appear more interesting.

"Well, it doesn't look like we will be going anywhere for a while," added Bill, with a gesture from his hands denoting their inability to leave the cage that they were all locked in.

Jim was still a little uncertain if this was what he should be doing. Nevertheless, relying again on what he had heard and seen in the movies, he was sure that sooner or later the word would get around as to what he was accused of. He paused for a second, thinking as he looked back at the three inmates peering at him from his left and across the table eager to hear him tell his story.

Not knowing him or anything about him, they would be impartial. Their judgment would be based strictly on what information he divulged to them, he thought. Maybe it would be best if he did tell them everything, instead of them finding it out through the grapevine piece by piece in a manner that would twist and distort all the facts.

"Well, it all started" he began, going back three years ago and beginning with their fist encounter with CYS. Step by step he explained the events that led up to his arrest. He tried not to go into too much detail, but at the same time he wanted to make sure that he didn't leave out anything, that would be of vital importance to his situation.

From time to time he was interrupted by one of his three cellmates, and asked questions as to a certain incident that took place. He stopped and satisfied their curiosity, then continued on completing the series of events that led up to his being in there.

When he was through, he added his own speculation and theory making sure he included CYS's critical involvement. In addition, Lieutenant Kotter, who for some reason he felt, judging from the different encounters he had with him, seemed to have an acrimonious dislike for him.

He appeared to have sparked some emotions, as Tom stood up and seemed to explode with a stream of words in defiance of the way he felt that the system had far exceeded its boundaries in their attempt to persecute him.

"Aw—that's bullshit, man! Are these people all to blind and stupid to see what is going on? I don't see how they could have arrested you without any evidence or proof of any kind."

"They said that they didn't need anything but her statement," Jim cut in. "Lieutenant Kotter said that it was all the proof that they needed."

"That don't mean nothing," Tom replied. "If all they got is her word and they don't have anything to back it up, there is no DA in the world that would take something like that to court."

"He's right," said Bill, adding his approval of Tom's summation. "I have seen cases a lot worse than this that never made it to court. From what you have told us, if all they have is her word, it shouldn't be too difficult for any attorney to discredit her as a witness and convince a DA that she is lying. Look," he said, nodding toward Tom and Henry "we are in here for robbery and possession of drugs, but man, you don't belong in here. Your whole case smells of a set-up and it sounds like someone wants you out of the way real bad."

"Do you have your own attorney?" asked Bill, "or do you have to wait for them to assign you a public defender?"

"Well, I do and I don't," replied Jim, thinking about the phone call that Lieutenant Kotter made from his office. "What I mean is, I had them call someone for me, but he wasn't in. He is supposed to contact me. However, until I talk to him, I can't be sure if he will take my case or not. I have got fifteen hundred dollars saved," he added, in an attempt to reassure them that he wasn't broke and at the mercy of the court to defend him.

"That's good," said Tom, clueing him in on the dismal facts that awaited him, if he was broke and couldn't afford an attorney. "You know, if you can't make bail that they can keep you in here for a year before they have to take your case to court."

"It's the worst that can happen," said Bill, adding a few words of reassurance. "In your case, as I can see it, they don't have a leg to stand on. If this attorney that you are supposed to talk to is any good, the chances are he will get you bail reduced to the minimum or even convince them to let you out on your own recognizance."

Judging from their conjecture on how the system works, Jim began to get the impression that this was not the first time the fellow inmates had been involved in the crime scene before. Since he knew little to nothing about the court system and how it worked, he had to consider that at least some of the things that they said were accurate.

Everything being pretty much said and not much else left to discuss until after seeing his attorney tomorrow, his attention turned to his stomach which began to growl, signifying its need for nourishment. He had not eaten breakfast or lunch, and his necessity for food was becoming painfully apparent as he felt a few hunger cramps.

"When do they feed you around here?" he said, still feeling like an animal locked in a cage.

"Not for a couple of hours yet," said Henry, speaking for the first time since Jim had entered the cellblock. "If you are hungry, we have got some cereal," he said, getting up and exiting from his cell within seconds with a big box containing dozens of snack packs of a variety of cereal.

"Anything that we have left over from breakfast Henry here throws in a box and we save it in case someone gets hungry later," Tom said, explaining the reason for the stockpile of cereal that Henry kept in his cell.

"Here, help yourself," said Henry, setting the box on the table in front of him. "Take all you want. We got plenty."

"Thanks" said Jim reaching in and grabbing a couple of boxes, feeling it to be sufficient to satisfy his hunger cravings until feeding time.

Sitting at the table, he looked up at the TV as he began to gulp down his snack. In spite of their conversation since he arrived, no one had bothered to turn the volume down, making it necessary for everyone to speak in an exceptionally loud tone of voice if they wanted to be heard.

He had thought about asking someone to turn it down, especially since MTV was not his best choice for entertainment. Not having much else to do, the TV was the main source of diversion that made their existence tolerable. However, considering the way that he had been accepted since he came in to their dominion, he decided that it was best to leave well enough alone.

The music videos, although not to his liking, he could cope with; it was the volume that began to get on his nerves. He got up and went into his cell, seeking a way to block out the high-pitched screaming voices that blasted out from the corner of his cage.

His eyes being a little better adjusted to the dim light as he sat on his bunk allowed him to see a few details that he had not noticed before.

There were pieces of a couple of pictures stuck to the wall that someone had made a lazy effort to remove. The concrete floor was painted a dirty gray, reflecting very little light and gave the dim enclosure an all the gloomier look. Other than the blanket and pillow he had brought in, the cell contained nothing else. There was no soap, towel or wash rag. There was not even a cup to drink out of.

He stretched out on the hard mattress and transfixed his eyes on the bunk above, trying to block out the noise. The outside door to their cellblock stood open, so not only did they have to contend with all the noises from the TV and the voices of his three cellmates shouting to be heard, but all the similar sounds from across the hall and other floors as well.

His head began to pound and it seemed like the noise was becoming louder by the moment as he lay there motionless. The last time he could remember lying in a cot surrounded by other men was in the Army, over thirty years ago.

Being a frightened, seventeen-year-old kid and away from home for his first time, he was scared out of his wits and never thought that he would survive the first night. Nevertheless, he did and the next night and every night after that. He was young then and knew very little about life, but his experiences over the years had taught him to cope with things far worse than he could ever have imagined.

He was just a scared kid and he had survived everything the Army had thrown at him he thought, as he put his hands over his ears trying to block out some of the clamor that seemed to be filtering in from everywhere in the building.

That was a long time ago and he was much older and wiser now. There was nothing he couldn't deal with if he put his mind to it.

That is, if this insensible noise didn't reduce him to a babbling idiot first, he thought, as the sounds filtered under his clasped hands and seemed to thunder inside his head.

He sat up, taking his hands off his ears. It seemed to have little effect anyway in deadening the noise. There was no way that he was going to be able to stop it, so he knew that somehow he was going to have to adjust to it, like everyone else in here.

Rubbing the stubble on his chin, he took his mind off the noise by concentrating on a few things that he was going to need if he were to spend any length of time in there.

There was nothing to drink out of, and cupping his hands under the faucet to get a drink of water seemed a bit primitive to him, even for a jail. He would need a razor and some soap and towels and since he was not allowed to bring anything with him, he assumed that these things were supposed to be provided for him.

He wished he had a cup of coffee as he sat there twiddling his fingers, thinking about the fresh pot he had made and was still sitting on kitchen counter where he had left it when they arrested him.

It couldn't have been more than three or four hours ago, but it seemed like days as he re-encountered in his mind all the events that had taken place since then.

What he wouldn't do for a cup of that now, he thought, as he became aware of his craving for caffeine. *And, maybe a cigarette,* forgetting that he had quit smoking and mindless of his kicked habit, reaching for his pocket and a cigarette.

His hand stopped in motion, as it triggered the nightmare that he had tried to forget and the reason why he had quit smoking over three months ago.

He had been in this jail before. However, it was not like this and he had experienced none of the things that were happening now.

It had happened the night that he was arrested and charged with allegedly beating his son Ron with a baseball bat three months ago. After refusing to release him in spite of any incriminating evidence, Officer Clancy proceeded to charge him and take him to a magistrate to set bail.

Jim was furious at his actions, contending they had no right to even charge him, based on the eyewitness testimony of at least three people that there was no evidence to what was supposed to be perceived by all of his accusers.

It was almost midnight when they arrived at the county jail, and the rage and contempt that had built up inside of him had prevented him from seeing or thinking about anything rationally.

Although his wife, kids and mother-in-law sat right in the next room at the township jail, he was not allowed to talk to them until after his bond was set several hours later, and he was taken to the county jail.

His fury became all the more intensified when he was told that she was not allowed to come down and post bail there. He would have to wait until morning when she could go the courthouse to make the proper arrangements before he could be released.

He had only two cigarettes left when he first arrived at the county jail. Having a nicotine fit being as it was the first time he had been allowed to smoke since he was arrested, he smoked them both. Overwhelmed by the continuing anger building inside of him since his arrest, he had great difficulty in thinking about anything beyond the present. He had assumed when he first arrived that Kate would be there at any time to bail him out.

As they led him to the cell where they explained he would be kept for the night, his anger subsided just long enough for his mind to form a vivid picture of what lie ahead.

He was out of cigarettes and Kate would not be here until sometime tomorrow morning. The chances of buying a pack off someone seemed very remote and as they walked down a very dimly lit hallway and the guard proceeded to open the door to a single empty cell, his chances of even bumming one seemed very slim.

The night that followed felt like some horrific dream that just seemed to be too real to be happening. He noticed as he walked by several cells on the way to his, that there appeared to be the remnants of someone's dinner lying in the middle of the floor. There were several pieces of chicken that looked dried and crusted as if they had been there for some time.

He wondered in disgust as he stepped around it if this was an example of what this place was like. He couldn't understand how anyone in their right mind would leave food rotting in the middle of the floor.

It was damp and chilly and goose bumps began to pepper his exposed flesh. He had nothing on but a tank top shirt when he left the house and he began to shiver as he entered the cell and the guard locked the door behind him.

It had been a long day and all the events of that evening had left him physically and mentally exhausted. He lay down on the bunk and felt around in the dark for a blanket or something to cover up with. There was no blanket or sheet, or even a pillow—just a hard thin mattress that separated him from the steel bunk attached to the wall by chains.

He had hoped that as tired as he was he would be able to fall asleep, leaving that much less time that he would have to suppress the craving desire for a cigarette.

He laid his head down and closed his eyes, attempting to surrender to his body's exhaustive state. In spite of his determination to sleep, the relentless noise that echoed through the halls prevented him from drifting into total unconsciousness. Every time it seemed as if he would drift off into an insensible state of mind, a loud noise of some kind would bring him back to reality and his urgent craving for nicotine.

The damp chill felt like it had penetrated his flesh all the way to the bone and he drew his knees up, curling into a ball in an arduous attempt to keep warm. Feeling a need to go the bathroom, he got up and bumped into the stool before finding it in the dark cell.

There were concrete walls on three sides of what he later discovered they called "the hole." The only light that entered was through the door from the single bulb that hung high overhead in the hallway. Even with his eyes becoming accustomed to the dark, it was still difficult to make out anything clearly.

The sink was a little easier to find, partially visible in the front corner of the cell, but he wound up wiping his hands on his pants after washing them, not being able to find a towel to wipe them on.

He grabbed a hold of the bars, peering through them, concentrating at what lay on the other side in a effort to suppress that nicotine craving that was stronger than ever.

There was a brick wall facing him instead of cells and to his left there was a steel door with a view slit in it that led to who knows where. He could not see far to his right, but the hall looked empty except for the food that was still lying on the floor when they came in.

He wondered what time it was as a crazy thought of counting the bricks in the wall in front of him to take his mind off a cigarette entered his head. They had taken his watch and he had no way of telling time.

The blind fury that had raged within him throughout the evening had dulled his senses and combined with the light-headed effects from the withdrawal of nicotine, he had lost all consciousness of time. He had no idea if he had been in here for twenty minutes or two hours.

He listened intently to the sounds that rebounded through the halls, trying to detect something among the chaotic confusion that would give his some inclination as to what time of the morning it was.

As he listened to the mumbling voices, the desire for a cigarette struck him so hard that he felt like slamming his head against the bars. Someone had lit a cigarette and the smoke drifted down the hall and entered his nostrils, making him feel like he was going to go completely mad if he didn't have one right away.

He had to do something, anything to keep his mind off smoking. Staring at the brick wall, he even considered counting the bricks again, no matter how insane it seemed.

His mind drifted back to early that evening when Officer Clancy arrested him. It was not only the neighbors that had caused all of this, but he was the one who was responsible for him being in here.

Suddenly he started to tremble, as he felt the anger slowly begin to envelop all of his senses. All of his thoughts began to focus on the scene that took place when Clancy arrested him at his house.

Clancy had become very belligerent when Jim told him that this whole thing was all nonsense and he couldn't just come to his house and arrest him. The hard line look on his face as he came toward him removing his handcuffs from his belt was enough to convince Jim that he had no intentions of listening to him tell his side of the story.

A few seconds ago he was trembling with a damp chill, but now he was trembling with rage as he gripped the steel bars with such a force that his knuckles turned white and the sweat began to drip off his forehead. There was no reason for him to apply the handcuffs the way he did, cutting off all circulation and causing excruciating pain. All he had done was ask him to let him call his wife and wait until she came home and straightened this whole thing out.

He had done nothing to deserve his arm being twisted behind his back and slammed onto the back of the police car. All of this happened in front of his kids as they stood trembling and terrified as they watched.

He released his grip on the bars, still trembling. With sweat dripping off his forehead, he turned and sat down on the bunk.

God, he hated that cop. He had experienced anger and hatred before, but nothing had ever affected him like this.

He lay back on his bunk and closed his eyes as a mental image of the detested cop came into view. He was in his middle to late twenties and about five eleven in height. He was a little on the stocky side, weighing what he guessed to be two ten, but carried his weight well and looked to be in top physical condition. His close-cropped hair cut and picture perfect appearance made him seem like he would make a very appropriate candidate for a poster at some Marine recruiting station.

It was his face that presented the clearest image though: the grin across his lips suggested to Jim that he was about to take great pleasure in what he was proceeding to do. There was never anything that presented itself as a gravity situation, justifying such adamant actions. Jim felt beyond a doubt Clancy had let his personal emotions take control of the situation rather than acting in the performance of his duty as a police officer.

Hearing a strange voice, he had sat up opening his eyes to see if he could tell where it was coming from.

"Do you want something to eat?" said a voice that he soon discovered was coming from a man standing outside in the hall in front of his cell door.

At first he thought he was dreaming, but the craving for a smoke brought him to a sudden consciousness.

"Yeah," he said, feeling that anything he ate or drank would help take his mind off a cigarette. "Hey," he said, standing up quickly as the man turned and started to walk away. "Is there any chance that you could get me a cup of black coffee too, if it's not too much trouble.'"

"Sure," the man said. "I will see what I can do."

"Hey, you got any smokes?" came a voice spoken from someone on his right.

"No" Jim replied, assuming the words were meant for him, and feeling strange talking to someone so close to him that he couldn't see. "I am all out."

"Yeah, me too," the voice said. "I just run out. Maybe I can bum a couple off one of the guards when he comes in."

"Hey," Jim asked, getting used to the feeling of talking to someone he couldn't see and trying to form a visual image of what he looked like. "Do you have any idea what time it is?"

"Well, man, I don't know exactly, but it's breakfast, so it has got to be somewhere around seven thirty or eight o'clock."

That's impossible, Jim thought as he turned away from the door and sat on his bunk desperately craving a cigarette. It can't be seven thirty; I just laid down a few minutes ago.

Then, it dawned on him what had happened: he had been standing at the door gripping the bars when he began thinking about Clancy. When he lay on the bed and closed his eyes, he blocked out everything in his mind and concentrated only on the unrestrained anger that he had let take control of his senses. That was the last thing he remembered until he heard the voice outside his cell that woke him up.

It was incredible, but frightening, he thought, as he again began to tremble thinking about the arrogant manner in which Officer Clancy had acted. Realizing it was what was firing his emotions, he was surprised that hatred could be so powerful as to control one's mind and spirit.

In spite of the danger of stimulating his contemptuous fury, it had led to some good. For over eight hours now, it had stymied his overpowering addiction for nicotine. It was the first time he had gone that long without a cigarette in over thirty-five years.

Hearing a shuffle of feet, he looked up to see the inmate trustee that had been there before holding a tray in his hands. On it was a bowl, a carton of milk and two small boxes of cereal, also, a large mug of steaming black coffee.

"Hey," said the faceless voice that Jim had not yet been able to attach an image to. "You got an extra smoke I can bum?"

"Yeah, I guess," he said, taking a pack out of his pocket and after shaking out a couple, reached over to his left out of Jim's sight. "How about you, bud?" he said, motioning toward the bars of Jim's cell. "Do you want a couple, too?"

Jim looked at the filter-tipped cigarette protruding from the pack a few feet away, desperately fighting the urge to jump up and grab one. He felt like a man dying of thirst being offered a drink of water. His throat was parched and the nicotine craving racked his body, reaching every nerve ending and causing him to fidget uncontrollably.

He picked up the cup of coffee in his shaking hands and paused a second, savoring the rich aroma before sipping it. Then, looking up at the man standing there patiently awaiting an answer, he said. "No thanks, mister—I think I just quit."

That was three months ago when he said those words and he had never smoked a cigarette since. Although he had kicked the nicotine habit he still enjoyed his coffee, and he sure wished he had a cup now as he sat there thinking about what he was going to do to get himself out of this mess.

It wasn't so much the accusations that Kate had made that worried him the most, because he knew they weren't true; it was the confident manner in which Lieutenant Kotter acted when he arrested him and up until the time they brought him to jail. The way he had told him what he would probably get when convicted left no doubt as to what he believed the outcome of his case would be. The way everything seemed so cut and dried left Jim hesitant to believe that there wasn't more to his being arrested than what there appeared to be.

Crazy as it seemed, Jim wondered if there could be some kind of a connection between the last incident in September. Although the charges were dismissed, nothing really seemed to have been settled.

After the hearing, which he had later discovered was postponed for three weeks while Clancy and Kotter made an arduous attempt to get his so-called "staunch" witnesses to testify, Clancy had profoundly proclaimed to Jim's attorney that he had done nothing out of line and he still believed that Jim was guilty as hell.

With the opinion that Clancy had asserted, and Kotter being present at the hearing and his superior, he had probably agreed with him. Adding to it the domestic dispute that Kotter had presided over involving the rent, it was not a wonder that Kotter was convinced that he could make Jim out to be a bad guy.

Still, there had to be something besides all this. None of those things could be proved and had no bearing on his case. He couldn't seem to shake the feeling that CYS was somehow behind this whole thing and the main reason for Kotter's assurance that he had an airtight case.

Of course he knew speculation was all he had to go on as he sat on the edge of his bunk mind searching, finding success in its distraction from the noise around him.

Hearing the rattle of keys, he looked up in the dim light to see the guard unlocking the door to their cage.

Glancing toward the window and the diminishing light from the outside, he guessed that it must have been around five o'clock and dinnertime. He was right, as a food cart similar to what he had seen in hospitals appeared in the doorway and an inmate took four trays out and set them on the table. He also set two large containers on the table, which Jim discovered were filled with juice and coffee.

Seeing as he didn't have a cup, he asked the inmate for one. In spite of his craving for a cup of coffee, he could only take a couple of sips. It was so laden with cream and sugar that it began to make him sick to his stomach.

The meal was quite satisfying, and after hearing all the stories about the way that prisoners were fed in jail, he was surprised at how good the food was.

After dinner they sat around the table engaged in idle conversation. Among other things, it was explained to him that they had a simple set of rules in their cellblock that had to abide by; they took turns sweeping and moping the floor, everyone took a shower every day, and made sure that they cleaned up after themselves.

Jim noticed as they chatted about almost anything that came to mind, that their conversation never centered around any one of the inmate's personal lives or the reason for their confinement. The only thing that he knew so far was what was mentioned when he first came in the cell, but he never knew how long any of them had been there or how long they still had to serve. He gathered from what he had seen and heard so far that these things were seldom discussed and he decided to leave well enough alone and not ask any questions.

Bill got up, looking at the commercial that had just come on and switched channels on the TV, announcing that it was time for his favorite show, "Marty Stauffer's Wild Kingdom."

Finally, Jim thought, something he liked, and anything besides MTV.

That was not the worst of it as Jim soon discovered.

Bill and Tom, being in there the longest, primarily controlled what was viewed on the TV. Toms craze seemed to be MTV, but when it came to basketball, Bill was an extremist. He watched every game that came on and even jumped back and forth from channel to channel when more than one game was on at a time. Wild Kingdom only lasted an hour and when it was over, basketball came on and stayed on until the cable was turned off at eleven in the evening.

Although Jim liked to play basketball, he never took much interest in the game on the national level and he picked up a deck of cards he found lying on the ledge on top of one of the cells and began to play solitaire.

Henry, seeing his interest in cards, came over to join him and was soon followed by Tom and Bill. While still watching basketball, they joined in playing cards and what Jim was finding out was another one of the their favorite pastimes.

Sometime during the course of the evening, Tom had gotten up and went into his cell. He came back out with a cup of hot water and a large packet of instant coffee in his hands.

"You want some?" he asked, noticing Jim eyeing up the bag of coffee.

"Thanks, I would sure appreciate it," Jim replied, as he got up and went into his cell and filled his cup with hot water from the faucet.

In spite of the TV and the card games time still seemed to drag on, but with Tom generously letting Jim help himself to his coffee, things began to become much more tolerable.

Later that evening when the card games broke up, Henry let Jim borrow a towel and Tom and Bill chipped in with soap and a razor.

The shower felt good, relaxing him after the exhausting day and he hoped that it would help him sleep. It was after eleven when he lay in his bunk, and he tried to concentrate on something that would block out the racket that continued after the TV was turned off.

The steel door to their cell-block was closed, but loud voices still echoed throughout the building, leaving little doubt as to whether some of the inmates stayed up until the early hours of the morning.

There was no "lights out," simply because they never turned them off. The single bulb that hung over their cell block stayed on, with the dim light filtering into his cell making sleeping all the more difficult.

All the events of the day were reeling through his head as he tried to drift off to sleep. The half dozen cups of coffee he had consumed wasn't helping matters any and he couldn't help thinking, as his head pounded with the noise that seemed to be all the more magnified as he lay down about what was going to happen tomorrow.

He wasn't even sure if Frank would represent him or not. In addition, if he did, then there was the question in his mind as to how much it was going to cost. Sure, he had fifteen hundred dollars and the check he still had at work, plus a few more hundred he could scrape up, it came to a little over two thousand. Nevertheless, he also knew how expensive attorneys were.

His main concern was getting out of jail. If he could get Frank to represent him long enough to get his bond reduced so he could get out of there, he knew that he would much better be able to deal with what was to come next.

As it stood now he was completely powerless. With no one to help him from the outside, he felt like his immediate fate rested in the hands of the man that he hoped was coming to see him in the morning.

With these thoughts on his mind he managed to surrender to a fitful sleep, tossing and turning and awakening with each new and strange sound.

Sometime during the night, he was awakened to full consciousness by the rattling and jingling of keys. Propping himself up on his elbow so he could see, he discovered the origin of the rattling keys coming from the guard unlocking the outside door to their cell block so he could come in and make his rounds. He followed him with his eyes as he walked to his left out of sight. Amid the other sounds, from the footsteps of his hard-soled shoes on the concrete floor and the shuffling of feet as he stopped at each cell to make sure a prisoner hadn't slipped away during the night, Jim sensed his almost exact location as he made his way around to his cell.

Laying his head back down on the pillow, he could feel the guard's eyes stare at him through the bars as he paused for a few seconds, and then, his being the last cell, continued on back through the steel door, slamming and locking it behind him.

Closing his eyes, he soon drifted off to sleep, only to again be awakened by the rattling of keys and the loud banging of steel doors. Only this time it was accompanied by voices.

CHAPTER EIGHT

"Hey, you want something to eat?" came a voice that he didn't recognize as one of his cell-mates.

"No," he said, not even opening his eyes and feeling the need for sleep far more imperative than food. Mainly due to sheer exhaustion, he drifted off again amidst the voices and the TV that had again been turned on.

He didn't know how long he had dozed off when a thundering noise awakened him with such a start that he sat up, banging his head on the bunk above him and imagining that the whole building was about to collapse around him.

Rolling out of his bunk rubbing his head, he stood up as the sound came again, seeming to shake not only the ceiling, but also even the floor under his feet.

Stepping out of his cell, he didn't get the chance to question the source of phenomenal racket before Tom seeing volunteered the information.

"The weight room is on the next floor, right over our heads," he said grinning, as if he was finding it amusing that Jim had been awakened in the manner that he had. "It goes on from nine to eleven every morning and two to four every afternoon," he said, pointing at the ceiling.

He sat at the table as another thump that sounded like it was coming right through the ceiling rumbled through the cell-block.

Shit, he thought. *Could things get any worse?*

There was a pitcher sitting on the table and thinking that it might be juice, he took the top off to check. It was coffee left over from breakfast and from the looks of it, no one seemed to have touched it.

"I don't know why they keeping sending it in here," said Bill, as he observed Jim looking at it. "No one drinks it and we just wind up dumping it down the drain. We just saved it in case you wanted some."

"No thanks," Jim said, picking it up and heading back into his cell to dump it down the stool. "I tried it last night."

He filled his cup with hot water and got the packet of instant coffee that Tom had given him, after he had drank a half a dozen cups, explaining the he didn't drink much and he could pay him back later.

Coming back out to the table, he sat down with his coffee and picked a deck of cards laying them out for a game of solitaire, while he waited to hear something from his attorney.

It was after nine, he guessed, from what Tom had said about the timetable they had for the weight room. How long, he wondered, would he have to wait for Frank to show up? That is, he thought as he shivered with the sudden realization of it being quite possible that it could happen, if he decides to show up at all.

He didn't have to wait long. He barely had a chance to start the game when he heard the familiar rattle of keys behind him.

"Mr. Hess, your attorney is downstairs to see you," the guard said, as he unlocked the door to their cage.

He got up and headed for the door, stopping when he realized he had forgotten his shirt and shoes, and stepped back into his cell to put them on.

He retraced his steps from last night and made his way back down to the first floor, again attracting the attention of the female inmates and drawing shouts and dubious remarks as he passed through the corridor past their cells.

Entering into the main hall, he spotted Frank across the room talking to one of the deputies. Recognizing Jim, he broke off his conversation with the deputy and ushered him toward a cell in the corner of the room with a table and chairs, where they could be alone to sit down and talk.

After sitting down and seeming to make himself as comfortable as possible, he explained to Jim the seriousness of the charges, then he proceeded to tell him the news that he had been waiting for. He would represent him for a minimum fee of seven hundred and fifty dollars. "But of course," he explained, "that was only for his services to get his bond reduced and to represent him at the arraignment hearing. If his case were held over for trial it would cost him considerably more. And' he added, 'if he still wanted to be represented, Jim would have to give him a check for the seven hundred and fifty dollars before he could discuss anything any further.'

Jim looked at Frank, astonished at the figure that he had quoted him. At the hearing when he had first utilized his services in a case that he felt was not much different than this, it had cost him three hundred dollars.

However, he thought, as he suddenly realized the situation that he was now in, *before he was recommended by CYS and actually acquired by them for his needs. Now he was implementing his services to oppose the same people that first recommended him.* Somehow he couldn't get over the feeling that he was being taken advantage of, but as he thought of the desperate situation that he was facing, it seemed like he had little choice other than to apply for a public defender.

"Okay," he said, feeling like he was trapped into making the only logical decision that was left to him. "What do we do now?"

"I am going to ask them to write me a check," he said, getting up from his chair. "Then I am going to bring it in here for you to sign. After that is taken care of, we can get down to business."

Now that his case had been settled temporarily from a financial viewpoint, Franco sat down and began with an opening statement that left Jim at first in total disbelief and then trembling in anger.

"Did you know that Lieutenant Kotter called your wife and told her that you had signed a confession?" he said. "I talked to Detective Kotter myself and he said that when he arrested you and took you down to the station, you made a complete confession."

Jim sat there for a few seconds just looking at Franco and thinking, so angry that he was unable to speak.

It was all a ruse: Kotter sitting there like Mr. Nice Guy wanting Jim to tell him the whole story so he could better understand what it was all about. Jim had told him nothing that would incriminate him in any way. He had taken everything Jim had said and used it in such a way as to look as if he had made a confession.

No wonder he seemed so convinced that Jim would be convicted. If his little scheme worked, it would be Jim's word against his in a court of law and he knew whose words would prevail.

"Franco, I didn't make any confession—all I did was tell him what I thought caused her to make the accusation that she did, which put me in here. And I didn't sign anything," he said, noting that Kotter had told Kate that he did.

"Jim, you didn't need to sign anything—this guy is a lieutenant on the police force, and well known and respected within the court system. Who do you think they are going to believe, when or if you go to court? You shouldn't have told him anything," he said. "At least not without a attorney present—that is why they read you your rights."

As Jim sat there and listened to Franco's depiction of Kotter, he felt that if his few words had spawned such a confession as he claimed existed, then it wouldn't have made any difference if he had said anything at all and he would have produced one anyway. He was far too confident for Jim not to have believed that from the moment he was arrested his destiny had already been predetermined.

"All right," he said. "We will have to deal with that when we come to it. Now, first things first," he continued, after agreeing that his bond seem a bit high considering that he had no record. "I will go to the judge tomorrow and see if I can have your bond reduced to ten percent so you can post bail."

Touching on everything that seemed relevant at the time, they parted, with Franco promising to get in touch with him as soon as he received a ruling from the judge, and Jim heading back upstairs to his cell.

He had spent one night in jail and survived, and with the possibility of getting out tomorrow to look forward to, he was sure that tonight would be a lot easier to cope with.

The guard unlocked the door to his cage and he stepped in, not quite feeling as bad as yesterday when the door shut behind him.

"Well?" Tom asked before he even had a chance to sit down at the table.

Henry had gone upstairs to the weight room and Tom and Bill were sitting at the table, eager to hear some good news when he walked in.

"You came back?" said Tom, almost seeming surprised that he had. "What happened—didn't the attorney take your case?"

"Yes, he took my case" Jim said, then explained about his attorney going to the judge to get his bond reduced tomorrow. He didn't go in to detail after that, nor did he mention the improvised confession that Kotter was supposed to have in his possession.

What followed was Tom and Bill's opinion as to what Jim could foresee in the future. Bill, judging from the way he interpreted the law, seemed to be the legal expert, reassured Jim by telling him that if he had any kind of an attorney, it would be a simple matter for him to get his bond reduced. Based on the fact that he had no record and there was no reason that he would be considered a threat to society, there was a great possibility that he even could be released on his own recognizance.

The last part sounded too good to be true and from what Jim had experienced so far, he had little faith in such a thing happening.

Jim was off Tuesday when he was arrested, but Wednesday he was on the schedule to work. He knew that he would have to get in touch with his boss Mark sooner or later and tell him where he was and why he would not be able to make it to work. The next most important thing next to getting out of jail was his job. It was his only hope in getting out of the mess he was in.

There was a phone in their cage, which at first he thought seemed a bit unusual. As he picked up the receiver and dialed his credit card number, it occurred to him that their freedom of movement was limited to the confines of their cage. Due to the fact that phone calls were one of the few privileges that prisoners had, it would be highly impractical for the guard to come and unlock the cage and let someone out every time they wanted to make a phone call.

As he waited for the operator, he tried not to even think about what would happen to his life if he were to get fired over this incident. Without any income, he would not be able to afford an attorney and his case would be turned over to a public defender. He began to get a grim feeling as he thought about all the stories he had heard about how people were represented by court-appointed attorneys.

The phone receiver had been resting on his shoulder and he put it to his ear as he heard the voice of the operator come over the line.

"I am sorry sir, but your call did not go through. Would you like to try again?"

He was sure that he dialed the right number, but it seemed obvious from the operator's response that he had made a mistake, so he dialed it again. He got the same reply, and knowing this time that he hadn't dialed the wrong number, he hung up the phone wondering what was wrong. His phone bill was paid and he knew that his credit card number was good, but, nevertheless, his number seemed to be invalid.

Very little goes unseen or unheard in a prison cell, and Bill, guessing the problem he was having, gave him the answer to his wonderment of the telephone system.

"If you are trying to use a credit card, it won't work," he said. "You can only call collect on these phones."

Now if that isn't a hell of a note he thought, as he thanked Bill and picked up the receiver again.

Although it seemed a bit odd that he would be calling him collect, he was sure that once Mark heard his voice he would accept his call.

"Hi Jim, what's up?" came the welcomed answer that he had hoped for. "What's with the collect call? Where are you, anyway?"

"Mark, listen," he said, hardly recognizing his own shaky voice, as he struggled to contain the emotions he felt when he heard him tell the operator he would accept the charges. "I am in big trouble—I am in jail. Kate had me arrested."

In the next few minutes, Jim recounted all the events as they happened since he had last seen Mark the day before yesterday. He had to stop several times to clear his throat, as the memory of his ordeal caused him tremble and choke up inside, making it difficult to continue.

"My God, Jim!" he said, after pausing a few seconds as if taking time to absorb the unimaginable story he had just heard. "It is hard to believe that Kate would do such a thing!"

It was the way that he answered that revealed what he felt. It left no doubt in Jim's mind as to whether or not he believed him, as he continued with his speculation of what he felt had brought this all on.

"I have a attorney," he told him. "I just finished talking to him and he is going to see the judge tomorrow and see if he can get my bond reduced. I really can't do much until then. And," he added, revealing a little of the feelings that he had been holding back, "I hope he can get me out of here soon, because I don't think I can stand it too much longer."

"Hey Jim," Mark said, sensing his depression and trying to raise his spirits, by reassuring him that he was tough enough to handle anything in spite of how dismal the days ahead looked. "Come on," he said. "Things will work out. You just got to give it time and hang in there."

He knew that Mark meant well; however, he couldn't help thinking that it was easy for him to say, being as he wasn't the one in sitting in jail in constant fear of the next day, or even what the next minute might bring.

"Mark," he said, bringing up the issue that he felt was most important if he was going to make it through this "I don't know when I am going to get out of here. It might be tomorrow and it might not be until after my hearing next week. But when I do, I am going to need money to pay my attorney."

Sensing what he was leading up to, Mark stopped him before he could say any more. "Jim, if its your job that you are worried about— don't. Whenever you get out of there, it will be waiting for you. Look, Jim, I have got to get set up, so I am going to have to leave you go, but I want you to call me as soon as you find something out. Okay?"

"Thanks, Mark," he said, wishing that there was something else that he could think of to say that would really express what he felt.

After hanging up the phone, he felt a little relieved as he sat down at the table and he announced to no one in particular that he had just spoken to his boss and he still had his job.

He sat there and watched TV for a few minutes, thinking about the next phone call he knew that he was going to have to make. He had to call Kate's mother. He didn't even know if she would accept the call, but he had to find out. Her family had known him for nine years and he felt that they couldn't turn their backs on him regardless of how the situation looked. They had to know the real truth and he was the only one who could tell it to them.

It was going to be a very difficult call to make; he didn't know what Kate had told them, or what they believed. As he went back over to the phone and dialed the operator, he somehow felt like he had to convince Kate's mother that she was a liar.

The operator asked him to say his name. Kate's cousin J. R. had answered the phone and there was a pause as he waited for his call to be accepted. Instead of hearing his voice after a few seconds, there came a loud click and then the dial tone.

He still held the phone to his ear, finding it hard to believe that this was his answer. His feelings sunk to a new low as an instant fear of desperation and loneliness began to overtake him.

He had to try again; there had to be some mistake. J. R. must have asked if it was okay to accept the call, and before he could get a response from anyone he had been disconnected. It had to be the reason. There was only one way he was going to find out for sure, and that was to call back.

Kate's mother answered this time. He held his breath, trying not to think about what he would do if she refused to accept the charges. There was no click this time; instead her mother's voice came over the line.

"Jim, I am sorry," she said. "I was in the bathroom when you called. I told J. R. he should have accepted the charges, but he said that he knew how Uncle Harley was about the phone bill and he thought he better ask me first. By the time he got back to the operator it was too late and he had already gotten the dial tone."

Jane and Harley had raised their two nephews, Don and his brother J. R. J. R. had a serious learning disability, which hindered him from thinking quickly or clearly and was currently receiving a monthly check from S.S.I. It was a little hard to believe at first, but after she explained it the way she did it made sense and he could understand how the operator might have hung up on him.

"Mom," he said, having got in the habit some time ago of calling her that.

His mother and father had been dead for many years and the rest of his relations were living in Iowa, far away. Since he had married Kate, he had always felt like he was part of her family.

"I didn't know who else to call," he said, his voice trembling as he tried to recover from the dismal feeling he felt after being hung up on. "After we got disconnected the last time, I didn't think that you wanted to talk to me and I didn't know what to do. Somehow I knew that there had to be a mistake and I had to try again."

"Mom, look, I am sorry—I know she is your daughter, but she is lying. I love my kids and you have got to believe that I could never do anything like that."

"Jim, you don't have to explain. I understand," she said. "I think that I can speak for everyone in the family when I say that we believe you. Ever since Kate came back from CYS that Friday a couple of weeks ago waving the papers around that they had given her, we have been suspicious of everything she has had to say."

As she started to explain what had happened, Jim realized that his denial to Kate's accusations had not been necessary, because if they believed for a minute that he was guilty, Kate's mother would not be talking to him now.

He stopped her when she mentioned the papers, hearing about them for the first time and wondering what she was talking about.

"Mom, what papers?" he asked her.

"Oh, I am sorry," she said, excusing her ignorance. "I guess there is no way that you could have known about them. Well," she continued, "I guess the reason she had the appointment with Mariane Mayer, that caseworker from CYS, was to discuss what was in the papers she was showing to everybody."

"Well, what was in the papers?" he said, anxious for her to get to the point.

"I gather from what I read," she continued, "that she was under suspicion from CYS for sexually molesting Ron.

"It seems that the in last foster home he was in, a couple of weeks before the meeting with Mariane Mayer, there was a problem. He was supposed to have exposed himself to one of the girls in the home and I assumed," she said, "according to the way I read it that he was playing with his penis. It did not mention the name of the people's home he was in or the name of the little girl, only that she told her parents what happened and when they asked Ron why he did it, he just said that his mother plays with him all the time."

There weren't any details as to exactly what happened, Jane explained, only that the parents thought it was serious enough to contact CYS and report the incident.

"Shit, that's crazy," Jim said, after hearing what he thought was the most preposterous thing he had ever heard. "What the hell is wrong with these people at CYS? Ron is only seven years old and I am sure that he doesn't have any concept of what he did or what it is all about. In addition, that business about his mother playing with him. I don't think he has any idea, either, what he said or what it means."

"I know, Jim, and we all agree with you," she said, acknowledging that CYS's suspicions had been a bit far-flung. "It doesn't make any sense. And naturally we immediately became suspicious when she came up with this story of how she came home one night back in November and found you playing with Naomie."

As Jane described to him what Kate said had happened, he slowly began to piece together what was going on.

Ever since that meeting, she had made numerous calls to Devlin, Ron's caseworker from mental health and other people at CYS, the extent of their involvement became quite clear and he was convinced that they were the ones responsible for him being in jail.

"I know that there is a whole lot that Kate is not telling, us," her mom continued, revealing a little more of how they all felt. "Harley and I both tried to talk to her and find out what was going on at CYS, but all she would tell us is that Devlin and James Ramour were the ones that told her to have you arrested. She said they told her that if she didn't go to the police and file charges, that she herself could be in big trouble."

Jim had heard enough. Regardless of the reason for him being in jail, he knew that in there he was helpless and he was not going to be able to find out anything until he got out.

"Jane," he said, changing the subject to ask her a favor. "Do you remember Franco, the attorney I had at the hearing with Ron? Well, I talked to him today and he is supposed to go to the judge tomorrow and see if he can get my bond reduced. I was wondering if Don or Harley could come down and pick me up if I can post bail and get out of here."

"I am sure that Don can come down and get you," she said, answering with out any hesitation, indicating that they were willing to do anything to help.

"Thanks, Mom," he said. "Tell Don I really appreciate it and I owe him one."

He would have liked to talk to her all day to keep his mind off of the place he was in, but it was a collect call and he had already been on there for some time. He told her he would call tomorrow, as soon as he heard from his attorney, and hung up.

He sat there on his bunk for a few minutes, thinking about the phone conversation, feeling much better than he had at anytime since he was arrested. If there were any doubts, they were all erased now. Her family was behind him all the way. It wasn't a question of whose side they were on. They knew her and judging from some of the things that she had said and done in the past, it was a simple matter of them reading between the lines to come to the conclusion that her story was unbelievable.

It was not the first time she had been caught in a lie. Her announcement to her mother several months ago that she had an affair with a neighbor in Massachusetts and she wasn't sure that their two year old girl Kristy belonged to Jim did very little to enhance her shaky credibility.

The rattling of keys and the clatter of trays signified the time of day, as the inmates brought their food trays into their cell.

The time had seemed to fly that morning and he knew that it was only because he was busy. He used to be conscious of time at work and at home, but in here, it was his worst enemy. There was little to keep him occupied and there was a constant battle in his mind, to avoid thinking about it.

After lunch, the four of them became engaged in a game of cards. They all knew a variety of games, but the most commonly played was spades, which they were presently playing, or euchre, his favorite game.

The rest of the day was spent much the same as the day before. Dinner came and went. After that was Wild Kingdom on the TV, followed by more cards.

After taking a shower, he went in and lay on his bunk and thought about tomorrow. If Franco went to see the judge and succeeded in convincing her to lower his bond to five hundred dollars as he indicated was feasible, he would have to get Don to come down and get his money so he could pay for him. If he couldn't get it lowered to five hundred and only ten percent instead, that would present another problem. Since he paid Franco seven hundred and fifty dollars, he would not have a thousand left and he would have to get Don to go to Five Flag pizza and get his check.

Mark knew Don, meeting him many times when he had stopped to pick up pizza, and Jim was sure considering the situation that it would not be a issue he would have to worry about.

He lay his head on the pillow and after tossing and turning his head from side to side finding it still difficult to fall to sleep, he got up and went out and sat at the table. Amid the music videos on MTV, he discussed with Tom and Bill the proper procedure he would have to follow if he were able to post bail the following day.

They both seemed to be quite eager to display their counseling ability by conveying to him how things worked in such a way that confirmed all his presumptions.

A short time later after he felt like he was further educated on how the court system operated, the TV went off, signifying what time of the evening it was.

He went back in and lay on his bunk with all the thoughts of tomorrow spinning through his head. He again tried the impossible task of falling asleep. All the sounds were still as persistent as the night before and the loud voices of the inmates intent on staying up until the early hours of the morning, continued to reverberate off the concrete walls.

Tonight was different though: the thought of posting bail also meant freedom from the hellhole he was in, making it much more bearable than the night before.

He closed his eyes and began to dream of walking down the country road near his house, taking deep breaths of the fresh air instead of the foul stale atmosphere he was becoming accustomed to. He awoke several times during the night. After opening his eyes part way to identify the guard making his rounds, he fell back to sleep.

Again he awakened, this time by clanging of breakfast trays and the voices of trustee inmates. He swung his feet off the bed and put them on the floor. It was the noise that had awakened him, but the appealing aroma that reached his nostrils was what made him put his feet on the floor. It smelled like bacon and eggs. He blinked and shook his head several times to make sure that he was awake, then slipped his pants on and hurried out to make sure that someone didn't eat his share.

After breakfast a guard came in and stuck a newspaper between the bars of their cage. He turned and stood up when he heard him approach, half expecting his name to be called, but then he sat back down again after he realized what time it was.

It couldn't be much after eight o'clock and even with his limited knowledge of the courts, he knew that they did not convene until nine. Assuming that they did, and his attorney probably not being the first one on her agenda, he was sure certain that he wouldn't have any news until after lunch.

He picked up the front page of the newspaper that someone had discarded and began to read to occupy the time. A guard again approached the door, unlocking it this time. He started to get up, but stopped when Henry headed for the door conveying his intentions. In spite of him being sure that it was impossible to hear anything until afternoon, his over zealous instincts were making him restless and every time a guard came near their cage he expected it to be for him.

Bill, who had been reading the police beat, handed his section to him pointing to an article.

"Here, you might want to read this," he said. "It is about you."

He stood up and took the paper from Bill, his hands shaking a little and he sat down to read it.

It wasn't much: just one short paragraph which identified him and stated the charges, arrested for molesting a four-year-old girl. It didn't say who it was, or go into any other details.

He felt sick to his stomach and he started to become angry as he thought about Lieutenant Kotter telling his attorney Franco that he had made a confession. He wondered who else he told about his alleged confession.

He held the paper in his trembling fingers and read it again. It's a wonder, he thought, that he didn't have the reporter print in the paper that he had made a confession.

Over the years, he had seen his name and even his picture in the newspaper, but never in the police beat before. His already bleak future looked even more depressing, as he thought about the thousands of people that read the paper every day and would see his name in the column under the police beat, accusing him of such a heinous crime.

He knew all about the "innocent-until-proven-guilty" element and how the courts seemed to enunciate to the public that we are all treated fair in a court of law. Somehow when the accused looks at his name in the paper as he was now staring at his, the "innocent-until-proven-guilty factor doesn't even come into view, and just the fact of being accused of something like this is enough to destroy the whole world around them.

Lunch came and went and Henry left to go to the weight room. Jim had read most of the newspaper by the time Henry came back, and it was not until then that he realized how late it was.

He had still not heard from Franco and it was four o'clock already. Even if he hadn't gone to see the judge until this afternoon, he still should have heard something by now. His gut instincts told him that something had gone wrong, and things had not went the way that he had hoped they would.

Reaching in his pocket, he took out the piece of paper with Franco's office number on it. After waiting the usual few seconds, he was astounded when he heard the voice on the other end of the line refuse to accept the charges.

He knew that there had to be some logical reason for them to refuse his call, but as he hung up the receiver it was still awful hard to accept. When he was locked behind bars and cut off from the outside world, and had just given his attorney seven hundred and fifty dollars to represent him, it became a little difficult to understand why they wouldn't even talk to him.

After the rejecting call, he had little hope that he would find out anything that day and he resigned to the fact that there was nothing left to look forward to except an agonizing wait.

He called Kate's mom to let her know what was going on. J. R. answered, and this time he accepted his call. He handed the phone to Jane, who was in the process of making dinner and said that she only could talk for a few minutes. It was all the time he needed, to tell her what had happened and receive the news that she had for him.

Kate had called, she said, and told her that she received a call from Kotter at the police department, telling her that Jim had made a complete confession. It was kind of puzzling the way she explained it, Jane said. She sounded completely surprised, and exclaimed that it didn't make any sense. She said that she knew you too well to believe that you would confess to anything.

So, he thought, after receiving the latest news, even Kate believed that Kotter was lying. On the other hand, was it just that knowing that nothing ever happened, she knew that it was impossible for him to confess to something that she had made up?

There were a few more words, which were nothing more than her speculation on Kate's unusual reaction to his alleged confession, then she had to get back to making dinner. He told her that he would call and let her know about what his attorney had accomplished as soon as he found out, and hung up.

After his big let-down that day, his cellmates gave him their little bit of encouragement, and added their opinions as to what had happened.

He knew that it was going to be a long night after what had happened, but he had not given up hope. It spite of what happened today, he was still a lot better off than the first day he came in there.

Following their normal activities of the evening, he lay on his bunk and tried to go to sleep. Several times he got up after tossing and turning in his bunk and made a cup of coffee. Finally, sometime early in the morning he dozed off. He was so tired he was vaguely aware of the guard as he came in to make his rounds.

CHAPTER NINE

Awakening to the usual morning sounds of breakfast, he stayed in his bunk and tried to go back to sleep. Although he was exhausted from the restless night, his anxiety of meeting with his attorney kept him awake. He got and went out to join the others.

When the guard came and opened the cell door after breakfast, he assumed that it was to let Henry out to go up to the weight room and he didn't bother to get up until he heard his name called.

"Mr. Hess," he said, startling him for a second. "Your attorney is waiting for you downstairs."

Franco was sitting at the table in the little room where they had been the other day when he got downstairs. The look on his face was enough to tell Jim that the news he had for him was far from encouraging.

"Franco," he said, deciding to get off his chest what had been bothering him since yesterday afternoon. "I tried to call your office and your secretary refused my call. What the hell is going on, Franco? You know we can only call collect in here, so how am I supposed to get hold of you?"

"Look, Jim," he said, sounding like he was trying to explain the ignorance of his secretary, "I have many different cases and my secretary wouldn't have any information that she could give you—that is why she didn't accept your call. I was busy yesterday and I just didn't have time to get back to you until this morning."

It was his explanation and Jim had little choice other than to accept it. For the time being there was no way that he could prove otherwise. Still, his actions had given him doubts as to his credibility: why couldn't he have just called his office and left a message explaining what had happened, instead of leaving him in the dark as he has done?

Now that Jim had gotten his personal feelings out of the way, Franco proceeded to explain to him what was going on.

"We have a little problem," he said shuffling,through the papers in front of him. "I have talked to the judge. She refused to lower your bond without a hearing."

He had expected that was why he hadn't gotten back to him, but it was still somewhat of a shock to hear him say it.

"But why, Franco?" he asked, dumbfounded at her unreasonable decision. "I have a job and no reason to go anywhere."

"Look, I know," he said, showing what Jim thought was little remorse for his impending situation. "But you can't argue with the judge. What she says goes. We have got a hearing scheduled for Monday morning at nine a.m."

"Monday" he said, again expressing his distaste for the decision the judge had made. "Franco, that is three days from now. You mean that I have to stay in here until then?"

"You don't have much choice," he said. "By the way," he added, still showing very little emotion for Jim's critical situation, "I suppose I should let you know that your wife is back at your house going through your things."

He had taken all the money he had saved, or he thought he had, until he suddenly realized he had left a couple of hundred dollars in change in his bedroom. It was sitting on the dresser, and he knew that if she was back there she was sure to have found it.

"Franco, she can't legally do that," he said, angry with her for coming back and stealing the change it had taken him months to save. "I mean, by whose authority can she just walk in and help herself without me being there?"

"Oh" he said, explaining the reason that she had ventured back to his house to help herself. "I guess she called the police department and Lieutenant Kotter told her that according to the law, as long as she was legally married to you, she had every right to go back to your house and take the things that she needed."

This cop again. For the last three months he had plagued his life. In every incident, it seems that he had become personally involved. His actions and even his advice as in this case were beginning to feel like a personal vendetta. Was why he was so intent on prosecuting him? Jim was sure that he was not naive enough to believe that even a fraction of the things said about him were true, and he wondered what it was that was motivating him.

Getting back to legal matters, Franco showed him the papers he had drawn up. They contained all the legal foundations required to give the judge reason to believe that he would not be a liability, and his plea to the mercy of the court to have his bond reduced so he could afford to make bail and return to society and his job.

Reading it and recognizing its intended purpose, he told Franco he understood and to go ahead with whatever he had planned.

Completing the matters they had to discuss, Franco had other things to attend to so he said good-by until Monday. Jim got up and headed back upstairs to his cell, where he would be spending at least the next three days.

When he came back to the cell, he was bombarded with the usual questions as to what happened yesterday and what his attorney had accomplished. After satisfying their curiosity, he called Mark at the store to let him know what was going on.

He wasn't happy about his bond hearing being scheduled for Monday, since the weekends were always the busiest and that was when he needed him the most.

They talked for a few minutes about what he planned on doing when he got out, with Mark ending their conversation encouraging him to keep his chin up.

Next he called Jane to let her know what the latest development was and what he hoped to expect for Monday. Of course she was as confused as he was as to why the judge had rejected Franco's request for a bond reduction and felt as he did, that there was something else going on that he didn't know about.

He told her about his attempt to contact his attorney at his office after not hearing from him yesterday. She agreed that something strange was going on, and when he got out that maybe he should think about getting another attorney to represent him.

Another matter had come to his attention as he talked to her and that was his clothes. He had been wearing the same ones since he got there, and he desperately needed something clean to put on. Don was there while Jim was talking to her and after explaining to her what he had to do, she repeated it to him.

Acknowledging the procedure required getting anything in to him, he said that he would go over to his house and get his things up to him right away.

He stayed on the phone a while longer and they talked about the kids. Naomie's birthday was the eleventh of December, which was Sunday. Kate was having a birthday party at her mom's house and everyone in the family was invited.

"She felt strange in a way," she said, "with him being in jail and Kate being the one responsible for him being there. But the birthday party had been planned for some time and in light of what had happened, it wouldn't be fair for Naomie to have to suffer for something she wasn't responsible for."

He got a lump in his throat as Jane mentioned Naomie's birthday. It would be the first time since she was born that he would not be with her on her on one of the most important days of her life.

The memories of sitting at Kate's side in the hospital when she was born were still vivid in his mind. Squeezing her hand with each contraction, he had wished it were possible for him to share in the agonizing pain that Kate suffered through her birth.

As the time became eminent, a sudden uneasiness began to creep through the both of them when they realized the doctor still hadn't arrived yet.

"Don't worry," he said jokingly, but in his mind feeling that he could do what was necessary. "If he doesn't show up, I am sure that together we can manage without him."

The doctor arrived in the nick of time, and within minutes he had cut the cord. Naomie lay on her mother's breast while they both smiled at the miraculous joy they had brought into this world.

Angel, he nicknamed her. She looked just like a little angel he thought, as she wiggled, squirmed, and squealed with her first little cry of life.

"Mom," he said, his lips trembling and feeling so choked up inside that his words were scarcely audible. "Tell Naomie I love her and wish her a happy birthday for me. I will call you later," he barely managed to say, feeling like he was going to burst into tears any moment as he hung up the phone.

He went in and sat on his bunk, wiping away the few tears that had started to run down his cheek. His emotions were so mixed up from the confusion of the last few weeks that he didn't know how to feel about anything anymore. One minute, he hated Kate for what she was doing to him; the next minute, he felt like he still loved her and to hate her without knowing what was behind all of her actions would be the same as treating her as he was being treated.

He had been through three childbirths with her and together they had shared the agony and the pain, and also the love and joy. He knew that in spite of what happened, he couldn't erase those feelings. Somewhere deep down inside she had to still have those feelings too and sooner or later they had to surface, revealing what was really inside of her and the reason for her erratic behavior.

The lack of sleep from the night before and the mental strain from the events that had taken place that morning had left him exhausted and he lay back on his bunk with the intention of taking a nap before lunch.

He had become accustomed to most of the noise by now, and he thought that he might be able to ignore the racket.

That idea became short-lived though, as what sounded like two hundred pounds of bar bells bounced off the floor overhead, making him wonder what moron came up with the idea of putting the weight room on the fourth floor instead of the basement.

Realizing that what he had intended to do was fruitless, he rolled out of his bunk and went out to join the others.

He had just sat down at the table with a deck of cards to play solitaire when the guard came up to the cell door with a plastic garbage bag in his hands.

"Mr. Hess," he said unlocking the door and handing the bag to him. "Someone dropped these off for you."

Taking out three pants and shirts and corresponding underwear, he set one aside, deciding to take a shower and change into something clean. Although he had taken a shower every day, his clothes still stunk from body odor.

There was a bucket and some laundry soap in the shower, so he took his dirty clothes with him and washed them, then hung them over in the corner of his cell to dry.

By evening, he was so tired he felt like he could have easily slept through an earthquake. Several times after dinner he found himself falling to sleep at the table while they were engaged in their nightly card games.

It was not his turn to clean up that night, so he excused himself early after finishing one of the card games, went in, and collapsed on his bunk. He did not toss and turn as he had the previous nights, or at least he didn't remember. When he closed his eyes, he seemed to slip into a state of oblivion.

They startled him when they brought the breakfast trays in. Thinking it was still the middle of the night, he didn't realize it was morning until he opened his eyes and glimpsed the dim rays of light beginning to emerge through the window at the end of his cell.

He couldn't remember what time he had lain down, but it was the first time he had slept through the night since he had been in there. He had slept so soundly that he didn't even hear the guard come in to make his rounds.

Feeling well rested, he slipped his pants on and went out to see what they had to eat.

Following breakfast and the reading of the morning newspaper, it was nearing lunchtime when he decided to call Kate's mom and let her know that he had gotten his clothes.

After talking a few minutes about the comments and speculation from other members of the family regarding his unfortunate situation, she told him that Don had asked her to find out what time visiting hours were.

He checked with Tom and Bill to see what the procedure was. After discovering it was a simple matter of giving the guard a list of the names of people that would visit him, he relayed the information to Jane, along with the designated times that he was allowed to have visitors.

"Just tell Don if he comes, to tell the guard who he was there to see and they would come up and get him," he told her before hanging up.

A few minutes after Henry had left for the weight room, the guard came in to tell Jim he had a visitor.

Don was sitting on the other side of the glass when he sat down, and tried to act casual as he picked up the phone and spoke into the mouthpiece.

"Hi, Jim. How's it going?" he said. "Is everything all right? Is there anything else you need?"

"No, I am fine," he said, feeling it unnecessary to tell him what he really felt like being locked up in jail. "Thanks for stopping by, and I sure appreciate you dropping my clothes off for me," he added.

"No problem," he said, acknowledging Jim's appreciation for his help. "I am sure that if the situation were reversed, you would do the same for me.

"We all believe in you," he said, sounding like he was accentuating his feelings. "We know that Kate is lying. Mom, Dad and I have tried to talk to her—she won't listen to any of us. The only person she listens to is Devlin from CYS. She talks to him everyday, sometimes a couple of times a day. It just seems that she is doing every single thing that he tells her to do."

"Hey, Don, come on—don't worry about it!" Jim said, reassuring him that he didn't hold anyone to blame. "You didn't know this would happen, and if you did there was nothing that you could have done about it."

"No one believes her, Jim," Don continued. "We have all talked about it and after listening to at least a half a dozen different stories that she has told, there is just no way that anyone can possibly believe that she is telling the truth."

They continued to talk until visiting hours were over. Among other things, they discussed what Don would have to do if Jim could post his bail Monday. He asked Don if would go to work and pick up his check for him. The way all the events seemed to be taking place so far, he had little hope that Franco would get his bond reduced to less than ten percent and he had the feeling that he might need the money to get out of there.

He thanked Don again for coming to visit him and then went back upstairs to his cell. Henry was still in the weight room and Bill and Tom were watching basketball. They were both embroiled in the game and he didn't feel like playing cards by himself, so he decided to sit down and join them for a while to pass the time. He always liked to play basketball, but for some reason he just never could get into watching the game like they did.

He was well rested from the night before, so he stayed up until the TV went off, playing cards with the other three inmates. When he lay down, he again had a hard time falling asleep. It wasn't so much the noise; rather, it was the thoughts of Naomie's birthday party the next day that kept him awake. It was the first time he had ever missed any of the kid's birthdays and it was just not going to be the same without him.

Sunday was much the same as the rest of the week, other than the newspaper. Considering its size, it meant that reading it would consume most of the day and help pass the time.

Later that afternoon, he called Kate's Mom. While she talked to him on the phone, he could hear Ron, Naomie, and Kristy and their cousins in the background. They were all laughing and talking and they seemed to be having a good time.

As Mom told him what Naomie had gotten for her birthday, he could clearly distinguish Naomie's laugh, Kristy's giggle, and Ron's exclamation of joy in as it sounded like they were playing some kind of a game.

"It sounds like they are having a lot of fun, Mom," he said. "I am glad that you still decided to have her party."

"We didn't talk about you," she said. "Well, what I mean," she explained, not wanting him to get the wrong understanding and clarifying what she meant. "None of us talked to Kate about you, or questioned her about your situation. We did not think that it was the right time or place to get into a big argument with her."

"Thanks, Mom," he said, thinking about Kate's erratic behavior the last few of weeks, sensing how Kate would react to being questioned. "You are right, and there is no need to spoil Naomie's party because of me."

"I wished Naomie a happy birthday for you. I told her that you loved her and missed her very much and I don't care if Kate heard me or not," she said, sounding as if she was reassuring Jim of her strong beliefs.

He stood silent next to the phone, resting his arm on the bars for a few seconds as he fought to contain his emotions.

Normally the laughter of children brought a special joy into his heart that made him feel good all over, but now, as he stood behind the bars forcibly separated from the ones that he loved so much, all he could feel was pain. It was a deep down pain that began somewhere inside and spread through his body, causing him to shake and his eyes to become blurry with tears.

"Mom", he said in a broken voice, as he fumbled with his shaking hand to hold the receiver to his ear, "Thanks again for everything. I will call you tomorrow."

He hung up the phone, went in to his cell and took out his handkerchief as he sat on his bunk. It would probably have meant nothing to Tom and Bill seeing him with tears in his eyes, but to Jim, it felt strange crying in front of others. He always felt if a man needed to cry that he should do it alone.

He lay in his bunk thinking after the TV went off that night and it was quite some time before he fell asleep.

Tom, Bill, and Henry seemed quite convinced, that Franco would get his bond reduced to no more than five hundred dollars tomorrow. After talking about it several times over that last few days, they all agreed that it seemed to be a reasonable amount and they couldn't see any reason why the judge wouldn't grant his request.

He hoped that they were right, but he found it hard to think about anything positive while locked in a jail cell.

CHAPTER TEN

He had gotten up for breakfast the next morning, not being able to sleep with anticipation of what lie ahead in such a short time. It was not yet nine when the guard came and unlocked the door and told him to go downstairs.

Expecting the guard to come when he did, he was already dressed and he reached in his cell and grabbed his jacket before stepping through the cell door. The county jail was right behind the courthouse, but they had to go outside and walk up the street to get to it.

There was a deputy waiting downstairs to take him to the courthouse and he removed his cuffs from his belt, instructing Jim to slip his jacket on.

Still a little unfamiliar with functionings of the court system and more just going through the motions than thinking rationally, he questioned the deputies' necessity of handcuffing him just to walk up to the courthouse. No more had he asked the question than he realized how simple-minded it was. He had seen enough on TV and movies to know that it was nothing more than standard procedure as the deputy that was applying the cuffs explained to him.

It was the middle of December and although the sun was shining brightly, the air was extremely chilly with a brisk breeze blowing. He wished he had zipped his jacket up inside before the deputy had put the cuffs on as he stepped outside and the frigid air penetrated his thin shirt, chilling him to the bone. He stopped, fumbling with his numbing fingers for a minute, having great difficulty with the handcuffs on getting the zipper on his jacket hooked. He didn't know how cold it was out, but he was glad that they didn't have far to go to get to the courthouse.

They entered through the basement at the rear of the building and after passing the guard posted at the door, had to ascend three fights of stairs before attaining the level of the courtroom where his attorney, Franco, was waiting.

It was Monday morning and County Court house being domicile to many offices, was bustling with its usual activity. He passed many people, not giving his appearance much thought as he pulled the sleeves from his jacket over his handcuffs, partially hiding them, until he came upon the woman and her two children on the stairs.

The reaction of the children was one incident that would be forever engraved in his mind. There was a little boy about nine and a girl about ten that kept staring at the cuffs peeking out from under his sleeves on his wrists as he passed. He overheard the inquisitive little girl ask her mother what he did and why he was handcuffed.

Their mother glanced at him, showing a slight, almost apologetic smile for the rudeness of her children as she motioned for them to stop staring and keep moving down the stairs. The woman did not appear moved by his handcuffs and he assumed that she had been at the courthouse before and was accustomed to the sight.

He wished that he could have thanked her for the way she handled the situation the way she did. It wasn't much what he overheard, but her words of explanation to her children that "just because he had handcuffs on didn't mean that he was a criminal," was enough to convince him that she was one person that believed in "innocent-until-proven-guilty."

He felt sick inside as he continued up the stairs. At first when he came into the building and people glanced at him as he walked by it never occurred to him what they were thinking and it didn't really seem to matter. Now, after what the little girl said, he wondered what the other people that had seen him were thinking. If they were all to speak as the little girl had, what would their opinions be and what would they have to say?

Suddenly he became paranoid. Never in his life had he felt so degraded and humiliated. He felt like he was naked and everyone in the courthouse was staring at him. He hurried up the last of the stairs and down the end of the hall to the courtroom.

Franco was outside the courtroom talking to another man when they approached him and he turned to greet him with a look on his face that instinctively told Jim that something was wrong.

The other man with the black hair and neatly trimmed beard dressed in a dark blue suit was the assistant district attorney, he explained, and he had some notably distressing news to tell him.

"Jim," he said, as if he were blindly searching for an explanation for the troublesome news he had just received. "Is there any reason why your wife and kids would have any reason to fear you?"

Jim stood there for a few seconds, finding it hard to believe what he had heard, and said nothing. It was then that he spotted Lieutenant Kotter standing inside the courtroom door, talking to the assistant district attorney. Instantly, he became suspicious as to why he was there.

"Franco, what the hell is going on, and what is he his doing here?" he said, motioning toward Kotter, sensing that presence had something to do with the distressing news that Franco had to tell him. After discovering about the matter of his made-up confession, he knew that Kotter being there could only mean more bad news.

"Oh, he is just here to testify for the state," Franco said in a very bland tone of voice, showing no concern for Kotter's undermining presence. "Jim," he said, underlining his main concern, "it seems that your wife has told the police department and the courts that you have threatened to kill her and the kids and she doesn't want you to make bail. She has stated that she is afraid if you get out of jail you will come after her and the kids."

Jim was shocked and confused as it was with what was all going on, but when he heard this it was almost too much to believe. He wondered seriously if she had really said it, or it was something else that Kotter had just made up.

"Franco," he said, sounding like he was defending her. "This is nuts! None of that statement makes any sense. I know Kate—she would never have any reason to say that. Her and the kids have never in their life had any reason to fear me."

"Well, I don't know for sure what she said or didn't say," Franco told him. "All I know is that the court has been so informed and that is one of the things that we have to deal with."

The assistant DA who had been talking to Kotter stepped into the open doorway of the courtroom and motioned to Franco that it was time to go in.

As they went into the courtroom to face whatever unknown fate awaited him, Jim had the strangest feeling that he was about to learn an abrupt meaning for the power of persuasion.

What had began last Friday with simple bond hearing to determine whether there was just cause to reduce his bond to an amount that his attorney deemed affordable, seemed to be turning into a complete fiasco.

They walked toward the front of the room and sat at a long table overlooked by the judge's bench. As Franco shuffled through some papers in front of him, Jim looked around, glancing from person to person to see who all had attended his hearing.

Franco sat next to him, and at the middle of the table facing the judge sat the assistant district attorney, that Franco had been talking to earlier. At the other end of the table, Lieutenant Kotter leaned back in his chair with a smile on his face that left Jim all the more puzzled as to his actual reason for being there.

Other than the judge in her long black robe overlooking them, and a few other individuals standing in the back of the room that appeared to be waiting to be heard next, the courtroom was empty.

"Do you have any witnesses in you behalf, Mr. Rambsy?" the judge said, startling him, as her voice seemed to echo, making him feel all the more like a doomed man.

The sudden feeling of loneliness was overwhelming and the perspiration began to bead on his forehead as he glanced at the rows of empty seats.

Panic struck him as realized what was about to happen. He turned to Franco and fiercely snapped at him for what he felt was his ignorance to the following proceedings.

"Franco!" he said, half-shouting as he tried to control his anger. "What the hell is going on? Why didn't I know anything about this? If character or credibility was going to be an issue, I could have gotten plenty of people to appear to testify in my behalf."

Now he knew why Kotter was here and why the statement existed about him threatening to kill his wife and kids. As he glanced at the judge sitting above them, who appeared to be more like a queen reigning on her throne and with Kotter at the other end of the table grinning, he had the feeling the he was soon going to discover what the term "Kangaroo Court" meant.

"Jim," Franco said, in a haphazard attempt to explain what was happening. "I just found out about this a few minutes ago. Our hearing was scheduled with the judge for nine o'clock, so I didn't have time to inform you or see about getting any witnesses. Besides, this is just a hearing and it won't matter anyway."

Won't matter? He couldn't believe he said that to him. He was the one going back to jail if he couldn't post bail.

Franco's explanation had done nothing more than enhance his already strong suspicions about the kangaroo court proceedings that were about to begin.

Franco began with his plea to the court to have his bond reduced, stating the reasons as his job and his lack of available funds. He asked the judge to consider his situation and his need to work so he could afford to defend himself against the alleged accusations.

The state then took its turn, with the assistant district attorney informing the court of the information he received about the alleged threat against his wife and kids. He recommended to the court that Jim should not be released on bail because his wife was afraid of him, and she felt that if he was able to post bail she would be in fear for her life.

Jim sat at the table and listened as if he was traumatized. He wanted to jump up and object to the assistant district attorney's recommendation. However, his arms and legs wouldn't move and when he opened his mouth he couldn't speak.

Kotter stood up next when the judge asked if the prosecution had any witnesses to testify in support of the assistant district attorney's recommendation. He began with Jim's first encounter with the police department, involving the accusations of the abuse of his son. Following that, he brought to the court's attention the domestic dispute at his residence between him and the neighbors. Finally, he described to the court the details encompassing his current situation, placing great emphasis on the so-called "confession" that he had allegedly extracted from Jim.

Adding to what Jim hated to admit without any opposition had to be a very convincing presentation of Jim's questionable character, he noted that Jim appeared to be a troublemaker and supported the assistant district attorney's recommendation.

The last part about the confession brought him out of his trance and getting his voice back, he lashed out at Franco in a attempt to get him to stop this one sided testimonial.

"Franco, for God's sake—don't just sit there! Do something! You know the situation about Ron; you were there. And that incident about the rent was all Kate's idea. It was even taken care of by CYS. I told you all about the alleged confession. I didn't sign anything and the whole damn thing is a lie."

"Look, Jim," he said, sounding almost as if he was convinced himself that Kotter's testimony was the truth. "He is a very reputable police officer and well-known and respected in the court community, and his word is taken to be the truth."

"Well, why don't you say something to him?" Jim said, desperate to defend his reputation. "Ask him some questions. Say something to the judge. Say something to someone."

He was frustrated now at his complete helplessness, sensing what the outcome of the hearing was going to be. Without anyone to testify in his behalf he knew that his only hope lay in the hands of Franco, his attorney.

His outburst had caused somewhat of a disturbance and Franco grabbed his shaking hands, calming him by reassuring him that they would get their chance. "Besides," he again reminded him. "This is just a hearing to post bond—it doesn't mean anything or have any bearing on your case." *Damm* thought Jim, fighting to control his anger. *Why does he keep saying that? How can he say it doesn't mean anything? If he can't convince the judge that I am not a risk, she will not reduce my bond. If she doesn't do that, then there is no way that I can come up with enough money to post bail. And that means I will go back to jail.*

"Mr. Rambsy," the judge said, addressing Franco again after Kotter had finished. "Is there anything else that you would like to add on behalf of your client, before I make a decision in your case?"

Her words cut through him like a sharp knife as she spoke and he began to shiver as he realized the absolute power she held over him.

"Yes, your honor," Franco said, getting up and walking over toward the bench to face the judge as he gave his plea in Jim's behalf. "I would like the court to take into consideration that Mr. Hess has a clean record and has not been convicted of any previous offenses. Aside from the allegations by the prosecution, Mr. Hess is not and never has been considered to be a violent man. He has a steady job and has proven to be dependable. In addition to being well liked by his manager and fellow workers, he is even supported by his wife's family."

Jim thought that Franco had given a reasonable testimonial in his behalf, but he knew that it would have little effect on the decision of the court. The assertion of Jim's non-violent nature and the backing of his friends and her family was nothing but hearsay. Without any witnesses to testify for him, it left nothing for the judge to base her decision on but his word.

"Mr. Hess," she said, looking at Jim after pausing a moment to glance through the papers in front of her. "I see here that you were married before and you are from Iowa. After leaving there twenty years ago, you have traveled all over the country and lived in many states before coming here. What guarantee does the court have that if you are released on bail you won't just pick up and leave like you did before?"

"Your honor," Franco said, sensing Jim's urgency to talk to him and explain why he had moved all over and lived in so many states. "Could I have a few moments with my client?"

Jim had given Franco a brief summary of his life in the little time that they had together, and it was included it the report that he had given to the judge. He was sure that he had told Franco what line of work he was in and why it was necessary to move all over. However, judging from what he had just heard, there seemed to be no mention of it.

Jim was angry. The way she read his report it sounded like he had just been running around the country hiding for the last twenty years.

"Franco, will you please tell her it was because of my job that I lived in so many states," he said, after the judge granted his request and Franco came over and sat down. "I have been living here in Pennsylvania since 1979. I left for a while to take a job in the northeast after I married Kate, but I came back when I got laid off. This is where my wife is from, and we decided to live here so she could be near her family."

While Jim and Franco were having their few words, the assistant D. A. and Lieutenant Kotter seemed to be having a little discussion of their own. When Franco had finished relating to the judge what Jim had told him, the prosecution had another short statement to add in its behalf.

"Your honor," said the attorney for the prosecution after being granted the permission to speak, "We feel that the evidence shows that Mr. Hess is very unreliable and a danger to society. We strongly recommend that he not be granted his request because we feel that he would be a threat to his wife and kids."

"Is there anything else?" the judge said, looking at Franco and then back to Kotter and the assistant district attorney. "All right then, we will take a ten minute break and I will give you my ruling on this case."

"What do you think?" Jim asked Franco as they sat at the table waiting for the judge's decision. "Do you think that we stand any kind of a chance?"

"Well, I don't know, Jim," he said. "With Kotter's testimony and your wife's statement, things don't look too good. However, you never can tell what the judge might decide."

"When I first talked to her and gave her the papers requesting to have your bond reduced to ten percent to one thousand dollars, things looked promising."

"Wait a minute, Franco," Jim said, puzzled by the new figures that he just quoted. "I thought you told me you were trying to get it reduced to five hundred dollars."

"Originally I was," he said, explaining the reasons for the change. "But considering your record and closeness to your wife's family after the allegations against you, I thought that the judge might see fit to comply with my new request to have it lowered even further.

"Now," he continued, "With these new and unexpected developments that I hadn't counted on, I don't know how much they will have affected her decision."

The judge had left the courtroom during the break and she came back in and called the two attorneys to the bench.

"I have reached a decision in this matter," she said, looking up from the papers in her hands. "Although I can not grant the defendant what he asks, I will partially come to terms with his plea. I will leave the bond at ten thousand dollars, but allow Mr. Hess to post ten percent of that for his bail.

"And in addition, Mr. Hess," she said, directing her attention toward Jim, who had stood up at the table when she entered. "The court orders that you do not go near your wife or kids until it is so ordered otherwise. If you do not comply with this order, your bond will be revoked and you will be arrested and incarcerated."

After hearing the testimony from Kotter and the alleged statement from his wife, it was almost more than Jim hoped for.

"Thank you, your honor," he said, after pausing a second, not sure whether he should address the court directly or through his attorney as he had been.

It was a lot more than the hundred dollars that would have been easy to pay, but when he thought about the ten thousand that it began with, the thousand dollars still looked a lot better. All he would have to do now was get Don to bring his check down so he could sign it, then get the money he had in the safe at the jail and go up and post his bail so he could get out of there.

While he was standing there waiting for the deputy to take him back to jail and thinking about how long it would take to have all this done, he was suddenly presented with another unsuspecting surprise. This time it was from Franco, his attorney.

"Jim," he said, after picking up his notes and placing them in his briefcase. "Your arraignment hearing is Thursday. I am pretty sure that I can get Molly Hill, the magistrate, to reduce your bond to five hundred dollars."

Jim looked at him, startled, finding it hard to believe what he had just heard.

"Franco," he said. "Am I hearing you right? Do you want me to go back to jail and sit there until Thursday?"

"Look, Jim," he said, explaining his reasoning for the suggestion.

"There is no sense using all of your money to get out of jail now if I can get your bond lowered. Besides, it is only four days away."

Only four days he thought. *In here, that seemed more like four weeks.*

He had to admit though, that in a way Franco was right. If he did use the thousand to get out, he would be flat broke. He had the couple of hundred in change at home when he was arrested. But Franco said that Kate was at his house going through his things and he was sure that she would have taken that and whatever was left in the checkbook.

"All right," he said, not liking the idea of having to agree with him, but feeling that he had little other choice. "I have made it this long. I guess I can last four more days."

CHAPTER ELEVEN

As the deputy escorted him back to jail to await his arraignment hearing, there was something else on his mind that began to bother him. He first thought about it when he paid Franco the fee to represent him.

When he was arrested, Kotter and the other officer had seen how much money he put in his pocket. Aside from them and the deputies that were there when they put his money in the safe, no one could have known how much money he had. Yet, Franco seemed quite certain that he had the money to pay the fee to represent him. Then the mention of him spending his last few dollars to get out of jail had begun to make him altogether suspicious as to how he seemed to know so much about his finances.

He assumed that there had to be some reasonable explanation, but he was sure that he would keep these thoughts in the back of his mind until his curiosity was satisfied.

Right now though he had other things to attend to as he entered his cell which would be his home again for the next four days. He called Mark at work to let him know what was going on. After assuring him that he would be available to work the weekend, he called Kate's mom to clue her and the rest of the family in on what had happened at the bond hearing.

As he had expected, Jane knew nothing about her calling and telling the court that he threatened her. She was not only surprised but also angry with Kate for her sudden accusations.

It was lunchtime when he called. Harley, Don and J. R. were there just sitting down to eat. She had held the phone away from her mouth to inform them about Kate's latest doings.

Don, being the first to react to the news, left no holds barred when it came to expressing his opinion.

"It's that dam Devlin—I know he has got something to do with this." Jim heard him shout in the background. "She is always on the phone with him and it seems like she doesn't do a thing or make a move without talking to him first."

It sounded to Jim like he was excusing her actions by holding Devlin accountable for what she said.

"I agree with you about, Devlin," Jim, he heard Harley say next. "She probably has reason to be a little afraid of Jim after having him arrested and thrown in jail, but that still doesn't explain why she would say that Jim threatened the kids."

"Look, Mom," Jim said, feeling left out of the conversation that was going on at the other end of the phone line. "I don't care what she said or who anyone thinks is responsible. The fact of the matter is, we all know that she is lying."

The cart appeared in the doorway with their lunch trays, so he told Jane that he would call her later and find out what was going on for Thursday.

Later that evening, they brought a new inmate to their cellblock. It was after dinner and they had all settled down to a four handed game of euchre, when the guard came to unlock the door and tell them that they had some company.

Bill and Tom both greeted Eddie by name when he entered their cage, which suggested to Jim that he was no stranger to jail. It seemed, as he soon found out, that Eddie had been in this same cell block just a couple of months ago and he was released and put on probation.

Jim didn't know why he was in there before, but this time he was arrested for drunk and disorderly conduct and assaulting his seventy-year old grandmother. He had been arrested the evening before and had spent the last twenty-four hours in lock up to sober up.

Eddie was in his early twenties, with a stocky build and weighing an easy two hundred pounds. He was a little shorter than Jim, with a noticeable muscular physique that he seemed to be quite proud of. Judging from his fair skin and smooth complexion, Jim found it difficult to believe that it could be the result of strenuous and hard work.

When Eddie sat down at the table, it seemed like a reunion between old friends as he talked to Bill and Tom about what had went on with him the last couple of months.

Jim's doubts about his build being due to life of hard work, were also confirmed as he overheard Eddie say that he still hadn't found a job yet. "He had been staying at his grandmother's," he explained "and continued to work out with weights everyday since he left."

The presence of Eddie in their cage seemed to interrupt their everyday monotonous routine. The next couple of days were spent getting adjusted to the new inmate in their cellblock. There was also the added variety in their everyday conversation, with new stories to be heard and to tell.

He had called Kate's mom several times to find out if there was any news pertaining to the hearing on Thursday.

"Kate has been stopping by with the kids every day," she told him, and her, Harley and Don had all had been trying to talk some sense into her.

She kept telling them that she didn't want Jim to go to jail and it was CYS that told her to him arrested. Kate said that after talking to her and Harley on Tuesday she had called James Ramour at CYS and told him that she wanted to drop the charges. He just told her that it didn't make any difference because the matter was out of her hands anyway.

"Look, Jim," Jane said, sounding apologetic for all of them not being able to do more than they had. "We tried to make her realize how wrong it was to do what she was doing, but it appears like it has already gone too far. I know how the system works: once they get their claws into something, they just never seem to want to let go."

Jim knew how Jane felt about CYS. She had talked to him about what had happened many years ago. Jane had her own problems when Kate was young and was not able to care for Kate and her brother and sister. They were taken in by the system and later adopted and raised in separate homes. Jane did not want to give them up and had begged them for assistance so she could keep them. The court rejected her plea and did what they felt was best.

He sensed the deep-down hurt and the touch of bitterness that still remained as she had explained to him what had transpired over thirty years ago.

It was Wednesday evening when he talked to her last and she told him that Don would be at the hearing in the morning. Afterward he would take care any of details required to have Jim released on bail.

He sat up late that night talking to the inmates about the hearing the next day. Again, they all assured him that things would work out and he would be getting out of jail. Feeling a little more confident now that his bond was reduced to one thousand dollars, he was convinced that tomorrow whether his attorney succeeded in having his bond lowered or not, he would be out of jail.

As he lay in his bunk that night trying to get some much-needed sleep, he couldn't help thinking about what Kate had told her mother.

"They told me that it was out of my hands," she said.

It sounded like CYS was using Kate like a pawn in some kind of a obnoxious chess game. *Only this game* he thought. Familiar with the game of chess and wondering what purpose their intended actions were leading up to, *this was not just an ordinary chess game*. They were playing a game with his life, and it was one he could not afford to lose.

He got up the next morning after being awakened by all the familiar sounds, hoping that it was the last time that he would ever have to hear them and got dressed.

It was shortly after they finished breakfast when the guard came in and announced that the deputies were waiting downstairs to take him the magistrate's office for his hearing.

He stepped into his cell to grab his jacket and paused a moment, looking at his belongings and wondering if he should take them with him or not.

The guard sensing the reason for his hesitation relieved him of any doubts as to what he should do.

"Just leave everything here," he said. "You will come back here after the hearing, while they post your bail and you can pick them up then."

He turned his back on his things, suddenly feeling as if there was nothing worth retrieving anyway and hastened through the doorway and down the circular staircase to the first floor, anxious to get to the courthouse and get his hearing over with.

A short time later as they pulled up in front of the old wood frame building with the sign, "Magistrate's Office" hanging on the front, an image came into view of the last time he was in her courtroom.

After Molly Hill had dismissed the charges due to lack of evidence, she had her own few choices words to say: they began to ring in his ears as he got out of the car and started up the sagging wooden steps to the entrance.

They were all there that day in her little courtroom when he had been accused of assaulting his son, James Ramour and the woman that had visited him at the township jail, along with Devlin, Ron's caseworker. He and Kate had both talked to them and they all agreed that there were no grounds for any kind of an investigation regarding abuse against Ron.

After Clancy's statement that was non-supportive by any witnesses, CYS and the attorneys went into the judge's office to discuss the matter privately. Kate's mom and the kids were there and they were all able to identify the raised voices of protest that were coming from the other room as they sat outside waiting for the judge's decision.

A short time later they came back out and returned to their seats. James Ramour, with the permission of the court, stood up and stated that as far as CYS was concerned the matter involving the accusations against Mr. Hess was settled. They were aware of the marks under Ron's eye he explained, being reported several weeks before the alleged incident. He felt that there was no evidence of abuse and therefore determined that it was not necessary to proceed with any kind of a further investigation.

Immediately following James's, statement, identifying CYS'S position regarding Jim's situation, Molly Hill announced that she had reached a decision in his case.

"Due to lack of evidence and the State's inability to produce any witnesses to these allegations, charges will have to be dropped," she said, looking at Officer Clancy and Detective Kotter, who was also present at the hearing.

The way she said, "have to be dropped" sounded to Jim like she was disappointed that the officers didn't have enough evidence to make them stick.

Next she turned to the table that Franco and Jim were sitting with a few more things to say.

"Child abuse is a very serious crime and we see far too much of it in our court system today, Mr. Hess," she said, looking directly at him. "You were lucky this time. The next time you come in front of me, maybe you won't be so lucky."

CHAPTER TWELVE

They went into the courtroom and after one of the deputies removed his handcuffs, he sat down next to Franco at the table in front of the judge's bench.

Molly Hill was sitting at the bench, and as he glanced up at her he thought about her last words. Well, here it was the next time and he had the feeling that she meant every word of it.

He seemed to be the last one to have arrived as he looked around and noticed that everyone else that might have something to do with his case appeared to be already there.

It was no great surprise to see Detective Kotter sitting at a table opposite of them and there wasn't much doubt in his mind as to why he was there.

James Ramour and Devlin were seated in the back of the room. Next to them, was a woman that he did not recognize as having seen before.

Kate was seated directly behind him with Naomie on her knee. She was holding on to her, but not nearly tight enough to stop her from getting loose when she spotted him.

It only took an instant to break free and cover the short distance between them. She reached him with her arms stretched out and a big smile on her face.

"Hi, Dad," she pronounced with a special glitter in her eyes that left an image in his mind that would last forever. "I sure missed you," she said, grabbing him around the neck and giving him a big hug.

He held her at arm's length, noticing a change in her even though it had only been a month that they had been apart. She had put on a few pounds since he last seen her.

"Hi Naomie," he said, cherishing the few seconds that he was sure they would only be allowed together and wishing that it could last forever. "I missed you, too."

He was correct about the few seconds, as the magistrate noticed that Naomie had come over to him and ordered that she be removed from the courtroom.

He felt like a part of him was being ripped away as the strange woman that had been sitting in the back of the room came and took her out of his arms.

"Bye, Dad," Naomie said, waving as she took her away.

"I'll see you later," he said, his gut feeling like it was tied in knots not knowing when or even if he would ever see her again.

Jim glanced over at Kate to find her staring at him. She had made no attempt to stop their brief reunion, but the loathsome look she gave Jim made him feel that she was not at all comfortable with what she had just witnessed.

He looked at the judge, feeling a sudden intense hatred for both Kate and her. What the hell were they afraid of? Naomie was just sitting there on his lap; she wasn't making any kind of a commotion or disturbing anyone.

Franco had been sitting next to Jim, taking in the little scene. He leaned over close to remind him of what he already knew, but his blind hatred had prevented him from seeing.

"Jim," he said, bringing him to his senses. "You are accused of sexually assaulting your daughter by your wife. I don't think it would look good for her or the courts if your daughter were sitting on your lap during the following proceedings."

The judge hammered her gavel on the bench, getting everyone's attention, and proclaimed that the court was now in session. She opened the proceedings with the testimony from detective Lieutenant Kotter.

He began, by explaining, "that on the recommendation of CYS, Kate had come down to the station and sworn out a complaint, alleging that she had witnessed her husband molesting their daughter Naomie. Based on the evidence, Mr. Hess was charged and later arrested for aggravated indecent assault."

Next he pointed out the piece of paper he had been holding in his hand and waving around as he spoke.

"I have here," he went on to say, "a statement by Mr. Hess. I talked to him after his arrest, and he confessed to the charges placed against him."

Jim sat in his chair feeling numb as Kotter finished his testimony. This was the third time he had heard about his so-called "confession." Once from Franco and now twice from Kotter. He had yet to see it and he was becoming quite curious as to what was written on that piece of paper that he was supposed to have said.

The woman who had taken Naomie out of the room had come back in and returned to her seat. She got up when the detective finished and with the permission of the court, proceeded to make a statement regarding CYS's involvement in his case.

"Mrs. Hess came to me with a statement disclosing what she had witnessed her husband doing to her daughter."

So, this is Mariane Mayer he thought. His suspicions about her were proving to be correct: the first words that came out of her mouth were lies. First of all, Kate didn't come to her with a statement. He had been with her just hours before that meeting, when she was ordered to appear with Ron. Also, Kate had revealed to her Mom and others through the papers that Mariane had given her that she was there because she was under suspicion of molesting Ron. He knew that when got out of there nothing was going to stop him from going down to Mariane Mayer's office and finding out what that meeting was all about.

"We feel that there is sufficient evidence to believe that Mr. Hess did in fact molest his daughter," she continued, "and support the allegations by his wife and police department."

By the time she had finished, Jim's anger had almost reached the boiling point and he was ready to explode.

Franco had been sitting there shuffling through his papers as if he was oblivious to anything that had been said since the hearing began. He looked at him, finding it very difficult to understand why he still hadn't spoken up in his defense.

"Franco, for God's sake," he said in a desperate voice, "Are you just going to just sit there? Aren't you going to do something? Tell the judge that the confession is all a lie. Tell her that I said he made it all up. Besides, I couldn't have signed something that I knew nothing about."

"Look, Jim," he said, reminding him about the credibility of a police officer in a courtroom and doing little to bolster his depressed state of mind. "It's still his word against yours."

Jim felt that he must have thought that he had gathered sufficient enough evidence to prepare his defense as Franco stood up and, after being acknowledged by the court, began to speak in his behalf.

"Your honor," he began, in a move that surprised Jim. After the way he kept talking about the credibility of a police officer, he never thought that he would question the confession issue. "Mr. Hess disclaims any knowledge of the confession that Officer Kotter has in his possession. He admits that he did have a discussion with the officer, but states that he only explained to him what he felt happened that caused his wife to accuse him of the things that she did. Never did my client feel at any time that he hinted or suggested to the officer that he committed any of the acts that he has been accused of.

"My client also states that he knows that there is no physical evidence to substantiate any of these charges, since they did not happen in the first place. He contends that his wife's testimony is nothing but a ruse to stop him from getting their kids in a custody battle.

"The defense feels, that a great injustice had been done toward my client, and at this time moves toward having the charges against him dropped before any more unnecessary harm is done."

It sounded pretty good and it might even have raised a few eyebrows, but Jim had little doubt as to its making any difference in the decision of the court.

They had Kate's statement which gave CYS all the provocation they needed. Jim also noted that Kotter's expression had not changed when

Franco disclaimed any knowledge of the confession. He sat there in his chair unmoving, confident as to whose word the court would believe.

Having concluded his plea to the court and receiving no further comments, the judge called Franco to the bench for a brief conference. He had noticed a large manila envelope lying on the bench when they had come into the courtroom, and now she was discussing the contents with him. After a few minutes, she asked Franco, Detective Kotter and members present from CYS that were there in regards to his case, to join her in her office.

There was no mention by the court the reason for the sudden break, and he felt bleak sitting at the table all alone. He assumed that their little gathering in the magistrate's offices office had to do with some documents that were contained in the envelope, and he figured that he would find out soon enough what it was all about.

He was right on both accounts, as Franco came back out shortly after they entered and sat down next to him at the table.

"Jim," he said, answering what was on his mind before he had a chance to speak. "The papers we were looking at" indicating the manila envelope "were the doctors report. There is no indication in his report that Naomie was molested in any way and after talking the matter over with all the parties involved, the judge wants to make a deal. I wanted to discuss it with you first and get your approval before I gave her my answer."

A deal! He didn't like the word at all, especially when it was in connection with the court system. He sat there for a few minutes before answering, thinking about what Franco was proposing. Images began to flash through his mind, of charged individuals confessing to their crimes and giving information about their associates to get off with a lighter sentence. "Franco, what the hell is going on?" he said, becoming more puzzled then ever. "You just told me that the doctors report showed no signs of any abuse. What am I supposed to make a deal about?"

"Well" he said, "after reviewing the evidence she feels that there is not sufficient grounds to hold you for court on the charges of aggravated indecent assault. However, she still thinks that you are guilty of something, and wants to hold you for court on a lesser charge. She proposed reducing the charge to indecent assault, victim unaware.

"Not only that, but if you agree to her proposal of having your charges reduced, she has also agreed to reduce your bond to five hundred dollars cash. "Here," he said, reaching in his pocket and taking out a sheet of folded-paper. "It is a copy of the charges. Take a few minutes if you want and read them over."

Jim scanned through the fine print, reading what he was already pretty much aware of.

"Franco," he said, looking up at him after he finished. "It seems to me, that if I agree to her proposal it means that I am admitting that I am guilty only to a charge a little less serious than the first one. What will happen, if I decide not to agree with anything she says?"

"Well, I hate to tell you this, but it looks like you have little other choice. It won't matter to her one way or the other. Chances are she will hold it over for court anyway on the original charges. Also," he noted, "There is a good possibility that she would not grant our request to reduce your bond, either."

So, this is what it boils down to, Jim thought, as he sat there staring at the paper in his hands, trying to assimilate all the facts. What she was offering sounded much more like an ultimatum: either he agreed to her little deal or he paid the price.

It looked like the police department had gone a little overboard on the charges, and she was trying to correct the over zealousness of the police officer by getting Jim to admit to something a little more believable to a prospective jury.

"She is waiting for your answer, Jim," Franco said, seeming to get a little impatient. "What have you decided to do?"

"Well I don't like it one bit, Franco," he said, feeling like he was being manipulated into doing something that was against his will. "But being as she leaves me little other choice, then I guess I will have to accept it."

Franco had asked for a little privacy when he came out of the judge's chambers to discuss the judge's deal, and the courtroom had been cleared, leaving them alone except for the deputy standing guard. After receiving his answer, Franco went back in to join the others.

Jim hardly had time to wonder about the decision he had made before the door opened again and everyone came out of her office. Franco came over to him, explaining that it would just be a few minutes while they had the proper papers drawn up and then he would be returning to the jail to get his things. "Don," he said, "after settling the matter with the bail, could pick him up there."

The outside door to the waiting room had been opened while they were talking and Jim, noticing Don standing next to Kate and Naomie, called him over to him and Franco to tell him what he needed to do.

Naomie had seen Jim when he called Don over. "Hi Dad" she shouted, as Kate pulled her out the door.

Franco had left while Jim and Don were talking and appeared a few minutes later with some papers and handed them to Jim.

Jim read over the new charges, he agreed upon then, he turned his attention to the terms of the bond agreement on the other paper. There was a stipulation added to the normal preconditions, stating that he would only be allowed to see his kids under supervision of CYS.

"What's with this, Franco," he said, wondering why Franco had omitted telling him about it. "There was never anything mentioned about me not being able to see my kids."

"Well, Jim," he said, accounting for the added conditions, while sounding like he was excusing himself for his own slip up in not telling him about it before hand. "The judge felt that due to the nature of your charges, it would be in the best interest of the children if you were not to see them unless it was under the direct supervision of CYS."

He knew that the decision was final, but as he handed a copy to Don to take up to the courthouse so he could post his bail, he couldn't help wondering how much CYS had to do with her decision.

The deputies took him back to jail. When he went upstairs to get his things, he was greeted with a minor surprise. He stepped into his cell to discover that these were not the few articles he had come back for, but someone else's.

"They are over here," Tom said as Jim stepped out of his cell with a puzzled look on his face, wondering what had happened to his belongings. "We all figured that you wouldn't be back. Eddie" wanted your cell. Everything of yours is in on his bunk."

"Thanks," Jim said, stepping into the cell feeling like it didn't matter if he retrieved any of his things or not. There was nothing of value anyway, and all he wanted to do was just get out of there as fast as he could.

CHAPTER THIRTEEN

Don, who had left the magistrates before them, was waiting outside for him when he got downstairs. After giving him his personal items out of the safe, one of the guards opened the steel doors and he stepped outside. He stood there for a minute, flinching as the last door shut behind him, hoping that he would never have to hear that sound again.

He took a deep breath of fresh air and a warm feeling spread through his body as they stepped out of the shadows of the building into the rays of the late morning sun.

God, he thought. He never could have imagined how good it felt just to be free.

"Are you okay?" Don asked as they headed toward the car seeing the serene look on his face.

"Yeah," Jim said, glancing over his shoulder. "I am fine, just fine."

As they drove back to Kate's mother's, Don described a little incident that had taken place in the waiting room of the magistrate's office. He had been talking to Kate when Devlin intervened telling her that she didn't have to answer any of his questions.

Having a great dislike for Devlin anyway, Don had told him to mind his own business and just butt the hell out.

Detective Kotter observing the minor disturbance between Don and Devlin, came over to administer what Don felt, was his unwanted assistance. He had gotten very angry when Kotter told him to sit down and leave Kate alone, and was blaming Devlin for the whole matter.

He was very upset at Kate also, for sitting by as if she was agreeing with the both of them. "After all the times that I helped her when she needed someone" he said, expressing what he felt about the incident. "She didn't have to treat me like that. Its that jerk Devlin. We all try to help her, but she turns around and does everything that ass tells her to do."

They had to pass his house on the way to her stepdad's, and as they neared the driveway Jim asked him to pull in.

"Uncle Harley is waiting for us," Don said, sounding as if he was a little bit reluctant to stop.

"Don look, I know, but I haven't been home in ten day's and I would just like to go in and look around for a minute," he said, assuring him that he wouldn't be long.

As he opened the basement door and stepped inside, the first thing he noticed was that all of the kid's toys were still there. He knew that Kate had been there while he was gone and since she had a place of her own, it seemed strange that she hadn't taken any of the toys with her.

He headed up the steps into the kitchen, trying to remember how everything looked when he left. Glancing around as he passed through to the living room, he noticed that the coffeepot was missing. She had taken one with her when she first left and as he stepped into the adjoining living room, he wondered why she had taken his.

The kid's table and chairs were still in the corner and their book bags and stuffed animals were strewn across the floor as before. Even the pictures were still left hanging on the walls. However, there was something noticeably missing, as he looked at the table where the TV and VCR were sitting. He was angry when he saw the empty table and yet somehow he was wasn't surprised. He had the feeling when he heard that she was here, it was one of the things that she had come back for.

He continued to the end of the hallway passing his own bedroom, finding the kids' rooms the same as when he had left. He returned, thinking about the rolled change he had saved and wondering if it was still there.

From what he had seen so far, he half expected things to be a mess, but the sight before his eyes made him sick to his stomach when he opened the partially closed door to his bedroom. Not only was his money gone, but the dresser that it had been sitting on. Everything that had been on the dresser and in the drawers was heaped into a big pile on the floor. The drawers in the other dresser were half-opened with clothes hanging out of them. Other clothes had been taken out of the closet and strewn across the bed. There was hardly anywhere in the room that he could walk without stepping on something.

He made his way to the bed and after moving some clothes, sat down. Feeling numb, he looked around the room not knowing whether he should scream or cry. Before he could do either one, Don appeared in the doorway.

"I didn't know she did this," he said, seeming to be shocked at the sight in the room. "She had the dresser and the drawers out in the living room and I just took them down to the truck. If I had known, I would never have agreed to help her," he said apologizing, after feeling partially responsible for the mess she had left.

"Come on, Don," he said, getting up off the bed, his head reeling with thoughts of what spiteful reason she would have for doing such a thing to him. "Let's go—I have seen enough for now."

He got into his own car and followed Don over to his mother-in-law's.

As he pulled up into the driveway, he couldn't help envisioning the last time he had been there. It was that Friday night when Kate had left him over a month ago. Don had gone into the house and he hadn't realized how long he had been sitting there thinking about the kids until he came back out and asked if he were coming in.

"They are all waiting for you," he said, making it sound to Jim like he was someone of notoriety.

"I will be right there," he told him. "Just give me a minute."

Why did he feel so nervous as he got out of his car and slammed the door?

There was a roaring fire in the fireplace when he walked into the back room. Kate's step-dad was there, along with Don, J. R. and Harley, Kate's brother-in-law. They were sitting at a table in front of the fireplace and he sat down next to them.

They talked about his situation and the experience he had gone through. He described to them what jail was like and how it felt to be on the inside.

Each one gave their account of the story that Kate had been spreading around, and gave their opinion as to why they thought Kate had done what she did. After a period of discussing what he was going to do in the future, the conversation began to center around his attorney, Franco.

Feeling that Franco was too closely associated with CYS and could not be trusted, they all agreed that it would be wise to find someone else.

As they spent the whole afternoon talking, there was a certain tranquillity Jim felt being able to sit next to the fire and just relax. When someone called down to tell them that dinner was ready, it also felt good to be able to get up and leave whenever he wanted to.

After dinner the topic of conversation continued to be about his arrest and the conflicting stories that Kate had told.

Kate's sister Rose was there, and it seems that the story she told her was not the same story that she told her Mom.

Kate had told her Mom that Jim had lain down with Naomie to get her to go to sleep, after she was supposed to have observed him with his hand in her underwear. After her Mom questioned her saneness in allowing Jim to do that after what she had allegedly witnessed, she later told her sister that she was the one that went in and laid down with Naomie. When questioned about her conflicting stories, she denied telling her mother that Jim had lain down with Naomie.

After listening to their conversation for some time, Jim slipped out of the kitchen and went back downstairs where he could be alone.

The fire had died, down leaving a hot bed of coals. He threw a couple of logs in the fireplace and watched as the flames lapped at the added fuel. Having camped out in the woods ever since he was a kid, he loved to sit by a fire. The heat felt good and he seemed to feel an inner peace of mind as the flames reached out toward the draft from the chimney.

The logs he had added were burned down to red-hot coals when he looked up and noticed Don standing in the doorway.

"How's it going?" Don said casually.

"I am all right," Jim said. "What's up?" He knew that something was on his mind just by the way he was standing there.

"Well, Uncle Harley told me to ask you if you wanted to stay here tonight, instead of going back to sleep at your house. He thought you might want some company instead of being alone."

"I appreciate his offer," Jim told him. "But I will have to make it some other time. I have a lot of things to do and the sooner I get started, the better."

A short time later after thanking his in-laws for the meal and their caring about him, he went back to his house. He went into the living room and sat on the couch, feeling heavy-hearted as he could ever remember in his life. He looked at the pictures of his wife and three kids smiling faces on the wall in front of him, and wondered hopelessly if there would ever be a chance of them getting back together again.

When Kate had admitted her affair to him several months ago, he was at first furious. He still loved her and forgave her, not being able to bear the thought of losing her and the kids. As for Kristy being his? Well, there was no doubt in his mind as he held her and heard her first little cry at birth as to who her father was.

He had tried to make it work between them. Many times he had compromised in situations that were against his better judgment, just so they would stay together. It was obvious that all of his efforts had failed though, as he looked at the pictures of his family torn apart, feeling the wetness of the tears on his cheeks.

They were gone. He was all alone now. He had nothing —nothing l but a few pictures and the heartbreaking memories of the happy times that they had spent together.

He thought about the ten years of his life that he had been single and began to again feel the pangs of loneliness. After being married ten years to his first wife, his divorce forced him into a life that he despised. He had lived alone, hating every minute of it, wishing many times when he went to sleep at night that he would never wake up the next morning.

Although he never felt that he had adapted himself to the single life, feeling he did nothing more than just exist, he somehow managed to survive by keeping himself busy.

Then one day he met Kate and everything in his life changed. They had many differences between them one being their age of seventeen years. Even that didn't matter though when they seemed to meet on common ground, and everything in his life began to take on a purpose.

He could never forget those first feeling he had for her, and there was nothing else in the world that could ever replace them.

Looking at Kate's picture on the wall he felt a sudden anguish, knowing that he would never have those feelings again! He got up and went into the bedroom and just threw everything off the bed onto the floor. He lay down, and sometime during the night he fell asleep, wishing as he had many times before in his previous single life that he would never wake up again.

Late the next morning he opened his eyes, bewildered at first sight of what lay before him. As it all started coming back, he turned his face toward the pillow and tried to go back to sleep. He lay there a while and after realizing how useless his behavior was, sat up and began to think about how he was going to face the day that lay ahead.

He went into the bathroom and took a shower. After shaving, he slid the scale out and stepped on it. He had noticed in the mirror that he had put on a few pounds and when he stepped on the scale, he discovered why he had so much trouble getting his pants buttoned. At one eighty, it meant that he had gained almost twenty pounds since he quit smoking in September.

After looking around and not being able to tell what was dirty and what was clean out of the pile of clothes in the bedroom, he just grabbed what he thought he would need and took them down to the basement. He was thankful as he loaded the clothes in the washer that she had left the washer and dryer and he didn't have to go to the laundromat.

Having accomplished that part of the things on his mental list, he went back upstairs to tackle the stack of mail on the kitchen table. When he opened the junk drawer looking for a letter opener, he also discovered to his surprise more unopened envelopes.

It was far worse than he had imagined as he opened bill after bill that had not been paid. The best he could figure after going through what he could find was that he was about three months behind in everything.

What amazed him was the fact that some of the utilities hadn't already been shut off. She must have been giving them just enough to keep them satisfied, with a promise to get caught up as soon as she could.

He still had five hundred dollars, which would take care of his rent, but that didn't leave much for anything else. He was going to see Mark today and he thought about asking him if he could work a few extra hours so he could get caught up. If he had to, he was sure that he could get back on at the Warrington store. It was Saturday and there was nothing he could do about the bills until Monday during business hours.

There was another thing on his agenda for Monday that he had promised himself he would take care of: he was going to go to see Mariane Mayer at CYS and find out about those allegations that they were supposed to have about Kate abusing Ron.

Even more important, he had to look into the matter of the visitation rights for his kids. According to his bond agreement, he was supposed to be allowed to see them under supervision. What he wanted to find out was when and where.

CHAPTER FOURTEEN

He called as soon as the offices of CYS opened Monday morning, and was given an appointment to meet with Mariane Mayer at one that afternoon.

They were located in the courthouse square building in downtown Warrington, at the end of Cherry Street in the same block as the county jail.

Knowing what traffic would be like at that time of the day, he left early, allowing himself plenty of time to find a parking place. This was one meeting that he did not want to be late for.

He parked in the metered lot up on Main Street and as he walked the several blocks down Cherry Street to the Courthouse Square, his route took him by the old county jail.

He shivered, a sudden chill passing through him as looked up at the bars on the third floor, and the remembrance of his imprisonment flashed through his mind.

Suddenly he felt tense as he pushed the button and waited for the elevator to reach the sixth floor. He knew why he had come here, and he was certain that the social worker knew also when she had made the appointment with him. It was his anger and hatred for the system that worried him: he hoped that his ordeal of the last month hadn't left him so bitter that he wouldn't be able to accomplish what he had set out to do.

He stepped into the office, closing the door behind him. As he made his way over to the receptionist's desk, he couldn't help noticing the few decorations hung around the room, as well as small tree with a few baubles with some presents under it.

After confirming his appointment, he went over and sat in chair to wait. He looked at the little tree in the corner of the room and thought about Christmas, which was only five days away. He felt none of the joy and happiness that he had felt in the past years; it had been replaced with a sad, empty feeling. He was at the mercy of CYS just to be allowed to visit his children and he was far from certain that it would be before Christmas.

Looking up as a woman entered the room, he recognized her as the one who had spoken in behalf of CYS at his hearing and had taken Naomie out of his arms.

With all the stress at his hearing, he had only taken quick glances at her, and had not had the chance to focus on her overall appearance.

She came over to greet him, wearing a bright green dress with a wide white belt drawn tight at her narrow waist. She wore a pair of heart shaped earrings and a beaded necklace. Although she was attractive, there was certain air about her that suggested this was just an outward appearance.

His intuitions seemed to be warranted as she addressed him in a very authoritative business-like voice.

"Mr. Hess," she said, as he stood up to greet her. "I am Mariane Mayer. Did you want to speak to me?"

"Yes Ma'am, I sure do," he said, almost shouting at her, anxious to get their little meeting started.

"Would you follow me please?" she said in the same tone of voice as before. She turned and headed toward an open door at the other end of the room. The anxiety in his voice was unmistakably clear and it was evident that she wanted to continue their discussion in private.

They entered a small office and she closed the door, assuring their privacy. He sat down on one of the two chairs facing her at the desk, that she had seated herself behind.

The room was bare, except for a few children's books and a toy box over in one corner. Judging from his initial observation, he assumed that its primary function was for meetings of his sort.

"All right, Mr. Hess," she said, after assuming a comfortable position in her chair. "Just what is it that you would like to talk to me about?"

"I came in here to find out just what the hell is going on," he said looking intently at her.

"Well, it's pretty obvious isn't it?" she responded, avoiding a direct answer. "Your wife came down here and made a statement saying that you molested your daughter."

He stopped her before she could go any further.

"Look, Ms. Mayer," he blurted out sharply. "Let's stop all this nonsense and get to the point. I know damn well that Kate didn't just come down her to tell you that I molested our daughter. I was with her less than three hours before that meeting you had with her. After that meeting, without any forewarning, she left me. The next thing I know, I am arrested, charged with molesting my daughter and she is showing papers around saying that she is under suspicion of sexually molesting our son. What I want to know is why you called her in here to see you and what that meeting was all about?

She had been sitting in her chair with a placid look on her face when he began. Suddenly she sat forward, her expression becoming more rigid, seeming to be taken aback by his adept knowledge. It only took her a few seconds to recover, and she answered him in the manner which he expected.

"Mr. Hess," she replied, as if her response had been perfectly planned and calculated to meet her specific needs, "The allegations against your wife have nothing to do with your situation, and her being under suspicion does not alter the fact that she has accused you of molesting your daughter. We had called her in here on the day in question," she continued, "to inform her that the allegations against her concerning Ron had been under investigation and were determined to be unfounded."

Wait a minute!" he said, more confused now then ever, finding her explanation hard to believe. "I don't get it. First of all, why wasn't I informed that my wife was under suspicion? From what I understand, she didn't even know what it was all about until she came in to see you."

"Well," she said, "it is standard procedure that the papers be sent to her house informing her of the suspicions and the impending investigation."

"Look" he said, sitting forward in his chair and making it clear that he was becoming angry at the game of hide-and-seek he felt she was playing. "I don't give a damm about your standard procedure. I was not informed that my wife was under suspicion of anything. Also," he said, beginning to tremble as he began to unleash the anger that had been bottled up inside of him. "I would like to know what gives you the right to investigate my wife on charges of such serious nature without personally informing me of what she is accused of. This is my son we are talking about—I should think that I would have a right to know what is going on.

"All right," he said, sitting back in his chair and taking a deep breath to calm himself. "You said that the suspicions were unfounded. I would like to see a report of this investigation."

"Well," she replied, seemingly undisturbed by his contempt for the way she was handling things and maintaining her rigid business-like expression. "I'm sorry, but I can't give you a copy of the report yet, because the investigation is still ongoing."

Now if that isn't a hell of a note, he thought. First she tells him that the allegations are unfounded and now she tells me that the investigation still isn't complete.

"Well, what about the papers she has been waving around that were supposed to be sent to me?" he shot back. "Do you suppose that I could at least get a copy of them?"

"I will make some copies of them before you leave," she said, with an expression that indicated her reluctance to do so.

"Mr. Hess," she said, changing the subject in an obvious attempt to avoid and further discussion about the allegations against his wife. "Your wife has accused you of molesting your daughter and we did just what we felt was necessary."

"Well, if that is the case, then why the hell didn't she go to jail?" he shot back raising his voice, still seething about what he felt was her attempt to cover up the real truth. "You didn't make any effort to investigate her any more than you investigated me.

"Look," he said, not wanting her to get the impression that he thought Kate was guilty of anything. "All I am trying to say is that if you had acted in the same manner regarding the allegations against her as you did me, then we would both have gone to jail. I would think that someone would have found it within them the decency to at least inform me of what was going on before resorting to such drastic measures."

"But, Mr. Hess," she said, upholding her actions that had subsequently resulted in his arrest and incarceration. "The significant difference in your case is your confession that you made to the police department."

He slid his chair back and stood up, taking a few steps toward the window and back, hoping it would help calm the silent rage within him. As he stood in front of her desk and prepared to answer her, he wished that Franco and Kotter and the judge were all here so they could hear what he had to say.

"What is it with you people?" he fumed. "Do you think that you have the right to justify any means of extracting information, even if it means falsifying a confession to attain your intended goal?"

"It states in your confession that you admitted to the charges that your wife placed against you, Mr. Hess," she continued, ignoring his declaration that it was all made up.

"The hell with your damm confession!" he suddenly shouted, unable to control his churning frustration. "I told you that I didn't make any statement to anyone. What he has on that piece of paper that is supposed to be my confession is not what I said to him—it is only what he wanted me to say. And" he added, finding it difficult to speak without shouting. "If you will note, I did not sign it, simply because I didn't even know of its existence until the next day."

"Please, Mr. Hess," she responded, her expression changing from the stern-faced businesswoman, to one of alarm from his outburst. "I know that you are a little bit upset and feel that you are unjustly accused, but there is no need to swear and carry on like that."

"A little upset! How in the hell would you know how I feel?" he shouted.

Now that he had started, he was finding it impossible to stop until he finished everything he had to say. One of the reasons he came there was because he held her directly responsible for everything that had happened since the meeting she had with his wife. He was not about to leave until he expressed to her in detail just the way he felt.

"Over a month ago," he reminded her, as he began pacing back and forth across the floor. "My wife came to you with my son for a meeting. As of yet, I still do not know exactly what that meeting was all about. Since then, my life has been a living hell. I have been arrested, put in jail and been informed that I had made a confession that I wasn't aware of. Not to my surprise, I was told at my hearing that there was no medical evidence to incriminate me on any of these charges. Then, I sat there and listened to you speak in behalf of CYS and give your support to Kate's accusations and Detective Kotter's fabricated confession."

Ms. Mayer, having recovered from the abrupt way he began to express his vented anger, returned to her adamant manner.

"We felt that with your wife's testimony and your confession it was more than enough to warrant the further actions that were taken against you, Mr. Hess," she said, defending her procedure.

"Bull!" he said, replying to her simple explanation. "If you hadn't been so incompetent in your investigation and had done your job the way you were supposed to, none of this would ever have happened. It would have been quite obvious after talking to any of our friends or relatives that there was no reason to be suspicious of me ever abusing my kids. And if you had made any attempt to follow up on any of her actions, after she claimed the alleged incident took place, you couldn't possibly be too stupid not to see that she made the whole thing up just to assure that she would get custody of our kids in a divorce.

"Also," he added, "If you had taken the time to talk to anyone that knew us well, you would have discovered that I was the one considered to be too lenient when it came to discipline. Kate was short-tempered, and quite often she would get carried away when it came to correct punishment."

"Well" she said, as if he had suddenly got her attention. "If you think that your wife has been witnessed abusing your kids, why don't you get statements from these people and we will investigate it?"

Jeeze, he thought, *don't these people ever let up?*

"Look" he said, "I didn't say that my wife was abusing my kids. It's just that I know she is under a lot of stress and she has been seeing a therapist for some time."

"Mr. Hess," she said, sliding her chair back and standing up as if she was content that she had divulged all the information that was necessary. "If that is everything, I have other things to attend to."

"Not everything," he answered, addressing the most important issue he had come there for. "I want to know when I can see my kids. It has been over a month and according to the bond agreement I am supposed to be allowed to see them under supervision. It is almost Christmas and I would at least like to see them before then."

"We are kind of busy right now, but you can call to set up an appointment," she seemed to mumble over her shoulder as she opened the door, showing little concern for his urgent request. "If you wait a few minutes, I will make a copy of the papers you requested."

He sat in the waiting room giving their meeting a brief thought as she returned to her inner office. He had not meant to explode the way he did, but the emotionless attitude vindicating her behavior had provoked him. It was very likely that she had felt threatened and he had a feeling this would be the last time they would meet face to face.

She returned and handed him two papers, standing in place as if waiting for some kind of a reaction after he glanced over them.

"Just who are these people that Ron was staying with when this was supposed to happen?" Jim remarked, seeing no mention of any names in the report.

"That is privileged information, and I am not allowed to give that to you" she uttered, displaying a rigid stone-faced expression that made him wonder why he had asked the question in the first place.

There was no explanation as to what had happened. It only mentioned that Kate was under suspicion from accusation stemming from an incident that had happened involving their son in a foster home. The other paper contained nothing more than the announcement that she was scheduled to appear with her son at her office.

He looked at the date in the upper right hand corner, shaking his head in amazement. No wonder she had called her that morning to inform her of the hearing. The paper had been prepared on the same day as it was scheduled.

Convinced that there was nothing else to be gained by hanging around any longer, and feeling frustrated by his lack of success, he turned his back to her and walked out the door.

CHAPTER FIFTEEN

Jim had gone back to work Friday evening and prepared to undertake the difficult task of going on with his shattered life. From previous tragedies that had occurred over the years he knew that the only way he was going to make it through what awaited him was to take one day at a time. Most importantly, he had to keep himself busy. Mark had been very sympathetic to his needs, and as had promised, kept him working long hours every day.

He got up Tuesday morning feeling that the new day would be different than the others. The anticipation of being reunited with his kids brought about a certain kind of cheerfulness in him. He had not felt that way since the last day he had taken the girls to school and came home later from work to find out that Kate had left him.

Although he had worked late the night before, he rolled out of bed early to make sure that he called Ms. Mayer just as soon as the office opened. When nine o'clock came, he called and a secretary answered. There was a brief pause after which he was informed that Ms. Mayer was not in her office, and she didn't know when she could be expected to be in. Assuming that the matter of the time for an appointment was only a minor detail, he explained to the secretary about their meeting the day before, and asked her when she could schedule an appointment for him to see his kids.

"Well, I am sorry, Mr. Hess," she answered, sounding somewhat dismayed at him asking her to do such a thing. "That is a matter that you will have to take up with Ms. Mayer. I will leave a message for her to call you just as soon as she is available."

He hung up the phone not only feeling a great disappointment but also somewhat puzzled after his brief conversation.

It didn't make any sense, he thought. He left her office yesterday believing that all he had to do was call this morning and find out when he could see his kids. Now he was told without certainty that it is a matter that only can be discussed with Ms. Mayer. Then he discovered, not only isn't she in, but her secretary doesn't even know when she will be available.

He didn't have any idea what was going on or why there was a delay in making an appointment for supervised visits. With Christmas on Friday, he could understand that they would have a busy schedule, but that was what bothered him. It would be a simple matter for her to look in her appointment book and set a date, even if it were not until next week. Although their actions seemed typical for what he was used to, he sensed that he was being ignored and his visits with his kids were being put on hold.

After waiting all day and not hearing anything from CYS, he felt more depressed then ever, and it took everything he had to concentrate on his job that evening. Mark and Judy, the new girl he had hired as assistant manager while he was in jail, tried to cheer him up, assuring him that things would work out. Even what they had planned for Christmas Eve did little to uplift his Christmas spirit.

Under normal circumstances, he would have been enthused about dressing up as Santa Claus to deliver pizza. However, these were not normal circumstances and after not receiving an answer to his phone call to CYS all day, he couldn't shake the overwhelming feeling that his call would not be returned. The thought of not being with his kids on Christmas was difficult enough without playing Santa and enhancing his already saddening feelings of the upcoming holidays.

"Look, Mark," he said, not sure if he would be able to handle the emotional consequences that he was sure would come about by playing Santa, "I think it is a great idea and I think it would be wonderful for all the kids, but after the news I received this morning, I just don't think that I am going to be up to it."

"I understand," Mark told him, after Jim explained about the telephone conversation that he had with CYS. "I am not picking the costumes up until Friday, so why don't you think about it and let me know what you decide."

By mid-afternoon Wednesday he had still not received any response to his phone call from CYS. Tired of waiting, he decided to call again. The same secretary answered with a textbook reply that sounded like she was reading programmed instructions identical to the day before.

"Ms. Mayer is not in, Mr. Hess. I do not know when she will be in, but I will leave a message for her to contact you as soon as she is available."

He didn't even bother to answer her. He just hung up the phone, having doubt in his mind as to whether he was being ignored or it was just a coincidence that she hadn't returned his call. It was quite understandable that she would be busy; On the other hand, how long did it take to make a phone call and arrange a supervised visit with his kids?

By Friday morning, still having received no word, he had given up hope on seeing his kids before Christmas. The thing on his mind now, was when would he be allowed to see them. It was evident that there was something going on, and decisions were being made regarding his visitation rights that he knew nothing about. The court had only stated in his bond agreement that he would be allowed visits that were supervised by CYS. That, he reasoned, meant the decision as to when and where would be left up to them. After the negative response from his calls to CYS the last couple of days, he couldn't help the gut-wrenching feeling that it was within their plans for him not to see them.

He went to work that Friday evening, feeling as dispiriting as he ever had on Christmas Eve. Earlier that day he had called Mark and agreed to the charade he and Judy had planned so he knew how many Santa costumes to get, but his heart and mind were not in it.

As he and the other two drivers dressed up, he was encouraged by Judy to keep his chin up. "Think of it as doing your own little part to spread joy and happiness on this special evening," she said. "Maybe, after you take a few deliveries and see how the kids react, you will feel a lot different."

In spite of his thoughts of his own kids and what kind of a Christmas they were having without him, he soon discovered that Judy was right. His appearance as Santa to little boy in the home of his first customer brought such thrill and excitement that he felt a warm glow overcome the depression he had felt the last few days.

Throughout the evening children sat on his lap while their parents took pictures of them with Santa. He stuffed his pockets with candy canes and passed them out to the children and even to the parents as he went from house to house making his deliveries. The delight he received from the children's exuberant smiling faces, along with the gratifying "thank you" from many of the parents, had turned an expected downhearted event into an evening that he was sure to never forget.

He was invited to his in-laws to spend Christmas Eve, but declined their offer. The last three years they had spent Christmas Eve at her parents as a family. Alone and depressed as he was, spending the evening at Kate's mom's with all her family was something that he just didn't think he could handle.

Things were different now though: his play-acting of Santa Claus had uplifted his spirits and he decided to call Kate's mom and let her know that he had changed his mind and would be stopping by.

It was shortly before ten when they closed the store, so when he arrived at her mom's everyone was still there exchanging presents. Mom, being concerned about him spending Christmas Eve alone, was glad that he stopped by.

As was common practice for Kate's family, being as there were so many different places to visit over the holidays, they opened some of their presents on Christmas Eve.

He attempted to join in and share the joy and happiness as his nieces and nephews opened some of their presents. "Look, Uncle Jim!" they shouted, showing him the new clothes or toys as their faces lit up with the opening of each gift. They sat on his knee as he helped them assemble some of the toys that they were having difficulty with.

His eyes became cloudy as he struggled to control the feelings that the joyous evening had brought upon him. He felt so happy, and yet so sad, as his thoughts drifted to his own kids.

He knew that Kate would have presents for them: however, it just didn't seem right for him not to be able to give them his presents and be there to see the expression on their faces when they opened them.

Jane, seeing the look on his face and sensing what he was feeling, called him over to the table away from the tree to talk to him.

"Mom," he said, feeling the wetness of the tears that had formed in the corner of his eyes and had started to run down his cheeks. "I miss them so much."

There had never been a holiday that he had been away from them before other than the post Thanksgiving, when she had been here with the kids at her parents. The thought of how they were spending Christmas revealed a dismal picture as he tried to imagine what it was like for them.

"Jim," she said, trying to alter the mood she sensed him slipping into by giving him some compelling news. "They are going to be all right. I had Don take all their presents over to Midge's. Kate came by there yesterday and picked them up, so Ron, Naomie and Kristy are going to have a good Christmas."

Midge was a close and longtime friend of Kate's family, and as Kate used her as a baby-sitter quite often, she kept in constant contact with Kate and her mother.

"Thanks, Mom," he said, feeling a little better knowing that they would have plenty of gifts to open.

Later that evening when the activities began to wind down and everyone left to take their kids home and put them to bed, he was again asked to stay the night. He felt uncomfortable staying at their house with the situation as it was. Maybe some other time he would take them up on their offer, he told them. Tonight he just wanted to be alone.

He went home and lay on the sofa staring at the pictures of his family on the wall, as he thought about what was happening to him.

Losing his faith in anything that represented the system was disturbing to him. Being raised in a Christian home, he had always been taught to believe in truth and justice. The happenings of the last few months or the last few years for that matter had undoubtedly convinced him that no one involved with the system could be trusted.

That was only part of it though: the other matter was his belief in God. Over the years his beliefs in the way things were and what they were meant to be were replaced with doubts and questions. If God was so good and all-powerful, then how could he be at the same time so cruel and heartless to let such evil happen?

Many times in his past life he wanted to believe, but he found it too difficult to be joyful and happy with God in his life while he was being told that he had to give up his home and his family because his wife had found another man and didn't want him anymore.

Having been raised a Catholic and divorce being against his religion, he had stopped going to mass after the breakup of his first marriage. Over the years, he had attended several different church services, but he had never returned to the religious way of life that he was raised as a child.

He still believed in God, but it was more in what he called a scientific way. He had taught his children what he believed in, the basics of the bible and the creation, and that God was the supreme ruler and governed everything in the universe. As for what religion they should follow? Well, he felt that teaching them right from wrong and good from evil would lead them on the right path, and one day they would choose what they wanted to believe in.

Sometime during the night he drifted off to sleep, thinking about what Christmas had been like when he was a child, and then with his first family, when he had still been living a Christian way of life.

Around ten A .M., he was awakened by a phone call from Kate's mom. She wanted to know if he would like to join them for religious services at the church that they attended. He felt it strange that she would even ask, since she knew that he rarely went to church.

"Sometimes when you are down and you feel like have no place to turn, God could be the answer," she said.

It sounded like she was preaching to him, but he knew that it was because she was concerned and she was only trying to raise his spirits by encouraging him to have faith.

"Mom, look—I appreciate your concern and I wished I could feel like I wanted to join you," he said, "but I am sorry—I just can't."

"I understand," she said. "Maybe some other time. Dinner will be ready around one," she added, before she hung up, explaining that they were ready to leave. "But you know that you are welcome to come over any time."

He waited until after one before going over to his mother-in-law's. He wanted to make sure that she was back from church services. It was a time for all the family to get together, and Jane's as well as Harley's family usually stopped by on Christmas day. He knew most of them from other family gatherings over the years, but he still thought he would feel a little uncomfortable if Jane were not there.

He tried to mingle with the others, but this Christmas was just not the same. Several minor incidents occurred during the day that made him wish he had stayed home. Not everyone was aware of his situation. Some had traveled from other nearby towns, and did not keep in constant touch.

Not being informed of what had happened, and noticing the absence of Kate and the kids, he was asked where they were. Luckily, each time Jane seemed to be near by and had overheard. Seeing the awkward position that he was confronting, she came to his rescue.

The following week brought several new developments. His phone calls to Mariane Mayer at CYS had never been answered. He had called again on Monday, receiving the same answer as before. By now he felt that his suspicions about CYS's intentions regarding the visitation of his kids were well justified. They had ignored the bond provisions, and it seems that they had taken it upon themselves to make their own stipulations.

He had also received a letter from Franco, his soon-to-be ex- attorney. It stated, in somewhat complex legal terms, that the fee that he had paid was for services rendered. In addition, it explained, the elaborate legal process required to continue to represent him in a case such as his would require an additional retaining fee of one thousand dollars. Furthermore it stated, making it quite clear that this was only a retaining fee. In the event his case could not be settled out of court and went to trial, it would cost him considerably more.

The letter, having been told earlier by Franco that there would be additional costs if he wanted him to continue to defend him, did not surprise Jim. Franco had also asserted the fact that he could not take any kind of payments and was to be paid in advance. He looked at the letter and what he felt was the extravagant fee. In addition to uncertain feelings he had about the manner in which Franco was handling his case, it was all the more reason why he had decided to find someone else.

Jane had called her attorney's office after he had discussed with them what he wanted to do. Although her attorney didn't handle cases of his nature, she had made an appointment with one of his associates who specialized in such matters.

The holidays were a busy time of the year for pizza shops and not only did he work every day, but also the customers were exceptionally generous. By New Year's Eve he had managed to earn enough money to catch up on his immediate needs, and began to put some away for the future.

He stopped by his in-laws, as he had promised after work on New Years Eve. After several hours and a few too many drinks, the alcohol's influence began to enhance his desolate feelings. It had been many years since he had taken a drink and the effects became apparent as his slurred words depicted his state of mind.

Against their wishes and his own better judgment, considering the inebriated state he was in, he decided to go home instead of spending the night. It was only a couple of miles down the road where he lived, and it was a good thing, because he barely made it to his driveway.

The following day, he awoke with a somewhat expected hangover wishing he had taken it easy the night before since he was not used to drinking. He was invited over to his in-laws for dinner, but still feeling a little queasy in the stomach, he decided to wait a while before attempting to eat anything.

Later that afternoon, he went over for dinner and to what was pretty much a repeat of Christmas day. Other than occasionally talking to Jane and Kate's cousins, Don and J R, he kept to himself spending most of the day in the basement by the fireplace. He knew that his actions made him appear unsociable, but he couldn't relinquish his feelings about the New Year's prospects. Also, his state of mind was such that he just couldn't deal with being around other people.

Monday morning brought another week and a snowstorm that the weather channel had been predicting. It had started sometime during the night, and he awoke to a beautiful blanket of white snow that seemed to cover everything in sight. Judging from his car and the way the snow level had almost reached the front bumper, he guessed that there was at least a foot of accumulation.

As he looked at the traffic off in the distance crawling at a snail's pace on the interstate, it was apparent that if it continued to snow much longer, everything would be at a complete standstill. Also, it meant that he would not be going to work.

Normally, he would have enjoyed a couple of days off. He almost felt like a kid again as he looked out the window and envisioned running and romping with his own kids in the snow drifts that were piling up in the front yard.

He looked away from the window, his blurred vision again reminding him that these were not normal times and it might be some time before he had the chance to play with his kids in the snow again.

It was late morning the following day before the blizzard was all over with, after dumping as much as three feet in some areas. Driving had become impossible, and all the roads were closed until they could be plowed.

It was kind of formidable, he thought, as he looked across the snow-covered pastures at the horses huddled under the open shelters and his car almost buried in the snow. Nature in all its beauty still has a way of making one mindful of its supreme power.

Only the main roads were open when he went back to work on Wednesday, and traveling the side streets had become treacherous from the deep snow.

The weather had caused the cancellation of many things, one of them being his appointment with his new attorney on Thursday. After some minor complications, due mainly to reaching the secretary, he was rescheduled for the next Wednesday.

CHAPTER SIXTEEN

With the weather as bad as it had been, they were busier then he could ever remember, and things were almost chaotic at work. They were short on drivers and he wound up working double shifts almost every day.

It was like a Godsend, he felt, as he gathered his things together and looked at the amount in his checkbook before putting it into his pocket.

The snow was piled at least six feet high at the curbs and he had stomped his feet, shaking the snow out of his pants legs as he entered the office.

He walked over to the desk where a woman about his age was sitting and introduced himself. He recognized her as the person to which he talked to on the phone, as she advised him that it would be just a few minutes. As he sat down on the sofa across from her desk and waited for the attorney to finish with a client in his office, he chatted with her about the record snowfall to pass the time.

Within a few minutes, the door to the inner office opened and two men came out. After a few words to the secretary, a man in a light gray suit came over to him and introduced himself as Tim Meyer, Attorney at Law.

Still feeling a little uneasy as he followed him into his office and sat in a leather recliner that made him feel like he was in a doctor's office, he handed him his paperwork.

His past experience had made him wary of everyone and everything pertaining to the law, and although he had come here seeking someone to represent him, this man was still a stranger and it included him.

Jim looked around the office as Tim glanced through his file. There were the usual diplomas hanging on the walls, but the thing that attracted his attention the most was the picture on his desk. It was of two little girls, about the same age of his own.

"Your grandchildren?" Jim asked, assuming his age to be around forty-five and motioning to the picture as the attorney looked up from his file.

"No, I have been married twice," he said. "The second time to a younger woman, and they are my own. I didn't have any children from my first wife and these are my first," he said, his face beaming with pride as he glanced at the picture on his desk. "You can't imagine what it felt like to become a father for the first time, after I turned forty."

He didn't know what it felt like to be a father for the first time over forty, but he did know what it felt like becoming a father at his age. All three of his youngest children were born after he turned forty.

He picked up the papers and shuffled them into a neat pile. "Mr. Hess," he said, changing the subject and getting back to the matter at hand. "Other than the accusations against you and a few of the details regarding your hearing, the information that we have here is kind of sketchy. Is there anything else that you can tell me about your previous involvement with CYS that could shed a little light on the picture and help me to better understand just what it is that we are dealing with?"

"There is plenty" Jim told him, and proceeded to explain. It seemed like Jim had been talking for hours, with Tim nodding his head in recognition to the different facts, before he held up his hand and indicated that he had heard enough.

"All right" he said. "I have been representing clients dealing with CYS for seventeen years and I can see a developing pattern. From what I have heard so far I think you have a pretty good case, and I will represent you if you want me to."

In the course of time, he had been pouring out his feelings and speculations about CYS and their involvement, Tim's recognition and seeming interest in his problems had not gone unnoticed.

Sensing this attorney's concern in his case not only as a client, but also as one who was unjustly being prosecuted, Jim felt that he had found what he had been looking for.

"What do you want me to do?" he said, standing up and holding out his hand to shake on his approval.

As he left Tim's office, there was a whole different air about his feelings. When they discussed his strategy in his office, he was honest and straightforward, never under-assessing the actions of the courts. It was the way he spoke that he credited his confidence in him, too. He spoke in a positive tone of voice, never relinquishing to defeat in spite of the odds they might be facing. Jim had a gut feeling that he couldn't have made a better choice.

The following Saturday he received a letter from CYS. He was sure when he took it out of the mailbox and opened it that it would have something to do with his visitation rights for his kids. Instead, it was about something that he had least expected and after reading its contents he became outraged. It was all about the accusations against Kate regarding the supposed incident with Ron in the foster home.

The way it was worded incited his anger. During the meeting with Mariane Mayer in her office, he was informed that there was an investigation being conducted. Now, according to what he had read in the letter, it stated that they had commenced an investigation on the ninth of January. That meant everything she told him regarding the investigation that she was supposed to be conducting over three weeks ago was a lie.

There were some instructions as for what he had to do if he wanted to exercise his right to see a copy of the report. Also, there was a phone number in case he wished to speak to someone in person. He recognized the phone number as Mariane Mayer's, the same one he had been trying to reach at CYS since their meeting.

In spite of what he was sure the answer would be, shortly after nine on Monday morning he called anyway to confirm his suspicions. After giving his name, he was greeted with the same reply that he had almost become accustomed too.

"She is not in, Mr. Hess, but I will tell her you called and she will get back to you as soon as possible."

Damm, he thought as he hung up the phone. *Just what in the hell was he going to have to do, if he wanted to speak to this woman again?*

Tim had told him to inform him about anything he thought important to his case, but since it was Saturday, he had to wait till Monday to contact him.

He left for work a little early and stopped by Tim's office to show him the letter. He briefly explained about the meeting between him and Ms. Mayer and the reason why he was so upset by its contents.

"Look, Jim," he said, after reading it. "I can understand your anger, especially after what you have told me about your meeting. I got the feeling that you probably pissed some people off. However, what we have here is not a legal issue. I might enter into the picture later in the future. As for now, I wouldn't be too concerned."

Jim sat in his chair and looked at Tim for a minute before he said anything. As his attorney, he was entrusting himself to his professional judgment. On the other hand, since this all began he had felt nothing but anger and contempt and it was consistently getting in the way of his own judgment.

"Thanks, Tim," he said, getting up from his chair and reaching out to shake his hand. "You are right and I guess I am getting a little too excited about things that I shouldn't. But I just get so angry at the arrogant manner in which some of these people conduct themselves that it is hard to control myself."

"I know" he said, "I assure you that after seventeen years of dealing with Social Service agencies I have seen and heard just about everything."

"Tim, I've got to go. I have to be at work in five minutes," Jim said, glancing at his watch. "Thanks for taking the time to talk to me and I will have all the information you asked for as soon as I can," he added, as he headed for the door.

Patience, he thought, as he drove the couple of blocks up the street to work. Tim had stressed the importance of having patience. "These things take time and you just got to have patience," he said. He had a lot of fortitude when it came to stressful situations, but when his life was being manipulated by his wife and the system, it was becoming very hard to remain patent.

CHAPTER SEVENTEEN

The snowstorm from the past week had left more than just a difficult situation when it came to driving on some of the hills and back streets. There was also a certain amount of beauty projected from its deep drifts that covered fences and left small pine trees and bushes half submerged. It had come so soon after Christmas that most people still had their lights decorating trees and rooftops, adding all the more to already majestic holiday scenes.

The long hours at work continued, making it possible to put some money away for the expenses that he was sure would eventually come. Still, as he drove around night after night, it didn't block out the suppressed memories and he continuously found himself thinking about his kids.

He was trying to be patent, but as the days went by with no news about his visitation privileges, he could feel himself slipping into a lapsed state of mind.

It was nearing the end of January, with still no answer to his repeated calls to CYS. Desperately seeking any kind of help available, he revealed to Tim his intentions of meeting with the Local State Representative.

Although he didn't think it would do any good, Tim didn't discourage Jim from seeking outside help, stating, that any help would be greatly appreciated.

The meeting with the representative revealed about what Tim had expected it to: there was no outright promise that anything could be done, but the State Representative did agree that there had been an infringement on his civil rights. Jim was assured that the matter would be looked into and he would be notified of the results.

Several days after the meeting with the State Representative at the end of January, he received another letter from the state. This letter was from the Domestic Relations Office ordering him to appear for a support hearing on the twenty-eight of February. Even though they were still legally married, Kate had been living on public assistance since she had left and he was being ordered to pay support for his children and possibly her.

He was not against paying support and there was no doubt in his mind as to his obligation to support his children. However, after recently going over his bank statements and discovering through the canceled checks and cash withdrawals that Kate had spent over eleven thousand dollars on bingo in the last three years, he seriously doubted that any money he paid for support would be used on his kids.

He knew it was an incredible amount that almost anyone would find difficult to believe, but he had all the data to prove it. Even that wasn't all of it, though: there were also thirty-eight returned checks for insufficient funds. It was all part of the report that he been preparing for his attorney. Tim felt that their financial status could be a key factor in proving her credibility, and he had put together everything he could find.

After receiving the letter from Domestic Relations, he gave Tim a call and an appointment was made to come in and see him. Several days later he stopped by his office with all the information Tim had asked him to gather to discuss his upcoming support hearing at the end of February.

Tim glanced over the figures Jim gave him, exclaiming that they could be very helpful at his hearing, then he broke the news to him about the attorney that Kate had acquired for the hearing. He had just been contacted that morning and presented with a proposal that Kate had her attorney prepare.

Jim sat and listened, contemplating each term as Tim read it to him.

Nothing that she asked for seemed unreasonable. Aside from some of the furniture, she also wanted the Plymouth station wagon back. Although he was still somewhat hesitant about giving her the car to use, he was about to agree to her requests when Tim mentioned an added comment by her attorney.

It was suggested if Jim were to agree to her terms, it could be quite favorable in regards to the charges against him.

Suddenly he became angry. His thoughts had drifted back to the arraignment hearing, and the deal he had agreed to so the magistrate would lower his bond. "Forget it, Tim," he mused. "I am not agreeing to anything."

Somewhat puzzled by his attitude, Tim sat forward in his chair folding his hands under his chin, as if he was waiting for an explanation.

"Look, I am sorry if I am seeming unreasonable," Jim continued. "I don't like their suggestion, and I don't see what this support hearing has to do with what she accused me of. It sounds to me like I am being threatened."

His emotions stirred up now, he began to blurt out the feelings that were bottled up inside him. "Tim, I am sick and tired of being told what is good for me, and what kind of deals I have to make to better my chances. This whole thing is crazy and never should have happened in the first place.

"All I want is the things that I planned for ten years ago: my wife and kids, a home, and a future to look forward to. I am fifty-one years old, Tim, and it is too late to start over. My kids need to grow up with me and not be supported through checks in the mail. Do you realize that I will be making support payments out of my social security check? What the hell kind of life do I have to look forward to after another divorce?"

He was almost in tears now as the memories of the past began to haunt him, and he began thinking about what it had been like after the breakup of his first marriage.

Twenty years ago he owned his own home, he had a good job at a meat packing plant which was only five minutes away, and the school his kids went to was almost directly across the street.

From the front porch, he and his wife could look out across the Mississippi River. He loved to fish and did whenever he had the chance. His wife Pat also liked to fish, and many evenings they spent on a barge overlooking the lock and dam, waiting for the catfish to nibble on their bait.

Not wanting to get stuck in a rut and spending the rest of his life working in the meat packing plant, he started his own cleaning business, trying to get ahead.

He worked long hours both day and night and things were just beginning to take shape when he was struck with the most devastating occurrence that was ever to happen in his life.

It was on the way back from the doctor when she informed him of her plans. Somehow he had dislocated his right shoulder at work and the doctor told him that it would take at least four weeks for it to heal. On top of news that he would be off work for four weeks, she picked that time to tell him that she had filed for a divorce.

Before it was all over, he had lost his home and part-time business, not to mention his family and everything he had strived for in the last ten years, and wound up living in a two-room apartment.

He had not even known that she had been seeing someone else. When he was forced to move from his home and another man moved in, it was almost more than anyone could be expected to bear and he still retained the feelings that he felt he would harbor forever.

"Tim," he said in loud whisper, slumping back in his chair almost as if he were ashamed of what he had done. "I am sorry. I didn't mean to get carried away."

"I understand," Tim said, seeming to be satisfied for the moment and not wanting to continue to discuss the matter. "It's still four weeks till the hearing, so why don't we just leave it go until then? If you happen to change your mind, we can deal with it at the hearing."

Now that the matter of the hearing had been settled for the time being anyway, he brought to Tim's attention the other thing on his mind.

"Tim, what is going on with the visitation rights that I am supposed to be getting? I have been calling these people since the day I got out of jail and no one will talk to me. I have called this Ms. Mayer at least a half a dozen times, and she is never available and will not return my call."

Trying not to be too dismal about the situation, Tim explained that it was not uncommon for CYS to act in this manner, although he did feel that they had gone to the extreme in not granting visitation rights or answering Jim's phone calls. He had been preparing a letter, he explained, asking that

CYS comply with the provisions in his bond agreement and schedule a visitation with his children.

"Thanks, Tim," he said. "I know they won't be able to ignore you like they have been me."

Now that his attorney had entered the picture, Jim felt sure that CYS could not continue to just look the other way—sooner or later they had to conform to the provisions of his bond.

One afternoon while in Warrington, he happened to notice Dee's van in the parking lot of Five Flags Pizza shop as he drove by. Dee Contrel was the owner of Five Flag Pizza where he worked. In case things slowed down at the store, he had thought about coming back to Warrington and work at both stores like he had done before. In the event that happened, Dee is the one he would have to talk to. Not in a big hurry to be any place, he decided to see if she had a few minutes to talk to him and turned around.

Having worked at the store for over a year, he knew most of the employees that worked there. As he stood in the back of the store and waited for Dee, he was greeted with a few nods of recognition and an occasional "Hi; how are you doing?"

Do they know about my situation? he thought as he detected something different in the way they spoke or even looked at him? He knew how word got around and he was sure that they had to know about him being arrested and what for.

He suddenly began to shift his feet back and forth, feeling uncomfortable and almost wishing he hadn't stopped. Dee walked in from the back room just as he was about to walk out the door.

"Hi, Jim—how are you doing?" she said with a smile that seemed to be a permanent part of her bubbling personality. "Did you want to see me about something?"

"Well I did, but if it is a bad time I can come back later," he said, still feeling awkward talking to her while standing out in the open with everyone listening.

"That all right—I have a few minutes. Let's go back to my office where we can have a little privacy," she said, sensing his uneasiness.

Her office was quite small, with barely room for two people to sit down facing each other. Being only a few feet apart, it was almost impossible not to notice each other's expressions as they spoke.

Knowing how busy she was he tried not to bore her with any unnecessary details and got right to the point of why he stopped. After finishing what he had come for, he told her that he would not take any more of her time and let her get back to work. As he rose to leave, he mentioned a few words about his present situation with the courts, and asked if it presented any problem in regards to his employment.

He felt like a fool and wished he could take back his words as he watched her facial expression.

Damn, he thought—why don't I keep my mouth shut until I stop and think for a minute? If there had been any doubt about the way she felt I wouldn't even be here.

Which was just what she told him.

CHAPTER EIGHTEEN

He knew it wouldn't help his problems, but he started to drink. He was not used to drinking much alcohol and had not been drunk in many years.

Everyone told him that he just couldn't just keep sitting home on his nights off. They all said that he had to go out and do something. "Go out, and have a few drinks," they suggested. "Relax, have some fun, enjoy yourself."

It began with just a few at first. Once or twice a week he would stop after work and drink a couple of beers and try to socialize. Soon the once or twice a week turned into almost every night. The couple had turned into as many as he could consume before the bars closed.

He could feel the change taking place, but he didn't care anymore. He was not meeting people and having a great time like everyone suggested, and he knew he wouldn't when he started drinking. There were many kinds of drinkers, and a party drinker he was not. He usually went to a quiet bar and drank alone.

Over twenty years ago he had gone through the same thing after his divorce from his first wife. Everything was different then: he was thirty and now he was over fifty, and too old to start over again.

He knew that he never should have started drinking again, but It was so hard to say no. Night after night he sat at the bars drinking himself into a stupor. After a few beers, he could feel the warm woozy feeling in his body and mind. Several drinks later, all the pain and hurt just seemed to drift back into his subconscious. He didn't care about what happened yesterday and he wasn't even capable of thinking ahead to the next day. All he cared about was that as long as he drank the alcohol made it seem like nothing mattered.

In spite of his drinking, the month of February still seemed to drag on. Tim had sent the letter he prepared to CYS but they still had not received a reply. Several days before the support hearing, not hearing from Jim, Tim called him asking if he had changed his mind about Kate's proposal.

His drinking only intensified his anger for the way the system functioned: He told Tim that he had not changed his mind and that he wasn't making any deals with anyone no matter what the consequences.

As they briefly discussed over the phone what was to take place at the hearing, Jim informed Tim of an unexpected death in the family.

Kate's great uncle had died and the funeral was the day of the hearing. Kate's mother had planned to be there in his behalf at the hearing in regards to their financial status, and she would not be able to attend.

The day of the hearing came and Jim came a little early as Tim requested. He wanted to talk to him about a change in his plans due to the inability of Kate's mother to appear.

"It was up to him to decide what he wanted him to do," he said. "It might seem a little bit unusual," he explained, "but there was no reason why the master shouldn't grant a postponement of the hearing for a later date. It probably won't make any difference in the outcome," he added. "It would just give you a little more time to think about what you wanted to do about her proposals."

"Okay," Jim told him. "Do whatever you think is best."

The hearing was held in downtown Warrington in a master's courtroom in a section of the Domestic Relations building. The courtrooms were much smaller then the ones in the county courthouse, containing a bench where the Master sat and a table with several chairs in the front of the bench where he and Tim, being one of the affected parties, sat. Aside from that, there were a couple of short rows of folding chairs, with the room not being designed to accommodate more than a dozen people.

He and Tim were the first ones in the room. After a few minutes, Kate and her attorney entered, followed by the Master.

They were sitting not more than ten feet apart and he couldn't help glancing at her. She looked like she was about to say something, when he broke the silence with the information about the death of her Uncle Pappy.

"Yes, I know," she said. "Mom called and told me and said that she was going to the funeral today."

She was about to say something else when the Master interrupted, announcing that he was ready to begin.

The meeting began with Tim handing the Master a paper containing the amount of his combined debts, his current weekly and monthly income, and his total assets. Then he asked that he be allowed to question Mrs. Hess so it could be revealed to the court how they had compiled such a monumental debt. After being granted permission, he began to question her about unexplainable cash withdrawals incurred by her and unreasonable purchases on his charge cards that eventually resulted in them being canceled.

At the insinuation that she was the one mainly responsible for his ruined credit, Kate became very flustered, answering some questions almost incoherently.

Jim did not understand what Tim was trying to do, until he noticed the effect his line of questioning was having on her. Tim wasn't even concerned about the answers he was getting; it was the manner in which she answered that he was interested in. He was trying to get her excited, so he could see how she would act under pressure if she were on a witness stand.

Following his third degree questioning, Tim was granted his request for a postponement after explaining the absence of his witness. The hearing ended as abruptly as it began, with both parties being told that that they would be contacted at a later date and everyone left the room without another word spoken.

CHAPTER NINETEEN

The drinking continued, and the days passed with him telling himself each morning as he awoke with a hangover that it would only lead to no good and he had to stop.

Tim sensed the change in him and having had a drinking problem himself at one time quite understood of his situation. Knowing, that to tell him the uselessness of trying to drink away his problems would do no good, he did warn him the consequences of getting charged with a DUI.

"That is the last thing that you need on your record right now," he told him. "With the way that Lieutenant Kotter feels about you, he would be sure to hang you for something like that."

March the ninth came and he sat in a bar after work, thinking about what meaning that day used to have for him. It was Kate's birthday and he had always bought her something special and personal on that day.

God he thought, as he ordered another beer. *It must be the alcohol. With everything that had happened he should hate her, but he still had some of the same feelings that he did the day he met her.*

The next day he got a call from Tim. He had received a response from CYS to the letter that he had sent over a month ago, and he wanted him to stop by for a minute before he went in to work. He did not say much else other than it was not what they had been hoping for.

It was certainly not the answer that he wanted to hear, as he soon discovered a short time later sitting in Tim's office, reading the letter that they had sent him. Not only did they continue with their relentless refusal to allow him the privileges as the court had prescribed, but now it seemed, according to their letter, that they had taken the liberty to deem any contact with his children detrimental and refused to allow visitations under any conditions.

Upon receiving the letter, Tim himself was a little upset. He had prepared a letter to send in reply, demanding to know how such a credential staff could have reached such a decision as they had.

CYS's response was almost immediate. Tim had sent the letter out on a Monday and by Friday they had scheduled a meeting for Tuesday morning of the following week. Jim, upon receiving the letter, called his attorney confirming his availability on that day and to see if he could give him a little insight as to what he could expect at the meeting.

Tim explained that it would be an informal meeting, with them facing one-on-one the staff of CYS, noting the names mentioned in the letter. There would be no court officials present and it would simply be a matter of CYS giving justification for their actions and him questioning their judgment in refusing to allow Jim his legal rights as a parent.

As Jim hung up the phone with thoughts of their upcoming meeting on his mind, he decided not to get his hopes up. Nothing he had encounter so far had ever been simple when it came to dealing with CYS and he had the feeling that this was not about to be any different.

Although he was early for the ten o'clock meeting Tuesday morning, Tim was already there waiting for him. Jim was surprised to see him there, but Tim explained that he had been to the courthouse already that morning and his business didn't take as long as he had expected.

The meeting was held in the courthouse square building, in the same office where he had his last encounter with Ms. Mayer. After a few words with Jim, in which Tim told him to let him do the talking and try not to lose his temper, Ms. Mayer came out of the inner office and asked them to follow her.

The room they entered appeared to be a conference room and much larger then the dinky little office where he had last met with Ms. Mayer. There was a table that was too big for the room in the center, with at least a dozen chairs encircling it. After maneuvering their way along the wall to the far end of the table, they sat down to wait.

They barely had a chance to pick up their conversation where they had left off in the other room, when Ms. Mayer, who had left, came back in the accompaniment of another gentleman that Jim didn't recognize. He was a short slim man, with dark hair and a neatly trimmed beard. Dressed in a dark gray business suit with a folder under his arm and appearing to be in his mid forties, Jim guessed that he was the other name mentioned in the letter, Ms. Mayer's supervisor.

As they prepared to sit down, the man introduced himself as Ryan Meric, Ms. Mayer's supervisor.

Tim began with a statement, demanding to know the reason that it was detrimental for Jim to see his children. He also pointed out that refusal to allow him visitation was a violation of his rights as a parent.

Jim could see by the unwavering expression on both Mr. Meric and Ms. Mayer's faces that Tim's insinuation of CYS'S wrongful doing had little effect. After pausing a few seconds to confer with Ms. Mayer, Mr. Meric answered with his prepared explanation.

"Mr. Meyer," he began, maintaining a rigid professional disposition that seemed to correspond with everyone that Jim had encountered from CYS so far, "after an extensive investigation, we believe that there is enough evidence to suggest that Naomie was molested. She is currently undergoing a psychiatric evaluation. It will not be complete until the psychiatrists at the Falk center in Pittsburgh, which is much better equipped to handle such cases, examines her. Until the examination is complete, we feel that it would be detrimental to Naomie and the other children as well if Mr. Hess has any contact with them."

The anger began to boil inside of Jim, and he felt a sudden urgency to just stand up and announce to the two individuals across the table what he thought about their investigation.

Tim, glancing to his side and noticing the look on Jim's face, laid his hand on his trembling wrist. "I know what you are thinking," he whispered, leaning close to him, "but I have been through this many times before, and it would accomplish nothing."

Following up with his line of questioning, Tim contended that the charges were alleged, and no court had established that he was the perpetrator of any crime.

Again they held steadfast to their convictions, this time Mariane Mayer being the one to voice her opinion.

"It could be psychologically damaging to Naomie," she said, "if Mr. Hess were to have any contact with her or the other children before the evaluation was complete. We are only doing what we feel is best for the children."

Mr. Meric and Mariane cited their reasons in what almost seemed to have become a heated contention.

"Being on top of this case and in close contact with Mrs. Hess," she explained. "In her opinion, she felt that Naomie was molested by Mr. Hess and in all probability the other children were subjected to the same treatment."

After calming Jim with a few words seeing the anger Mariane's insinuation had incited in him, he answered her with his own disapproval of her actions.

"Ms. Mayer," he said, in a slightly raised voice that was not typical of his normal speech. "My client is not on trial here and as I have said before, it had not been proven that he is anything like the individual you have been presenting such a image of. There has never been any evidence to suggest that he has ever been involved in anything of this nature in his past life, and I don't think that it is fair to him or to his children to just presume that he is guilty."

As Tim continued to argue the necessity of taking such actions, Jim began to wonder what the real reason was for them stopping him from seeing his children.

It didn't make any sense, he thought to himself. How could his seeing his children under the supervision of one of the caseworkers of CYS possibly be detrimental to anyone? Just what in the world were they afraid of, with one of their staff sitting there observing everything that was happening? After several more minutes of debating the matter of when visitation would be allowed, Jim's attorney finally came to terms with CYS on an agreeable arrangement. It was decided that just as soon as CYS had completed their evaluation of Naomie he would be allowed his visitation rights.

Tim had said that it was supposed to be an informal meeting. Maybe that was what it was supposed to be, but the way things turned out it was far from that. It reminded him a lot of what he had gone through at the arraignment hearing. There was no-one-on one with Mariane Mayer and Mr. Meric: the outcome of the meeting seemed to have been predetermined. CYS had already made up their mind as to the way they were going to proceed with his case.

Jim left the meeting angry and frustrated. They could not even give him an approximate date as to when all these tests and evaluations were to be complete, only that he would be notified. Tim had done his best and Jim commended him for his efforts. The question was where did he go from there.

"Tim," he asked him as he walked down the steps toward the street, feeling like his world was coming to an end, "Isn't there anything else we can do?"

"I am sorry, Jim," he said, apologizing for not having accomplished anything at the meeting. "Dealing with CYS as much as I have, I had hoped to make some headway. However, it seems that in your case, they have a one-track mind and are not easily dissuaded. There are always other alternatives," he said as they crossed the street and Tim suggested continuing their discussion over a cup of coffee in the drug store that they were approaching.

Over the next half-hour he explained another option, a long slow drawn-out process: they could appeal CYS's decision in court which would require a ruling by a judge. If his request was granted, it could take six months before a hearing could be scheduled with the courts caseload backed up the way it was.

"Look, Jim," he said. "I don't want to discourage you, but we have to look at the facts."

"In the event that you decided to go this way," he warned him, "you have to remember that you still have some very serious charges pending against you. Even if we have numerous witnesses to testify to your character, the court is not going to take these charges lightly and there is a great possibly that in spite of all our efforts the results could be the same as today."

"I am not telling you what to do or what not to do, but before you decide to spend the time and money to pursue this issue of visitation rights, I think that you should think about the most important matter at hand."

He knew that he was right, as Tim glanced at his watch announcing that he had another appointment and had to get going. Jim missed his kids and although he wanted to see them more than anything, he couldn't let his anger and resentment for the system confuse the main issue, the reason why he couldn't see his kids was because his wife had accused him of molesting his daughter.

His drinking became more intense after the meeting with CYS. Feeling his chances to see his kids remote and distant, he began to drown his grief every night after work. It seemed like all he had was memories, and the only way to contain the gloom of his future that persisted throughout the day was to dull the pain in the bars in the evening.

March twenty seventh came and as he spent Kristy's birthday in a local bar, the vivid recollections of the last year's birthday party especially took its toll. The tears rolled down his cheeks as he drank beer after beer trying to eradicate the ache he felt deep down inside that just didn't want to go away.

With the coming of April came the much-welcomed warm weather and the melting of the snow and ice that had accumulated over the harsh winter. There were many things that he needed to do that he had been putting off all winter because of the weather, but nothing was getting done.

The drinking had taken control of his life and occupied most of his spare time. He seldom stopped by his in-laws anymore. Frequently he received phone calls from Kate's mom, asking if he was all right, saying that they were worried being as they hadn't heard from him for awhile.

With Easter a short time away, he was asked to come over and spend the day with them. He didn't give a reply and just told her he would let them know.

It was noon on Easter Sunday when his mother-in-law called. Even after her insistence that he come over and join them, he declined her offer to spend the day with her family.

Since he had started drinking, his life had taken on a different perspective. He did not like being around people anymore unless he was drinking, and his in-laws were no exception. He knew that Easter would be like Christmas and New Year/s and with alcohol so readily available as it was at her mom's, he would get drunk and make an obnoxious fool out of himself. He just wanted to be alone and not be a bother to anyone.

His life sank to a new low as the days passed. Other than the communication with his attorney and his in-laws who called when they didn't see him for awhile, he avoided going anywhere in public. Other then his job, where contact with people was necessary, he kept to himself. Even in the bars where he spent most of his time when not at work, he isolated himself from crowds, talking only to the bartender now and then when ordering another drink. Life had little meaning anymore and the only thing that he looked forward to during the day was the time he would get off so he could go to the bar. Many times he came home and awoke the next morning, not knowing how he had got there, his last thoughts being at a bar somewhere in a drunken stupor barely able to keep his eyes open.

On the weekends he worked late and only having time to drink only a few beers before the bars closed, he would take a couple of six-packs home with him. The pictures of his family still hung on the wall and even the alcohol couldn't block out the remembrances of the way things used to be. He would sit there looking at them, with the tears running down his cheeks, drinking beer after beer thinking about the family cookouts on the grill on the front porch. Nothing could block out what he felt when visions of his kids laughing and playing in his front yard flooded his memory.

April passed and the month of May slowly seemed to drag on, until another important date appeared on the calendar. May the tenth was Mother's day in 1987, but what made it even all the more special was the birth of their son, Ron. Not only was it Ron's birthday, but it was also the birthday of another of his sons, from his first wife. James Michael Hess was born on May tenth, 1967.

Ron was their first-born, his and Kate's. Although each one of his children were special to him, the harrowing experience they had undergone with him as an infant had implanted a memory that would never be forgotten.

When Ron was three months old, he had lain in intensive care in a hospital in Harrisburg Pa., in what he and Kate feared was near death. For nine days they took tests and monitored his vital organs, assuring them both that everything was normal and he was in no danger. Finally one of the several doctors who had been caring for him discovered the reason for his skin discoloration. It had been hard to give a diagnosis, because Ron had a rare condition with an unusually high rate of met-hemoglobin in his blood. Although its symptoms were similar to heart problems and lack of oxygen, it was not the reason, and according to the few known cases that were recorded, his condition was not considered dangerous to his health.

He had gotten off work early that evening and by six o'clock was sitting at bar in a local tavern. He showed his pictures to the bartender, proud of his children as any father could be. After trying to socialize with a few of the local patrons and realizing the futility of his efforts, he retired to a quiet corner at a table and began to drink alone.

With more drinks came more memories and he began to think about the promise that he had made to himself and to his son. As Ron lay in the hospital bed, helplessly strapped and taped to the monitors, he swore that he would never leave his side and if he ever needed him he would always be there.

He had broken his promise, he thought. With his son's attention disorder and hyperactive condition, he needed him now more than ever and he wasn't there to help him like he had promised.

All evening he sat by himself, drinking himself into oblivion as he wrestled with thoughts of how he could have prevented the occurrences that resulted in the broken promise to his son.

He couldn't remember what time he left the bar. His condition was so questionable, it was possible that the bartender had just refused to serve him. Several times he remembered stumbling in the dark and almost falling down, as he made his way to his car.

He lay his head on the steering wheel as he started the car and then raised it, squinting his eyes as he tried to bring the spinning objects in his view into focus.

As he pulled out of the parking lot, his attorney's words flashed through his blurred senses:

"If you get caught driving under the influence, Lieutenant Kotter is going to take pleasure in prosecuting you and it is sure not going to make the charges against you and easier to contend with either."

He knew the consequences if he got stopped, but in his inebriated state of mind he had lost all ability to reason and he didn't care about anything.

It was a constant struggle to keep his eyes open and several times he found himself slipping into unconsciousness as he drove down the deserted back road to his home. Each time he would awaken suddenly to find that he had crossed the centerline or had drifted on to the shoulder of the road. As he rounded a curve a little too fast, almost losing control, a suicidal thought crossed his mind as he rapidly approached a concrete bridge.

It would be so easy to just end it all right here; all the pain and grief would be gone in an instant.

Even in his crazed state of mind he knew that it was not the way and he eased back onto the road, making it the rest of the way to his house.

He awoke the next morning fully clothed, lying where he must have passed out. The last he remembered was turning the TV on and laying on the couch with the room spinning overhead, making him feel like he was going to be sick to his stomach.

His head reeled as he got up to go to the bathroom, reminding him that he had greatly exceeded his limit the night before. His head hurt like hell and his stomach felt like it was on fire. Far from sober, he still had a little difficulty walking as he made his way into the kitchen to put on a pot of coffee.

A short time later as he sat down at the table sipping his coffee, trying to sober up, he began thinking about the night before.

"This is it," he said to himself. He knew that he would have to stop drinking, because sooner or later he wouldn't swerve in time to miss a bridge.

He had to go in to work at eleven that morning. All the coffee he drank did a good job of waking him up, but he still felt like hell. Mark, having felt that way many times himself, recognized the symptoms as soon as he walked in the door and seized the opportunity to aggravate him about his horrendous condition.

"God, you look like shit!" he exclaimed with a grin on his face. "You must have really hung one on last night."

"I feel like it, too," Jim mumbled, leaving the door open as he stepped into the bathroom and splashed his face with cold water. "It's the last time, though," he muttered almost incoherently as he looked into the mirror at his bloodshot eyes and resisting the urge to throw up, reminding himself that he never wanted to look or feel like this again.

He didn't break his promise to himself and instead of stopping at the bar when he got off work, he went over to his in-laws. With it being a warm evening, Harley, Don and J. R. were sitting out under the big maple tree at a picnic table when he pulled up in the driveway.

"Hi, stranger," remarked Don as he came within earshot. "I am glad that you finally stopped by to see us."

"It has been so long I had almost thought that you had forgotten where we lived," added Harley before Jim had a chance to say anything.

"Yeah I know, but things are going to be a lot different from now on," he said, realizing how much better he felt being around people that cared as he joined them at the picnic table.

It was around eight when he arrived and they sat there till some time after dark discussing what Harley was going to plant in the garden he was preparing to put in, until the chilly evening air persuaded them to go inside.

The days slowly passed and although he occasionally drank a couple of beers at his in-laws, he never went back to the bars that he had so frequently visited over the last few months. He began working on his cars and giving them the much-needed maintenance that he had been putting off because of his drinking.

He was invited over to his in-laws for their annual Memorial Day picnic. Every year the family friends and neighbors gathered for a cookout. He felt strange being there without Kate and the kids, and the uncomfortable feeling it gave him prevented the enjoyment that the day would normally have brought.

As the month of June slowly slipped by, the tension of the upcoming trial increased with each passing day. He had been keeping in close contact with his attorney and Tim had been explaining to him how he was preparing his case in the event that the DA would decide to take it to court.

Although character, was not normally a main issue in a criminal case, Time ruled, in his situation the credibility of Kate as a witness could be a major factor. That was why he told him that it was imperative that he tell him everything about Kate. In addition, it was also important to keep up with what was going on with Kate at the present.

Her mom was doing a very good job of keeping him informed of what was happening with Kate and the kids, as they had kept in constant touch since she moved out.

Kate was also concerned about the trial, as she revealed in a troubled phone conversation with her mom.

"I wished I had never went to CYs" she told her. "I wished I had never told them anything. All I wanted to do was leave Jim and I didn't mean for any of this to happen. I called the DA and asked him when this would be all over" she told her mom. "They told me at his office it could be a year before the case goes to court."

Six more months, he thought. He didn't know if he could take six more months of waiting. CYS had still not gotten back to his attorney about his visitation rights. It had been six months since he had seen his kids and now he was informed that it could be six more months before he would even know if his case was going to be held for court or not.

There were other pieces of information he had been receiving from his mother-in-law about Kate that were quite interesting. It seemed, not to his surprise, that Kate had managed to get herself in considerable financial difficulty. Not only was she three months behind on her rent and forced to move, but she owed nine hundred dollars on her long distance phone bill and her service was cut off.

She had been living in a different township and now she had moved back to Warrington with her adopted brother, Don. Kate had been adopted by Don's parents when she was five years old and lived with them until she married her first husband.

Don had been born with cerebral palsy, leaving him physically handicapped. After his mother died, alone and depressed, he had been living with Jim and Kate for periods of time over the last several years. When Kate had left, Don had been staying with them and he continued living with Kate and the kids, adding part of his SSI check to Kate's income to help make ends meet.

Kate's phone calls to her mom had been long distance, which was why she had run up such an outrageous phone bill. In spite of her unpaid bill, somehow she managed to get her phone reconnected. Since her calls were now local, she talked to her mom every day and often several times a day. Many times Jim stopped by before going to work in the afternoon and came in while Jane was engaged in a conversation with Kate.

On one occasion around the first of July, he stopped by for coffee and couldn't help overhearing a conversation between Kate and her mom. From the few words and the expression of on Jane's face he gathered that something drastic had happened between her and her brother Don.

Jane was in the process of preparing dinner, and also feeling that it was important to tell Jim what was going on before he had to go to work, she told Kate that she would talk to her tomorrow.

"Something very strange is going on over there," she said as she hung up the phone. "I have never known Kate to act this way before."

"Mom, what the hell is going on?" Jim said, becoming all the more confused by Jane's reaction.

"It's about Don," she said. "I guess her and Don got into a big fight about something. She told him to pack his things and then she took him back to his apartment in Bridgewood."

Don lived in an apartment building in Bridgewood, when his mother died. His handicap had not hampered his ability to function in society and his mother had seen to it that as he grew up he learned to take care of himself. Although living with Kate and the kids he had still kept his apartment, which was costing him very little to maintain because of his disability.

Jim was all the more confused now as Jane passed along the information that she had received from Kate. She had not gone into too much detail and the only thing that her mom could gather from her conversation with Kate was that something very serious happened between Don and the kids.

It didn't make any sense, Jim thought. Kate and Don had always got along well. He had been a big brother to her and had looked out for her all through her childhood. What could have possibly happened to make her say that he was not welcome in her house and in fact, she never wanted to see or hear from him again as long as she lived?

Over the next few weeks Jane had received bits and pieces of information from Kate, suggesting that Don had done something to the kids. Kate never explained what happened, and the exact reason for her banning her brother from her house still remained a mystery.

There were other things going on that he was slowly becoming aware of through Kate's conversations with her Mom. Ron had made several more visits back to Southwood Hospital where he had last been treated for his A.D.H.D. condition, and now two social workers affiliated with the hospital were stopping by once a week to check on his progress.

Ron had been going to summer camp at the townpark for the last several weeks and would be gone for the duration of the summer. Naomie was also going to special classes at summer school.

Jim or his attorney had still not been contacted by CYS, and as of yet Kate had never mentioned to her Mom any scheduling of visits for the kid's psychiatric evaluations.

It was going on the second week of July. Almost four months had passed since the meeting with CYS, raising an increasing amount of doubt in Jim's mind as to whether they had any intentions of keeping with the program as planned.

They are stalling, he thought. He didn't care how busy the doctors were, It was just not feasible to believe that it would take that long just to get an appointment.

The big question in Jim's mind though, *was why were they stalling? What could they possibly have to gain?*

CHAPTER TWENTY

On the morning of Tuesday July 12, he was over at his mother-in-law's discussing with her and Harley the possibility of moving in with them. With the constant harassment from the neighbors, add with the eviction notice that he had been ignoring since this whole ordeal began, he knew that it was just a matter of time before he would be forced to find another place to live.

He had to agree with their discovery about the senselessness of paying four hundred and fifty dollars a month rent, plus utilities. There was no reason for him to stay in a place where it was quite obvious that he was not wanted.

He and Kate had been looking for a house last fall, when this whole nightmare began. In spite of the tremendous odds, the last few months he had been desperately clinging to the hope that this matter could be resolved and they could find a place to live together as a family again.

"Don't be a fool," Kate's sister, Mary, told him when he talked about the possibility of getting back together. "After what she did to you, how could you ever trust her again? What she did was evil Jim, and nothing is ever going to change that."

He had decided to accept their offer and Jim was discussing the arraignments with Harley when the phone rang. Harley had suggested, since he had a three-bedroom house full of furniture to put everything in storage and just bring over the few things that he would need.

Jane had answered the phone and after a few minutes, Jim's attention was turned to the conversation that she was engaged in with Kate at the other end. It seemed that the kids had outgrown their clothes and with school coming up in six weeks, she didn't know where or how she was going to get the money to buy them what they needed.

"Tell her I will buy the kids any clothes they need, Mom," Jim said, overhearing enough of the conversation to understand what they were talking about. "Wait a minute," he said as Jane started to reiterate his message to Kate. "Just tell her I want to talk to her, and I will tell her myself."

Although hesitant, Kate agreed and Jane handed the phone receiver to Jim.

It was the first time they had talked in over seven months except for the few words at the support hearing.

"Jim" she said. "I am not asking you to do anything for me—It's just that the kids have nothing to wear that fits them anymore. You should see how much they have grown."

It was not the harsh tone of voice that their last conversation ended with that he heard. He didn't know if it was a put on, or if she was sincere about the way she was coming across to him.

"That is what I want to talk to you about," he said. "I want to see them. Look, can we just meet somewhere and talk?"

"But what about the court order?" she said, reluctant to meet in public. "What if CYS should find out that we were seen together?"

After explaining to her that there was nothing in the directive stating that the two of them could not meet, she agreed to meet with him after the bus picked Naomie up for school at one o'clock. She would arrange for the neighbor to watch Kristy and they would have until four o'clock before she had to be home.

She was waiting by the front door of Eat-n-Park when he pulled in the parking lot. "Can we go somewhere else?" she said, coming over to the car as he shut it off and prepared to get out. "I live near by and I am afraid one of the neighbors might get suspicious," she said, citing her reasons for not wanting to be seen there.

She began talking before they even left the parking lot. Since she seemed to have the most to say, he listened as they drove someplace where she felt more comfortable.

"I am sorry, Jim," she said, in a pleading tone of voice asking for forgiveness. "I am so sorry. I never meant to hurt you. How could I have ever thought that you would do something to Naomie?"

Now, if this isn't a sudden turn of events! he thought. After seven months of telling everyone that he molested his daughter, all of a sudden she decides that she didn't mean to do it. What in the world could have happened that was drastic enough to make her change her mind?

"It was Don," she said all of a sudden, with an intense look of hatred in her eyes. "I can't prove anything, but I am sure that he did something to the kids."

"Kate, what is going on? What the hell are you talking about?" he said, more confused now than ever as he turned into the parking lot of a little restaurant in Hunston.

The Pike Inn where they stopped was almost deserted. They sat at a quiet table in the back of the room sipping coffee as she began with the day of the meeting with Mariane Mayer.

"I picked up Ron from school and went up to her office as she requested," Kate said. "As soon as I sat down, she laid some papers on the desk in front of me and started asking all kind of questions about what was going on in our home."

Jim sat and listened as Kate went on to explain all the details that were left out in his conversation with Ms. Mayer in their meeting back in December. It was reported to CYS by the foster parents of the last home that

Ron had spent the weekend in, that Ron had exposed his privates to one of the girls of about his age while they were playing. As the case in an occurrence such as this, the names of the other people involved remained anonymous. It was then revealed to her the particulars following the incident that had induced the people to report what subsequently resulted in her being under suspicion of molesting their son.

"There was nothing in the papers they gave me that explained about what happened," Kate said. "It only said that I was under suspicion."

"Yeah, I know" Jim replied, sitting across from her stunned, as the shocking discovery of the real truth slowly unfolded. "I saw the papers myself."

"At first, I was angry when she told me that Ron had said I played with his penis all the time. I told her that it was all a lie and no such thing ever happened. Then, realizing that it was not the first time that Ron had fabricated a story and later told us that he lied and had made it all up, I told her about Ron's vivid imagination."

Kate was right, he thought, as she gave her explanation of what she felt happened. Ron may be diagnosed with A.D.H.D., but he was also very bright for a six-year old. More than once they had witnessed his little make-believe stories that were later proven to be untrue.

She told Mariane that she had been raped as a teenager and just the thought of someone molesting one of their children was unbearable, especially she told her, since she had been having flashbacks of something else that happened when she was very young. She was certain, although she could not recall any of the details, that she was molested as a child.

"I told her," Kate continued, "about that night I awoke seeing you with your arm around Naomie and how the sight of her snuggled up against you triggered something terrible and frightening in my past.

"All of a sudden she seemed to forget all about me," she went on, after pausing to take a sip of coffee, "She began to focus her whole attention toward you lying on the couch with Naomie."

Jim listened in awe as she went on to tell how Mariane bombarded her with questions regarding his intimate association with his children. How many times did he lay down with them? Was he alone with them often? Did she ever witness anything strange or unusual before? Did she ever witness him touching them in an unnatural way before?

"Jim" she said, starting to tremble now as she spoke. "I got angry and told her that what she was insinuating was crazy. When I got up, getting tired of her questions, she told me to sit down, stating that I wasn't allowed to go anywhere. Then she declared that they had enough evidence to place them both under suspicion of child abuse and have the children removed from their home.

"I was so scared Jim, that I didn't know what to do."

After being frightened out of her wits that CYS was going to take the children from them, she sat back down and listened while Mariane dictated to her what she felt had happened and what she wanted her to do if she wanted to keep her children.

As he sat there assimilating the incredible story that Kate was telling him, he tried to see if he could detect something that would suggest that she was making it all up. As much as he wanted to believe that everything she said was true, it he was still finding it hard to imagine that CYS had gone so far as to threaten to take the kids from her.

There was nothing in her trembling voice, and with the tears smearing her make up running down her cheeks, it was hard not to be convinced that she was telling the truth.

CY's had her bring Naomie in to the office on the following Monday after the meeting so they could question her. Even after receiving no information that would suggest anything had happened to her, Kate was told that they were still convinced that she was molested and she would have to go to the police department and make out a statement.

It was CYS's contention that she was lying to protect her husband. They believed that she had made up the story about something possibly happening to her when she was a child, and she was only saying that to cover up the real truth.

Kate, appalled at CYS's insinuation that she was lying to protect her husband, told them she refused to cooperate and was not going to accuse him of something that he didn't do. She was reminded that she too was still under suspicion, and in no uncertain terms that was still grounds to have the children removed from her home.

Angry, frightened and confused, she went to the police department as told, and revealed to them what had happened. She was sure that she made it quite clear to Detective Kotter that the only reason she mentioned Jim lying on the couch with Naomie was because it triggered a flashback of her childhood.

She was enlightened somewhat on the laws regarding child abuse by Detective Kotter, noting that it was her duty to report anything suspicious. She was also reminded that it was not a matter for her to decide what was right or wrong and that should be left up to the courts.

Kate paused for a few seconds while the waitress filled their cups and asked if they needed anything else. "Oh God, Jim," she said, after she left. "I have hurt you so much. For all these months I have put you through hell. Will you ever find it in your heart to forgive me?"

"But why?" Jim questioned after the shocking effects of her astonishing story began to sink in. "Why didn't you just come and talk to me and tell me what the hell was going on?"

"I couldn't Jim, she said, still trying to apologize for the hell she had put him through. "Don't you see? They told me that if I ever came near you or the kids, they would take them away and I would be under suspicion the same as you. That is why I was so scared when I came by the house and you were there. Mariane and Steve told me not to tell you anything about what was going on. They said it was their job to inform you of the accusations, and they would tell you everything that you needed to know."

"No wonder they didn't want me to know anything," he said, feeling the anger rise in him when he thought about how they had kept him in the dark all this time.

"Kate," he said, still angry at the way he had been treated and not quite ready to accept all the facts of her story. "Just why the hell did you go around telling everyone that I had molested Naomie when you knew that I didn't do anything? I know that you didn't believe that concocted confession Detective Kotter said I made because you told your mom that it was a lie. You even told her that you knew that I couldn't confess to anything."

"Oh, Jim," she said again, pleading for his forgiveness. "I am so sorry that I ever listened to any of those people."

"What people?" Jim asked with anger in his voice, wanting to make sure he knew just who he would hold responsible for persuading her to turn on him like she did.

"Well, it was all of them," she said, sounding like she didn't know in particular who to put the blame on. "I guess it was mainly Devlin and Didi Hargrove, though. They were the one's mainly responsible for implanting the doubts I had about you."

Didi Hargrove, he remembered, was the therapist that Kate was having regular visits with for the last several years. He did not have a high opinion of her or her methods, having gone to her once himself with Kate.

Devlin, being Ron's caseworker, was always in close contact with Kate and he could see how he too could affect her judgment.

"At first it was Mariane and James," she said. "They told me that I was lying and I was just covering up what really happened to protect you. Then they said that I wasn't having any flashbacks and just suppressing the things that I had seen."

She went on to tell how she began going to see Didi Hargrove every week, and sometime twice a week. At every visit, she was told the same thing: the nightmares she was having were not due to something happening in the past, but her refusal to accept what was happening in the present.

"She knew that she had witnessed her husband molesting the children," Didi repeated at each visit. "It was only a matter of time before she faced the truth and told them everything that happened."

"I felt like I was going crazy," Kate said, holding her hands to her ears and closing her eyes as if she was trying to block out all the sights and sounds around her. "I was so confused that I didn't know what to do. With talking to Devlin every day, and all the visits by Mariane and James, who kept telling me the same thing over and over, I began to believe that something did happen."

"If you were so convinced that I molested our kids like they said I did," he replied to her reason for her actions. "Why then the sudden change of heart?"

An enraged look came across her face as she spoke. "It was Don. Those flashbacks and nightmares that have been haunting me were caused by something in my past that I had blocked out for all these years. I know now what happened. It was Don all the time," she continued. "He molested me when I was eleven years old and I think that he might have done something to our kids."

So it's true, he thought: the reports about her and Don having a bitter disagreement and her taking him back to his apartment in Bridgewood was not just a idle rumor.

"All right," he said, not wanting to jump to conclusions before hearing the whole story, but finding it hard to control the anger fired by the mention of someone they trusted molesting their children. He sat forward in his chair, and tried to prepare himself for what he knew was another story that he was sure he was going to find hard to believe. "Tell me what happened."

The incident that took place, which caused Kate to relive the nightmare of her past, happened on a Thursday, almost two weeks before. It was the following day that he had heard from her Mom that she had taken Don back home to his apartment.

Naomie was not in school that day and Don was watching her and Kristy that afternoon while Kate went to the store. She came back a couple of hours later to discover that the girls were not there with Don.

Panic, being her first instinctive reaction to not finding her children where she left them, became replaced with confusion when Don told her that Dottie came by and took them to the park.

Dottie was a next door neighbor and was used by Kate as a baby-sitter from time to time, well-liked by the kids. It still did not explain, though, why the girls went with her to the park when they were left in the care of her brother.

The park was only several blocks away, so she left her car in front of the house and walked over to find her and the girls.

She was met by Dottie, who stopped pushing Naomie and Kristy on the swings when she seen her coming. She had an expression on her face that could only mean that something alarming had happened.

"I would get that son-of-a-bitch out of your house as soon as I could," she said, her face still beat red with anger from something that she had witnessed. Then she told her what had stirred her emotions, to cause her to be touched off the way she was.

She had just got home about a half-hour before Kate, and when she walked by the house she heard the girls screaming. At first she thought that they were just fighting, but something told her by the sound that it was more then that. When she knocked on the door to find out what was going on, it became quiet and no one answered.

After knocking several more times with her threatening to kick the door in if Don didn't open it, he came to the door, opening it a few inches and asked her what she wanted.

She pushed the door open, more suspicious than ever that something very strange was going on. As soon as the girls saw her, they started crying again and came over to her, grabbing onto her legs.

"There was no doubt, that he had done something to the girls to make them afraid of him the way they clung on to me," Dottie told her.

After questioning Don and not being satisfied with his answer that he wasn't doing anything and they were just being bad, she told him that she was taking the girls to the park and when Kate got home to tell her to meet her there.

She began asking the girls on the way to the park about why they were so afraid of their Uncle Don. It was what Naomie told her that caused her to be as angry.

"Don had been touching them," she had said, indicating where by pointing between her legs.

"That's when it all started to come back to me," Kate exclaimed. "I started to remember everything that happened. I know that you are going to find it hard to believe this, Jim," she said, as if she was shameful of what she was about to tell him. "I was molested by Don when I was eleven years old."

She hung her head, not looking at him as she recalled the horror of the events that took place over twenty years ago. It had gone on for several years, until Don found a lady friend. She was scared to death and never told anyone. She had begged him to stop and threatened to tell his mom. He told her to go ahead, saying that it wouldn't do any good because she wouldn't believe her anyway. She began to block it out of her mind and forget it ever happened. All this time it had worked, until the nightmares started to return a couple of years ago.

It all makes sense, Jim thought. The times he attempted to awaken her by making love and she had screamed and told him not to touch her made sense now.

"I almost went berserk when I started to think about Don doing to the girls what he had done to me," she said, raising her head and also her voice a little. "Dottie went with me back to the house," she went on, working herself into a frenzy as she vividly recalled the scene that had taken place. "He was sitting at the table when I walked in, and I told him to pack his things and get the *fuck* out of my house."

Kate looked around, realizing what she had said and how loud she said it.

If anyone was listening, they didn't seem to care, as it appeared that she hadn't attracted any special attention.

With everything that was taking place that day, she continued, she had completely forgotten that it was Thursday and the day that Mack and Dana stopped by for Ron's home visits. When Ron got off the bus that brought him home from summer camp at four o'clock, Mack and Dana arrived about the same time.

Don was getting his things together, and Dottie kept the kids occupied while she went outside with the two social workers from Southwood hospital to explain what was happening and why she wanted to cancel that day's visit.

They did not seem the least bit moved by Kate's recollection of her appalling childhood experience and simply stated as they were leaving, they would mention it when they got back to the office.

After they left, she helped Don pack his things, wanting him out of her house as soon as possible. The girls were afraid to ride in the car with him, so Dottie watched the kids while she drove Don back to Bridgewood.

The following week Mack and Dana came by for Ron's regular in-home visit. She asked them what was happening with her account of being molested by her brother and her suspicion that he had done something similar to the girls.

They still did not seem to find her story to be of any importance, and just said that they had informed CYS and Mariane and James were aware of her situation.

For over two hours they sat drinking warmed-up coffee as Kate unveiled the astounding tale of what had controlled the events of the last seven months. He listened to every detail as the pieces seemed to fall in place and confirm the suspicions he had since the whole ordeal began.

He desperately wanted to believe everything that she was telling him, as the overall picture came into view.

Then, the days and nights he spent in jail came to mind, and he knew that no matter what kind of an explanation she had, there would always be a doubt deep inside him that would never go away.

There were thousands of questions that he wanted to ask her, but as he looked at his watch he realized that they were running out of time, and he brought up the matter of seeing the kids.

"Jim, they talk about you constantly," she said, "and they want to see you, too."

It was then she told him about the little incident with Kristy when she left the house to walk down the street to meet him. Kristy had overheard their conversation on the phone and when Dottie, turned her back for a second, she slipped out of the house and attempted to follow her.

When Dottie caught up to Kristy, she exclaimed that she was going with her Mom to meet her Dad.

They discussed several possibilities of getting together where they would be inconspicuous, like one of the malls or grocery stores. Finally, as they prepared to leave, it was decided that he would stop by her house after work. No one knew him in the neighborhood. They had never met any of her family either, and if he should happen to be seen she could always say that it was one of her brothers. It would be after midnight when he got off, but with the court order denying his right to see the kids he knew that he would still be taking a great chance.

Still, he thought, as he pulled into the parking lot at Eat-n-Park to drop Kate off where he picked her up, *it was worth the chance.*

"Jim," she said, handing him a piece of paper she had scribbled her number on, hurrying, so she could meet Ron when he got off the bus. "Call me before you leave, so I can have the kids up and ready when you get here."

CHAPTER TWENTY ONE

He called her when as soon as he found out what time he expected to get done. They talked for a few minutes, and she explained what happened when she told the kids that their dad was coming to see them.

"You should have see them," she said. "They kept jumping up and down and running back and forth to the front door, wanting to know when they were going to be able to see you. They calmed down a little after I told them that you weren't coming until late tonight when you got off work."

It was just after midnight when he called back and told her that he was leaving in a few minutes. He was familiar with the street she lived on, having delivered pizza many times in the area and he tried to visualize the house as she described it to him. "There would be a light on and the kids would be at the door waiting," she told him.

As he made the twenty-minute drive to where Kate lived, all kinds of thoughts began to enter his mind: *It had been so long since he seen them, what was he going to say?. Kate said that she had talked to them, but how much would they understand?*

There was enough light to see someone standing in the doorway of the blue house she described as he pulled up to the curb. He got out of the car, looking around as he closed the door, still feeling a bit uneasy about being there.

"It's Dad!" he heard Ron shout and three figures began jumping up and down in the doorway as he approached the house.

Kate was standing behind the kids when he got to the front steps and she swung the screen door open to let him in.

"Guys, will you please get out of the way so your father can get in?" she said, putting her hands on the girls' shoulders and gently moving them out of the way to make an opening.

He stepped inside what appeared to be the living room, and paused for a few seconds waiting for his eyes to get adjusted to the dim light. The TV was on and the only other light was coming from a lamp on a table next to the door.

He looked at his kids as they stood in front of him like they were waiting for inspection. Ron had grown at least a half a foot since he last seen him.

Kate said that he was in summer camp, and it was evident from the dark tan how much time he had been spending out in the sun.

Kristy had grown too, although not as much as Ron. She had a big grin on her face, as she shifted from one foot to the other, impatient to get on with their reunion.

Kate had warned him what to expect from Naomie, saying it could take a little time for her to get used to him.

She stood there in her pajamas that were too small for her, with a slight smile on her face, the tight waistband attesting to the pounds that she had gained. He noticed that her long hair had been cut and she also had grown much taller. The gleam in her eyes that he remembered was gone, and as he knelt down the smile turned to an unfamiliar frown.

"No, get away from me. Don't touch me. I hate you," she said in a frightened voice, backing away as he held his hands out to her.

"God, Kate—what have they done to her?" he said as he stood up, horrified at her reaction.

Kate explained that Naomie had been acting in such a manner since she started seeing the CYS doctors.

"I don't know what they have done or said to her, Jim," she said. "It is not just you that she is afraid of—every time she gets near any man, she acts like this."

Those bastards! he thought as images of some doctor alone in a room with his little girl poking a rubber doll and asking her all kinds of confusing questions began to appear in his head. CYS tells everyone that the procedures they follow are designed to protect the welfare of the children, but what they have actually done is turn his little daughter into something that resembles a zombie.

"Give her time, Jim," Kate said, suggesting that he leave things as they were for the moment. "She loves you and she will remember you."

"Come on," said Kristy who had got tired of waiting and grabbed Jim's hand. "You want to see our house?"

"Yeah," said Ron, as Kristy began leading Jim toward the stairs, "and then we can play some Nintendo."

A short time later, after being given a grand tour of their house, Jim sat in a chair sipping a cup of coffee Kate had made while Ron and Kristy entertained him by doing somersaults on the living room floor.

Naomie, who had been standing off to one side, came over to Jim with a little smile on her face. Jim also noticed that gleam in her eyes returned as she spoke to him.

"Dad" she said in a soft voice that was just barely audible. "I can do that, too. Do you want to see me?"

"Sure" he said, his eyes becoming blurry with the sudden emotion that overtook him. "I would love to."

Kate was right, he thought, as Naomie became herself again. It was only a matter of time before she would feel left out and want to join in with her brother and sister.

"See?" she said, as she did a headfirst somersault and landed on her back with a loud thump. "I can do it just as good as they can."

It wasn't long before they became tired from their little workout, and started to show the effects of being woken up in the middle of the night.

As they sat down on the couch to get some rest, Ron decided that it was time to play some Nintendo. His mom cut that idea short, though, by reminding him that he had camp in the morning and Naomie had school, so they should all lay down and get some sleep.

Her explanation seemed to satisfy them and they remained content to just sit and talk. One by one, with Ron first, then Naomie, and Kristy last as she lay her head on his leg they drifted off to sleep.

"Jim," Kate said softly, after a few moments of silence, assuming that the kids had fallen asleep. "What are we going to do now?"

"I don't know," he answered, as he slid out from under Kristy's head and went out to the kitchen where they could talk without disturbing the kids. "I had never really thought about it until now when you mentioned it."

He was sure that Mike and Dana hadn't lied to her about telling CYS her recalling the horrifying experiences with her brother Don in her childhood. It was also certain that CYS had been made aware of her suspicions, of Don doing something similar to her children.

She had not heard anything from Mariane or James yet, which still did not seem unusual. Considering the speed that Jim and Kate were accustomed to, when it came to CYS acting on anything, it could be that they just hadn't got around to it.

Then there was the other alternative that he wasn't sure he wanted to even think about it was quite possible that CYS had chosen not to believe anything that Kate said.

Mariane had not listened to anything he had to say at the meeting he had with her in her office. Even with his attorney present at the encounter with her and her supervisor, they continued to reject any possibility that Jim might be innocent of any of their allegations.

Now with the new evidence that didn't seem to fit with their program, it would be much easier to disregard anything she said as not being true and continue with things as they had planned.

As heartless at it seemed, he was sure that sooner or later they would find out that that was exactly what CYS had done.

For the next couple of hours, Jim and Kate sat at the small table in the kitchen discussing what they were going to do. Lacking clear-cut knowledge of the law, it was difficult to know just what CYS was going to do when they found out that Kate had a change of mind. It also made it hard to imagine what was in store for them in the future.

The one thing they did come to an agreement on was that they would not tell anyone what had happened there that night. Kate was going to do her best to emphasize to the kids how important it was for no one to know that their dad had been there to see them.

"Kate," Jim said, in the only solution he could think of for their current situation, "I am going to call Tim, my attorney, as soon as I get home and ask him what we should do. Once he gets over the shock when I tell him that I have seen you and the kids, I am sure he will have some suggestions."

It was after four o'clock in the morning when Jim decided to go so Kate could get at least a few hours rest before she had to get up with the kids.

"Jim," she said as he got up and tried to rub the cramps out of his legs from sitting in one place too long. She came around the table and taking his hands in hers and looked into his eyes. "Please don't go. I want you to stay here with us tonight."

He knew that if he had any common sense he would leave while he had the chance, but there was something about the way she looked at him that made him forget about common sense.

"The kids would be so happy to see you when they wake up in the morning," she said, making it all the harder to refuse. "You can stay in the house until they leave and no one will see you."

She wrapped her arms around him, pressing her lips against his, assuring him that the kids weren't the only reason that she wanted him to stay.

They took a quick shower together, enhancing the fervor that had stirred in them. When they retiring to bed to make love, it was not just lustful sex; instead, they released the emotion which had been building since their separation, and it seemed to explode with their intimate contact.

They had not been to sleep long before they were awakened by Kristy crawling into bed with them. The excitement she showed at still seeing her dad was enough to convince the both of them that it would be useless to try to go back to sleep.

It was seven thirty, and time to wake up Ron and Naomie when they stopped playing games with Kristy and went downstairs. Kate put some coffee on and got the kids clothes together while Jim sat down at the table with Kristy, who insisted that her dad eat some cereal with her.

Jim went over with Kate and stood at her side as she awoke Naomie lying on the sleeper couch. She sat up yawning and rubbing her eyes, until she seen her dad.

"Hi, dad," she said, with a big smile on her face, reaching up with both arms and grabbing him around the neck and giving him a big hug.

Ron, who had been stretched out on the sofa, began to stir, awakened by the little bit of commotion that had been going on. He sat up somewhat startled, but also showing a great delight at Jim being there.

"Dad," he said all of a sudden, surprising the both of them. "Are you going to come and stay with us now? We got plenty of room. Dad can come and stay with us, can't he Mom?" he said, looking at Kate, as if he were pleading for her to say yes.

Kristy who had finished her breakfast and come over to join them, added her few words, "Yeah, Dad, will you come and stay with us."

Jim, somewhat taken aback by their sudden pleas, sat there for a moment not knowing what to say. He knew that what they were asking for was impossible, but he was finding great difficulty choosing the right words to explain why.

Kate, seeing the spot that the kids had put him in, spoke up, bailing him out of his predicament.

"Look, kids," she said. "I know that you want your dad to come and live with us, but he just can't right now. We can still talk to him on the phone though, and maybe he can stop by and see us once in a while.

"Come on now you, guys" she said to Naomie and Ron, changing the subject. "You have to get dressed, and I want you to get something to eat before it is time to go."

With their dad's help, it wasn't long before they were all dressed and ready. Ron even found the time to show Jim how good he was at Nintendo before his bus came.

Again Kate cautioned Ron and Naomie as it was time for them to leave how important it was to keep their secret about seeing their dad. She told them that if anyone found out he would not be able to come and see them anymore.

She wasn't too worried about Ron and Naomie she told Jim, as they talked for a few minutes after she put the kids on the bus. "They are old enough to understand how important it was not to say anything."

It was Kristy, they both agreed that would bear watching, as she stood there listening and grinning from ear to ear, looking like she just couldn't wait to tell someone all the exciting news.

He kissed Kate, and after giving Kristy a big kiss and hug promised that he would be back to see her soon. Easing out the front door, he glanced around, still feeling nervous as he headed for his car.

It was not yet nine o'clock when he arrived home, and he knew that Tim wouldn't be in his office yet. Afraid he would fall asleep if he waited, he called and left a message on his answering machine.

He didn't bother to go into the bedroom to lay down. It was already hot and it looked like the day was going to be another scorcher, so he slipped out of his pants and shirt and lay on the sofa with the fan turned on him.

Just as he was about to doze off, the phone rang.

"Jim," said the voice at the other end. "I knew that you were tired when you left, and I just wanted to make sure that you got home all right."

"Kate, I am fine," he said. "Now, what else is on your mind?"

He knew her well enough to know that it wasn't the only reason why she called. There had to be some news she felt was so important that it couldn't wait.

"You will never guess who I just talked to," she answered, confirming his suspicions. "Your landlord and favorite neighbor, Jean. She called to inform me that you didn't come home last night."

Jean's son owned the property they were renting when they first moved in. Due to serious financial difficulty, namely money owed to back taxes, the property was put up for public auction. Jean, along with monetary help from her daughter's boyfriend, purchased the property and now Jim had to contend with her as the landlord, or at least until he moved.

She was just being sarcastic about Jean. There was no doubt in either of their minds as to what he thought about her.

"Kate, what the hell is going on?" he said, astonished that she would even be talking to Jean. Then the thought crossed his mind as to how Jean would have gotten Kate's phone number. "How did she get your number, and why would she care if I came home last night?"

"Jim," she said, trying to apologize for the surprise. "You have got to understand how I felt after all the coaxing and prodding from CYS. I had called Jean and asked her to be a witness for me if I needed her."

I wonder how many more surprises I will have in store for me he thought at his sudden realization that he was being spied on by his neighbors ever since Kate's departure.

"Jim, I am sorry," she continued. "I was so mixed up and confused I didn't know what to do." Then she went on to tell him about some of the things Jean had told her: he was allegedly witnessed drinking and entertaining women on several occasions. Every time one of her grand kids or the neighbor's kids came outside when he was home, he was supposed to have been seen peeping through the curtains staring at them like some kind of a pervert.

"Kate," he said, wondering what kind of sick deviate minds were required to have the audacity to spread such rumors. "How could you be stupid enough to listen to that two-faced bitch, after what she has put us through with her lies and accusations?"

What had begun last evening with a very emotional and tearful reunion and seemed to have hopes of developing into a promising future, suddenly began to leave his mind full of doubts.

It was a horrible and depressing thought, but it was hard to think positively when given the news that Kate was being informed of his every move by someone he believed that she detested.

"I swear to you that every thing I have told you is the truth" she said, sensing his doubt as he had paused for a few seconds, not saying anything while he gathered his thoughts.

"Kate," he said in answer to her assurance that she wasn't lying, "I don't know what the hell is going on, but I am too tired to talk about it now. I need to get some sleep before I have to go to work this afternoon.

"As soon as I got home, I called and left a message on Tim's answering machine" he said, changing the subject. "I will call you this evening if I hear back from him, and let you know what he says."

CHAPTER TWENTY TWO

It was around four o'clock that afternoon when he was awakened by the phone ringing.

This time it was Tim, his attorney, returning his call. After overcoming the shock from the news Jim had for him, he agreed that they should get together as soon as possible and made an appointment for nine the next morning at his office.

Jim called that evening from work as promised, and after talking to the kids, informed Kate of his morning meeting with his attorney. He did not go into detail about his conversation with Tim, just saying that he was surprised and showed a great concern for the new turn of events.

For two hours the next morning he sat in Tim's office spelling out the details.

After listening for some time, Tim interrupted Jim with a few questions of his own.

"How does Kate feel about all of this?" he said.

Describing briefly her feelings from the night before, Jim went on to answer his next question of what she wanted to do about it.

"She wants to talk to you, Tim" he said. "We didn't know what kind of legalities were involved and she was hoping that you would be able to give her some suggestions."

It was a bit unusual what Jim and Kate were suggesting, since she had been the one who accused him in the first place, but Tim couldn't see anything illegal about Kate coming in to see him.

"What about CY's" Jim said, seeking some kind of a reassurance for Kate that she wouldn't get into big trouble for turning on CYS like she was intending to do.

"Legally, I can't see anything they can do," he said. "They might threaten her with legal action, but it would be nothing but a bluff to try to get her to change her mind. In the meantime," he added, as they ended their meeting, "I would strongly advise not to say anything to anyone before Kate talks to me."

He had to start at eleven thirty that day, so when he finished with Tim it was almost time to go into work. Later, in the early afternoon when things slowed down, he called Kate and told her what Tim said about the chances of CYS making an attempt to get her to change her mind.

After giving Kate his attorney's phone number and repeating Tim's instructions as to what he wanted her to do, Kate told Jim she would call him back as soon as she finished talking to him. It was not much more than fifteen minutes after he hung up when Mark answered the phone and shouted over the noise of the dough mixer that his wife wanted to talk to him.

"I have an appointment to see him at nine in the morning" she said, sounding a little bit nervous about their meeting.

"Relax," he told her, sensing the uneasiness in her voice as she explained about Tim wanting her to come in and make out a deposition, recanting her statement that she had made out to the police department and exonerating Jim from any wrongdoing.

"There is nothing to be afraid of," he assured her. "When you go in there to see him, just tell him everything as you explained it to me."

"I know there is nothing to be afraid of," she said, still with a little anxiety in her voice. "After the treatment he gave me at the support hearing, I didn't know what to expect though."

Jim laughed to himself as he thought about Tim's expressiveness at the hearing. "That was just a put-on," he chuckled. "He is really not that kind of a guy. You'll see when you talk to him."

It was Friday night and after volunteering to work a double shift, it was after two thirty when he got home. He was still sleeping when Kate called him the next morning.

"You were right," she said when he answered the phone. "He wasn't that kind of guy."

After giving Jim the details, she mentioned the possibility of him stopping some time over the weekend to see the kids.

He had to work late Saturday evening and he didn't want to risk coming over in the daytime. Having off all day Sunday, that evening seemed to be the best time, with less chance of him being seen.

They were all happy to see him and expressed their delight as soon he appeared at the front door, except for Naomie. As before, she was a little shy and not as hasty to respond to his presence. She stood aside with a questionable frown on her face, as if she was trying to decide whether she wanted to participate or not. Her decision was only momentary though as she soon joined Kristy struggling desperately in her losing battle of tug of war.

Ron had Jim by one hand trying to steer him toward the TV to play Nintendo with him while Kristy had his other hand, and having other ideas wanted her dad to play with her first. The matter was soon settled, and the next several hours were spent with Jim engaged in the joyous task of attending to his kids continuous demanding needs.

Later after joining together to accomplish the monumental task of putting the kids to bed and managing, in their excited state, to get them to go to sleep, Kate and Jim settled back to talk more about the rapidly changing events of the last week.

Kate told Jim what she felt like when she first entered Tim's office, and how she began to relax and feel more comfortable once they began to talk.

Now that Kate had seen Tim and signed a statement vindicating Jim of any criminal acts, there would be a lot of things that Jim would have to go over with Tim about their immediate future.

He had a brief discussion with Tim on the phone Friday after Kate's meeting with him.

The charges against him were still pending, Tim explained, and would continue to be until the DA reviewed his case and made a decision in the matter. As for CY's; Kate was their only witness, and without her it would be next to impossible to take his case to court without any evidence of a crime being committed.

When it came to the matter of his alleged confession, Tim explained, they could try to use it as some kind of leverage, but again without Kate as a witness and nothing else to go on, he rather doubted that it would have any effect.

With so many things to talk about, it was two in the morning before they realized what time it was. He had to work in the morning, so he suggested that they continue their conversation later.

They were sitting on the sofa in front of the TV talking. As he made a motion to get up, she put her arms around him, embracing him in such a way that left little doubt as to what her following intentions were.

A thought flashed through his mind about what happened that chilly day back in December at the end of his driveway, when he told her if she filed for divorce, he was going to fight for custody of the kids.

"I hate you, you bastard, and I will make sure that you never get our kids," she had said to him.

Could he trust her after that? Was it possible that the constant coercing by CYS had instilled in her such a fear that she had just lashed out, not meaning any of the things that she had said?

Unsure as he felt about Kate after what he had been through, there was one fact that still remained: this was the woman that he had promised to love and cherish, in sickness and in health, and for better or worse.

Kate was not the woman that hated him and wanted to destroy him, he thought, as they walked toward the stairs with his arm around her shoulder. *She was his wife, and the woman he had loved for ten years and somehow felt would always love, no matter what happened. She had given birth to their three beautiful children, and the feelings they had shared was something that would never be forgotten.*

Awaking shortly after daylight, he slipped out of bed and got dressed. He wanted to stay and be there when the kids got up, but his intuition told him that he was already pushing his luck.

They had talked about it before they went to sleep, so it was not a surprise when she awoke seeing him preparing to leave.

"I love you," she said, looking at him with her eyes half open as he bent over to kiss her.

Ron stirred a little, as he stepped into his bedroom and kissed him on the forehead. Both of the girls managed a little grin as he tiptoed into their room and kissed them on the cheek. He eased out of their room, being careful not to awaken them and headed down the stairs.

When, he thought, as he opened the front door and looked around to see if anyone was in sight. *When, would he be able to wake up with his kids, and not have to sneak out of the house, afraid of being seen?*

Things were quiet the next couple of days, and even Kate was amazed at how good a job the kids were doing at keeping it a secret about Jim being at their house, up until Thursday, that is.

It was late afternoon and Ron was due home from summer camp soon. Jim had been at home packing all day, preparing to put his things into storage so he could move in with Kate's parents. He had just gotten dressed for work and having a few minutes before he had to leave he called to see how things were going and to talk to the kids.

It hadn't dawned on him what day it was until he heard voices in the background. "No, it is not your Daddy, Kristy," he heard Kate say when she answered the phone. By the way she said it, he was sure it was a signal that someone else was there, and she didn't want them to overhear their conversation.

"Kate, call me later at work and let me know what is going on," he said, sensing her urgency to discontinue their conversation as soon as possible.

He had forgot about it being Thursday and the day Mack and Dana came for Ron's evaluation. Those had to be the voices he had heard in the background. It was not a wonder, then that Kate had told Kristy that it was not her Daddy on the phone.

There was a message that his wife had called when he got back from one of his delivery runs, several hours later.

"Oh, Jim," she said. "I am so scared. Mack and Dana were here when you called. Kristy thought it was you I was talking to, and she didn't believe me when I told her it wasn't. After that, I couldn't get her to shut up."

Jim knew what Kristy was like once she got going, and it wasn't even necessary for Kate to explain what happened after that. Mack and Dana started asking her questions, and in spite of Kate's efforts to keep Kristy quiet, they soon came to the conclusion that Jim had been there to see the kids.

Kate denied that Jim had been there, but did admit that the kids had been talking to their dad on the phone. She had tried to explain to them, that after the recollection of the flashbacks, she felt that she had been pressured into blaming Jim for something that didn't happen. Now that everything had come out into the open and she realized what she had done, she hoped to rectify some of her wrongdoing by letting the kids talk to their Dad and establish the loving relationship that they had been deprived of.

Mack and Dana were very disturbed at her declaration of Jim's innocence, exclaiming that she was confused and didn't know what she was doing and should not be so hasty in dealing with the welfare of her children.

"The big blow came," Kate said, "when they handed me some papers to sign pertaining to Ron's in-home visits. I had picked up the pen and having the feeling that something wasn't right, I decided to read the fine print. Having taken for granted the reason why they were there to see Ron, I couldn't believe what I was reading. The fine print said, "Post Traumatic Syndrome." They felt that Ron was sexually abused. Are you ready for this?" she asked, pausing for a second. "They felt that the perpetrator was his father. That's why they were coming to see Ron, not because of his A.D.H.D. problem."

"God," Jim thought, as Kate went on to tell him how angry she became at the discovery of their real intentions. *"Is there any limit to just how low, sneaky, and underhanded these people could be?"*

Mack and Dana had no explanation for the deception, exclaiming that they had been hiding nothing, and they had assumed that Kate knew why they were coming to see Ron.

Acting almost as if annoyed by their discovery, they proclaimed to Kate that everything that they had seen and heard there today would have to be reported to CYS.

"I know that I am going to get a call from them first thing in the morning, Jim," she said, the anxiety showing in her trembling voice, "and I just don't know what I am going to tell them."

"Don't tell them a damm thing," he said, seething from the double-dealing steps being taken by CYS. "At least, not about me and you and the kids. They are going to find out about your statement that you made to Tim, if they haven't already, but just don't let them con you into telling them anything that they don't already know."

Things started to get busy and he had to hang up. Before he did though, he told her that if she was called in to talk to anyone at CYS to make sure that she called him.

It was early the next afternoon when Kate called back. He was not surprised when she told him that she had just gotten back from a meeting with Mariane and James at their office.

It was just the way they worked, he thought. After two weeks, Kate had still heard nothing from them about her suspicions of her brother Don molesting her kids. Then, the next morning following their discovery of him communicating with his kids, she was immediately called into their office to explain what was going on.

"Boy, were they pissed!" she said, enunciating their reaction to the statement recanting her allegations.

"I had to show it to them," she said. "Mariane and James were both there, and they started in on me about how I was so confused I didn't know what I was doing. When they told me that their only concern was doing the right thing for the children, I got angry and showed them the statement that I had signed."

What followed then was a confrontation between the three of them, in which she told them just how she felt about all the assistance they had been giving her.

Ever since her meeting with Mariane on that fateful Friday back in December, she felt like they had pushed and prodded her into every move that she had made. Now that the truth had been brought out into the open, she realized the terrible mistake that she had made, she now wanted them to get off her back so she could go about the business of trying to put the pieces of their lives back together.

Of course they did not see it her way: their contentions were that there was still enough evidence to substantiate their beliefs that her husband had molested their children. Besides, believing that she was still lying to protect Jim, they felt that his alleged confession was all they needed to continue with their case against him.

Since she had first heard about the confession that Jim was supposed to have made she knew that it was a lie. She had told her mom that she didn't believe a word of it, simply because nothing had occurred. With the mention of his confession being used in their attempt to prosecute Jim, she exploded with her resentment toward their intentions.

"That trumped-up confession is nothing but a bunch of bull!" she told them. "I read it, and knowing my husband quite well after ten years, it was obvious that not one word of it was his."

After of arguing with Mariane and James, who seemed to be unmoved by anything she had to say, she became frustrated, feeling like they were trying to back her into a corner. She told them that after talking to Jim's attorney she knew that no matter what they said, without her as a witness they had no case.

She was warned before she left their office that any communication her husband had with the kids would be considered to be a criminal act and would be dealt with accordingly.

Jim was well aware of the position that CYS took regarding the visiting of his kids, but at some point in time since their joyous reunion he had ceased to care about what they thought.

He talked to the kids every day, not seeing where it stated anywhere that he couldn't speak to them over the phone. In spite of being warned about the danger, he still stopped by in the evening on several occasions. He couldn't help it, after Kate continuously told him over the phone how she had noticed the transformations taking place since he had re-entered their lives.

Ron's schoolwork had been improving in giant leaps and bounds. His attitude had taken on a whole new perspective, and what was barely passing grades had changed over the last weeks into A's. He was proud of his work and showed his papers to his mom every day after school, exclaiming that he wanted his dad to see his papers too.

Naomie had become a different person, since the first evening when she stood back frightened and trembling. The sparkle in her eyes returned, as well as the smile, laugh and giggle that was all part of her bubbling personality. Her school bus driver had even become surprised at her sudden change and had asked Kate what had happened.

Kristy never stopped talking about her dad, and every time Jim called Kate she made sure that she got her chance to talk to him on the phone.

Everything seemed to be going smoothly or as well as could be expected considering the situation, until the day that Kate came home one evening to find the message on her answering machine. It was CYS, and they said that it was important that she get hold of them as soon as possible.

She had heard nothing from them for the last couple of weeks since their last meeting. It wasn't their call that was surprising, but the fact that they had called her after business hours that she was quite disturbed about.

It was Sunday evening and he had just got home himself when she called to tell him about the message. As a matter of fact, he had just left her and the kids at the Dairy Queen where, as Tim suggested in case they were seen, "he had accidentally bumped into her and the kids." The first thing that came to mind was that someone had seen them together.

He could feel his own pulse began to beat faster as he tried to calm Kate down. "Relax," he told her, while trying to assure himself that he knew what he was talking about. "If CYS wanted to arrest me, I think I would already be in jail. They wouldn't have bothered to leave a message on your answering machine."

It would have been just like before, he thought, as vivid recollections of his previous arrest came to mind.

Since it was Sunday evening and she couldn't call them back, it meant that there was nothing they could do but wait until they opened in the morning. It was clear from the message CYS left that as soon as she called in the morning, she would be told to come in and talk to them.

It was almost noon when he heard from her the next day. She was almost frantic as she attempted to describe what happened over the phone. "Oh God, Jim," she began between sobs. "What are we going to do? They want to take our kids."

She had just gotten home, and had not yet recovered from the trauma she had undergone at her meeting with CYS.

"Whoah Kate, relax, take a deep breath, and try to calm down a minute" he said, trying to comfort her. "Just take your time and start from the beginning."

After assuring her that he was never going to let that happen, she calmed down enough to tell him the whole story of what went on at the meeting.

As they both had expected, as soon as she called CYS she was told to come right down to their office to discuss her problem. Someone, it seems, had reported that not only was he seeing the kids, but he had also been staying overnight at her house.

As usual she was told that the source of these allegations was privileged information, making her wonder if it wasn't a lie and just a way of getting her to come in there.

After Kate flatly denied that Jim was staying overnight, they brought up what Kate felt was the real reason for her being there.

Shortly after Jim's reunion with the kids, Kate had decided that it was not necessary to have the kids seeing the doctors that CYS had been scheduling them to see every week.

Naomie had come out of the shell that she had been in, and one of Kate's answers to her dramatic change was her renewed association with her father. They both noticed the difference in her as soon she stopped seeing the doctor they felt had been brainwashing her.

She had canceled Ron's in-home visits by Mack and Dana, which she felt was the primary reason for the change in his whole attitude.

There was no sense in her going to Didi Hargrove, her therapist, since she felt that continuing to see her would do nothing more than further damage her relationship with her husband.

Kristy had been seeing one of the doctors along with Naomie at C.A.R.E., which was another government-funded program available to minorities. She canceled the doctor's visits for Kristy along with Naomie's, never quite seeing any sense in them in the first place.

She was right about their real reasons: this was why they had called her in. It was to discuss all the issues that they felt were so important to the welfare of her children. Of course, they were not at all happy about her defying them.

When she removed the children from all the programs that had been prescribed by CYS, Mariane and James felt that she was depriving them of their suited care. They informed her that they were recommending her children become dependents of the court, to ensure that they get the proper treatment they needed.

Those bastards! Jim thought as Kate told him what happened. *Is that all these people think of? How many agencies they can recommend his kids to,* or how many programs they can enroll them in? Didn't anyone have brains enough to even think about going to her house, and see for themselves the change in the kids?

That was just what she told Jim, as she continued with her account of the meeting.

"It wasn't necessary," they told her. They still believed that Jim had molested his kids. It was imperative that her kids continue to see the doctors, and, for her to continue with her visits to her therapist.

Kate's insistence that none of these programs were necessary was in vain, as CYS dictated to her the actions they were preparing to take to ensure that her kids continue to get the treatment that they had prescribed.

"Jim, what are we going to do?" she said as she began to sob again. "You can't let them take our kids."

"I am not going to let them take our kids," he said, hoping he could back up his words, considering his own precarious situation. "Give me a chance to talk to Tim and see what he has to say. I am sure that this is not a situation that he has not encountered before. I am certain he will be able to tell us what to do."

Tim was out to lunch when he tried to reach him. When he returned and heard Jim's urgent call on his answering machine, he called him right back.

"Hi, Jim," he said, in a calm unwavering voice. "Why do I have the feeling that what you are about to tell me is not going to be good news?"

"If all I had was good news, I probably wouldn't need an attorney" Jim answered in return to his comment. "Tim, look—we got more problems. You know that Kate stopped taking the kids to the doctors and stopped going to the therapist. CYS called her in to see them using the excuse that someone had reported that I was staying there. When she went in there, they told her that they were not at all happy with her refusal to keep the kids in the programs they had prescribed for them. Now they are planning to make them dependents of the court."

"Jim," Tim said after pausing for a few seconds to digest this new information, "If it is possible, I want you and Kate to meet me here in the morning. Let me think about this overnight, and I will have some kind of a answer as to how we will proceed with this then."

"We will be there," Jim said, and hung up the phone.

Jeeze, what a mess, he thought to himself. *Could things ever get more complicated?* He hired Tim to represent him against allegation presented by his wife. Now, the tables had turned in such a way that he was asking him to side with the same one who had accused him to prevent their children from being made wards of the court.

Kate had to wait until she got the kids off to school, and after dropping Kristy off at the baby-sitters, she met Jim in Cantonville at Tim's office.

Together, they sat in Tim's office and filled him on the details of what had been happening since their last meeting.

After listening for some time, Tim finally held up his hand in a gesture to signify that he had heard enough.

"It is going to be difficult," he said, "but I think that there is a chance that we might be able to come out ahead in this."

Jim wasn't sure just what he meant by "coming out ahead," and he was just about to ask him to clarify his last remark when Tim proceeded to explain what they were up against.

Although Jim retained the right to contest any decision CYS had about making his kids wards of the court, the fact remained that he was still under suspicion of molesting his children. This was not a matter that the court was going to take lightly, and was not exactly a mark in his favor.

The next problem they had to face was Kate. In regards to the case that was still pending against Jim, she could still be used as a potential witness by the state. Even though she had recanted her statement about her allegations, she could still be put on the stand to testify about her original accusations. If that were to happen, Tim might not be allowed to represent her, on the grounds of conflict of interest. In that case, it would be wise to have her represented by another attorney.

Then, there was the matter of witnesses: they would have to prove that by taking the children out of the programs recommended by CYS, it had done them no harm, and in fact, made a substantial improvement in their attitude and behavior.

There was the thing about their suspicions of Jim seeing the children, which Tim did not think was too important. He mentioned, as he had before when Jim first told him, that if it really mattered to them, they would have done something about it long ago. He did remind them, that it was only common sense to heed their warning, and be very cautious about their meetings from now on.

"If you would like a few minutes, to talk it over," Tim said, sitting forward in his chair, as if he was preparing to get up and leave the room.

"No, that's all right," Kate replied as she glanced at Jim. "I believe we already made up our minds before we came in here."

"I think that means go for it, Tim," Jim said, taking Kate's words as a suggestion that she was prepared to do whatever was necessary to keep her kids.

"All right then!" Tim exclaimed, sitting back in his chair.

"Do you mind?" Kate asked as she took her cigarettes out of her purse, and fumbled nervously as she removed one from the crumpled pack. "By all means," Tim replied, sliding the ashtray over to share, as he reached for one of his own.

Jim blinked his eyes, blocking out the powerful urge, as the enticing odor of freshly lit cigarettes filled the room.

Simply mind over matter, he told himself, as he had thousands of times over the last year since he quit smoking.

"Kate, you can be a big help," Tim began, "if you can get me a list of people that would be willing to testify to the change in the kids' behavior and attitude."

After thinking about it overnight, Tim had formulated a plan as to how he was going to deal with Jim and Kate's situation. Assuming that Kate had been accurate in her description of CYS'S intentions, he wanted to make sure that he would be ready for any surprises they had for him.

It had been over two months since his attorney had given Kate's statement to the DA and they still had received no word. Tim was certain that he would be contacted by CYS shortly, and one of his main concerns was that they would be scheduling a hearing with a Master as soon as possible. Since the charges were still pending against Jim, this was something that he did not want. He was going to do everything possible to postpone the hearing as long as he could in hopes that the charges would be dropped before then.

It was only ten thirty when they left Tim's office. Kate had told her baby-sitter that she might not be back until noon, when Naomie came home from school. Since Jim didn't have to go to work until that afternoon and she didn't have to be home right away, they decided to stop for coffee and talk for a few minutes.

His future had begun to look much brighter with the reunion of Kate and his kids, and he felt that it was only a matter of time before their imminent problems would be solved. This sudden development had become a devastating blow to what he perceived happening in the months ahead.

Kate was still quite shaken, and she fought to hold back the tears as she thought about the possibility of her children being taken away from her.

Jim comforted her the best he could, reminding her that it was not her kids they were fighting for, but their kids. He felt that for seven months CYS had manipulated and controlled his wife and his kids. For the last two months, they had been seeing and communicating with each other, and Kate was showing significant signs of returning to the woman he remembered and still loved.

He had never given up hope, and the cunning maneuvers being employed by CYS at the present were all the more reason why it was so imperative that he stand by her side.

Kate had always put her trust in him, except for that fateful day last year when she confided in CYS and nearly destroyed everything that was important in their lives.

He was confident that with his attorney, they would win this crucial fight against the system no matter what obstacles they had to face.

CYS didn't waste any time. They must have already been in the process of drawing up the papers when they called Kate in to see them. On

Wednesday, only two days later, they all received a letter with CYS's proclamation of the actions they felt were necessary to be taken. It was also noted, not to Tim's surprise, that a hearing was scheduled in two weeks.

Tim didn't waste any time either: that same afternoon he filed a petition with a judge at the courthouse in Warrington. He was granted a postponement to allow him time to prepare his case.

Jim wished that they could be that expedient when it came to other matters that he felt were important, like scheduling visitations with his kids.

Aside from the few things that Tim had asked them to do in helping him prepare his case, there was little else that Jim and Kate could do now but wait.

Jim's attorney had checked with the DA to see if he could get any indication on when his case might be reviewed. Although the DA did not give him an official answer, he did say that he was familiar with his case, and Tim seemed to think that after reading Kate's statement he was having a tendency to decide in his Jim's favor.

The fact still remained though that there were still a number of cases ahead of his, and he would have to wait his turn. There was no telling how long it would be. The only positive note was the year deadline, which was up on December the seventh.

Kate's role regarding the rest of her family began to take on a whole new meaning now that her and Jim were communicating again. She had never lost touch with her mother, but the majority of her family had looked upon her as a cruel, evil person.

It was difficult to accept the notion that she was not responsible for her actions. They had never believed anything she said was true, and warned Jim not to trust her.

The recanting of her original statement seemed to change their feelings, though, especially after Jim and Kate joined together in their fight against the system to retain guardianship of their children.

CHAPTER TWENTY THREE

It was the middle of September now, and Jim was finally getting the last of his things out of his house and into storage. With everything that had been going on, it had taken two months after accepting Harley's offer to get moved. He was glad to leave. With the hostile environment that existed over the last few months, he was certain that the building tension was about to explode at any time.

He had several heated arguments with Jean after she told him that she was not returning his four hundred and fifty dollars that he had given her son as deposit when he moved in.

Still bitter about the events of last September that had cost him a night in jail and over six hundred dollars, he told her to go to hell when the rent was due.

That had happened at the end of July. Since then, every time she had seen him outside she had come out and started screaming and shouting that she was going to have him arrested.

He had been staying over at his in-laws the last few days after putting most of his belongings in storage, and the day he came by to get the last of his things she called the township police.

She also called her other son Derick while Jim and Don were loading the remaining things in his father-in-law's pickup. He came over and parked his pickup in the driveway, blocking their only exit.

After a very vicious exchange of words in which Jim made an extreme effort in making known just exactly how he felt about Jean, her sons, daughter and the neighbors, the police arrived.

What followed, was pretty much a replay of the last time the Chantilly Hunston Police Department had been called to investigate a disturbance at his residence.

Jean and the neighbors swarmed the officer's car as he pulled into the driveway. After a short time, the officer told Jean's son to move his pickup, then came up to Jim and Don. He told them that if they had everything they came for to leave and not to return to the property under any conditions.

Jim had put everything in storage except his clothes and a few personal things that he thought he might need. Although he was all settled in at his in-laws now, he still felt that it was only a temporary move, and sometime in the near future they would find a place that they could all live together again.

With the way things were going with his situation, he was positive that Tim would succeed in stopping CYS from taking the kids from them.

The DA had hinted that without Kate as a witness, it would be almost impossible to build a case against him. Kate had assembled a number of witnesses willing to testify for her regarding the kids improved behavior.

His hopes were beginning to build as the days passed, and they began talking about their plans once these matters were all settled. Kate even began looking in the newspapers, noting houses that were for rent.

Together they talked it over with her mom and step-dad about the possibility of Kate bringing the kids over to see them.

Harley had barred Kate from his house when she had Jim put in jail, but after seeing their effort to make amends, he did agree that it would be good to see his grand-kids again.

No one at CYS was aware that Jim was living at Kate's mother's. They also knew, that Kate had been barred from her parent's house. Since Kate and Jim started communicating again, no one had given CYS any indication that the situation had changed, so there wasn't any reason for them to be suspicious or believe any differently.

There were no close neighbors at her in-laws, and none of the neighbors that did live in the area felt that it was any of their business what went on at their house.

What it came to, when they put all the facts together, is that her mom's seemed to be about the safest place they could meet without them being detected.

Kate had bought a car from someone in her neighborhood that she thought she could trust. It wasn't long before she realized that it was a piece of junk and would cost her a fortune to keep it running.

Jim, meeting with her problem and feeling much different than he did at the support hearing, decided to let her have the station wagon so she could have a dependable vehicle to get around in. He also felt that if anyone was aware of his living at her mom's and drove by while Kate was there they would only see his car in the driveway.

The next few weeks seemed to drag on. There was still no word from the DA about dropping the charges, and CYS had not made any attempt to reschedule a hearing date. No one seemed to be making any move to resolve their problems, and everything pertaining to their situation appeared to come to a complete standstill.

The time waiting was not wasted though: now that Kate had been accepted again by her family, she began stopping by her mom's with the kids on a regular basis. Most of the time Jim was working, but occasionally he was home when she came over. When the situation presented itself, he spent as much time with the kids as he could. After all the time they had been apart, he felt like he had a lot of making up to do.

It was into the first week of October and the weather remained quite warm, adding to what Jim felt what was the most beautiful time of the year. Growing up in the country as he did, he loved the outdoors.

Living in the country as he was now presented him with the opportunity that he had been fortunate enough to have in his youth. Most of the time with his kids was spent outside, enjoying and learning what he felt growing up in the city was depriving them of.

It was around the second week of October when things began to heat up again. Kate called one afternoon shortly after Ron came home from school. She was angry almost beyond belief, stuttering as she did sometimes in such a state.

"THOSE BASTARDS," she screamed over the phone. "THOSE ROTTEN BASTARDS! IS THERE NOTHING THEY WON'T DO?"

"Kate, what is wrong?" Jim said, sensing that something very serious must have happened to cause her to act this way.

"It's Ron," she said, after pausing a few seconds to try to calm herself so she could tell Jim what happened. "They have been questioning him at school."

"Who's been questioning him, Kate?" Jim snapped, the anger showing in his voice as he began to envision his frightened son being interrogated.

"James," she went on. "James Ramour has been to school to see Ron. Jim, why do they have to be so damn sneaky? I have invited James and Mariane to come to my house any time they want. Instead of coming here, they go behind my back and start asking our son all kind of questions at school. And if that isn't bad enough," she stammered, "they even try to hide it from me."

Jim began to get the picture as Kate started at the beginning and explained what happened when Ron came home from school that day.

She sensed that something was wrong the moment he came in the door. He was not his usual happy self, and he began to mope around like he had something on his mind that was terribly upsetting him.

He was very reluctant to talk to Kate, which in itself was unusual. The last few months Ron had been very open about his problems, and was always anxious to tell his mother when something troublesome was bothering him.

After some coaxing, she finally got him to reveal what had happened to cause him to be the way he acted.

His first words were, "Mom, they told me not to tell you anything."

It seems that he was being teased by other kids at school about not having a father. He was overheard by one of the teachers bragging to them that he did have a father and they were all going to be living in a big house together very soon.

One thing led to another, and his comments to his fellow students soon reached his school counselor. Being aware of his situation at home, she felt it necessary to call CYS to report what was going on.

Jim thought about Ron's situation at school as Kate continued. He knew how cruel other kids could be when it came to be raised by a single parent.

In spite of the problems it had caused, it still made him feel proud that his son loved him enough to defend him.

The damage had already been done and there was nothing they could do about it now. They were sure that Ron would continue to be visited by CYS.

After the incident with Ron, a call came from his attorney, informing him of more surprises that CYS had in store for them. Tim received a notice that the court hearing had been rescheduled for November eighth.

This still left him ample time to prepare his case. Although he would like to have it postponed until later, it was not the thing that concerned him the most: it was the three attorneys that CYS had appointed to represent his children.

Not only was Jim confused by the lasted move, but Tim also seemed to be quite disturbed by this unexpected development. It was not to say that he changed his position on their chances at the hearing. What it meant was that there would have to be a change in his strategy.

He did have one good piece of news for Jim, though—in a brief conference with the DA, he was told that his case had been reviewed and it was decided not to hold it for court. It would be a while before the paperwork would be processed, but the word was official that the charges were being dropped.

Tim felt that this would be a big help, having this information to take to the hearing.

The next thing on Tim's agenda was for the three of them to get together to discuss just how he was going to proceed at the hearing.

Several days after receiving the latest news, Jim and Kate went out to Tim's office to keep their appointment.

Just recently, Tim had moved his law practice to a location nearer his home. The area he had been working out of was temporary he had explained. Practicing in three different counties as he did, his new location saved him a lot of driving time.

To Jim it was a slight inconvenience, meaning long distance calls and a forty-minute drive to his office.

Tim went over the list of names with Kate, seeming pleased as she identified Naomie's bus driver and teacher, among others, as ones willing to testify.

Following a brief terminology of subpoenas, he touched on their importance, regarding the issues they were dealing with. Then after an explanation in general of what CYS's surprise approach of introducing their three new attorneys meant to their case, he asked to see Kate alone.

"Go have a cup of coffee, Jim" he told him. "I need about twenty minutes to go over some things with Kate."

I wonder what that is all about, thought Jim as he left Tim's office, and headed toward a restaurant he noticed a block up the street.

He gave them a half hour instead of twenty minutes and they appeared to be just finishing their meeting when he rapped on the half open door to his office.

"Come on in—we're just about through," Tim called, assuring Jim he was not interrupting anything.

Having covered everything they could think of, Tim told them both to go home and try to relax. He would inform them if there were any changes.

Tim was done for the day, and as they walked out together, he motioned for Jim to lag back a little as Kate headed for the car.

"I have a hearing next Tuesday with another client at the courthouse in Warrington," he informed him. "I should be done about eleven, and if you are not busy I would like to meet with you to discuss some things."

As they made the forty-minute drive back to her mom's, they talked about the upcoming hearing. Jim, curious about their private meeting, asked her what their discussion was all about.

"Oh, it was nothing" she said. "He asked me some questions about CYS and the accusations I had made against you, but it was nothing important."

She didn't want to talk about it anymore and changed the subject to Ron, and James Ramour visiting him again at school.

All of a sudden, Jim began to get the strange feeling that he knew what Tim wanted to discuss with him. He was certain it had something to do with the contents of their meeting that Kate was so reluctant to talk about.

James Ramour's visits had begun to have a negative effect on Ron's behavior. His school grades began to drop off and he began to take out his frustration on his sisters. Kate had tried to get him to tell her what James and the school counselor was talking to him about. He would only say they asked him about his dad. Then he would get upset, fidgeting and becoming angry as he told his mom that he loved his dad and he didn't like it when they asked him all those questions.

It was Monday evening when she called him at work to tell him about Ron's reaction to CYS's latest visit that day.

As he listened to Kate, he began to seethe with the burning anger that CYS seemed to be constantly fueling since the whole ordeal began.

There was just no way he could justify the reasoning behind the latest methods that were being employed by CYS. Ron had been improving with remarkable fervor over the last three months. What they had done was to disrupt his life, not to mention being cruel, and most importantly, Jim felt they were in complete disregard for the well-being of his son.

He had not mentioned to her the appointment he had with Tim in the morning. After thinking about it all weekend, he couldn't get the thought out of his mind that their discussion was going to be about Kate. If **he** was right and it was then he didn't want to arouse any unnecessary suspicion.

He got there early, just in case Tim would be finished before he expected. Luck seemed to be with him as a car pulled away from the curb on Main Street, leaving an empty parking space in front of the courthouse.

After joining several others sitting on the concrete rail of the court house steps enjoying the warm October morning, he decided to go in and browse around while waiting.

Reaching the top of the four flights of steps he almost bumped into Tim coming out the door.

"Are you going somewhere?" Tim said, stopping before they collided with each other.

"Yeah" said Jim with a grin. "I was coming in to see if you needed any help."

He was right, he discovered, as they walked down the steps and headed across the street toward the drug store. It was Kate that Tim wanted to talk to him about.

As they sat in a booth and ordered coffee, Tim spelled out the purpose of their meeting. He began with the intuitions he had about Kate, and then followed up with the conclusion he had come to after the discussion he had with her in his office.

"Jim," he apologized, "I don't mean to discourage you, knowing what plans that you and Kate have for the future, but speaking as your attorney, I must warn you that I don't feel that she can be trusted."

"But, Tim," answered Jim, seeking to differ with the opinion that Tim had about his wife's reliability. "She told us everything that happened. And what about her deposition? Doesn't that prove that she is not lying and she means what she says?"

"I didn't say that she was lying, clarified Tim. "I just said that I didn't think that she could be trusted.

"Look, Jim—you have got to face the facts: she was pushed and prodded by CYS and when threatened with losing her kids, she complied with their wishes and had you put in jail. Think about it for a minute: she is facing the same situation again. If she is put on the witness stand, and the three attorneys for the prosecution start hammering her with questions, what do you think she is going to do? Especially if she feels that her only option to keep custody of her kids is to tell them what they want to hear."

Jim sat forward, his elbows on the table, hands pressed to his forehead, as the sudden realization of what Tim was telling him began to overwhelm his thoughts.

Tim was right: Kate might not have meant for this to happen, but what Tim described was what she did.

"All right," breathed Jim, still finding it hard to accept but feeling he was left with little choice, "Assuming that you are right, and there is a possibility of this happening, what do we do now?"

"If I knew what CYS'S real plans were for you, Kate, and the kids, it would make things a lot easier, but all I know for certain is what they told her.

"I wish that there was some answer I could give you, Jim," he said, sounding disheartening, "but there is not a whole lot else to do but prepare ourselves the best we can and wait."

He left Tim and drove back home pondering the thoughts that were inundating his mind.

So Tim thought he was making a big mistake. He was happy for him, regarding the way things had turned out with his case. Still, after talking to Kate several times, his experiences with such matters seemed to reveal several dangerous flaws in Kate's character, making him wary of her intentions toward him.

Tim's advice to him was to be very careful about any decisions he made regarding the two of them, and not to make any commitments until all the affairs with CYS were settled.

CHAPTER TWENTY FOUR

He never told anyone about his meeting with Tim, especially her family. Although they had seemed to accept her explanation and began to communicate with her again, Jim couldn't help noticing their reluctance to believe everything that she said as being true.

Kate stopped bringing the kids over after their meeting with Tim. Her explanation was. She was afraid that CYS might find out she was letting him see the kids.

Although he could understand her concern, it still seemed strange that she never worried about it until after her private meeting with Tim.

Each day he talked to her the last week and a half before the hearing, he began to get the strangest sensation that she was hiding something from him. He asked her several times what was wrong.

"Nothing" she said in a way that gave him the impression that she was disturbed by his asking. "I am just nervous about our court hearing."

He let it go at that. Whatever it was, he had the feeling that it would come out sooner or later.

The day finally came. Kate stopped by early to pick up her mother and he was getting dressed when they left for Warrington. They didn't have any time to talk, and he told her he would see her in a few minutes at the courthouse as she went out the door.

His attorney had mentioned that the hearing would probably be in one of the smaller courtrooms in the basement floor. He had passed through the metal detectors and had entered the main hall trying to decide which way to go, when he remembered where to go. Reaching the bottom of the stairs, he headed toward a small crowd gathered at the end of the hall.

Some of the faces became familiar as he approached them, making it apparent that one of the nearby rooms was where the hearing was about to take place.

James, Mariane and Devlin were standing off to one side, talking to several other people that he didn't recognize. He could feel the anger arise in him, and he tried to ignore their gaze as he made his way to the end of the corridor.

It wasn't just the devious staff of CYS that began to make his blood boil. There was another individual standing quietly off to one side that was mainly responsible for the renewed hatred in him.

"What the hell is he doing here?" were his first words to Tim as he rounded the corner and came upon his attorney talking to his wife.

"Your guess is as good as mine," replied Tim, looking up as Jim spoke and glancing over his shoulder at Lieutenant Kotter. "I would say that CYS requested his presence to testify for the state."

He didn't like it one bit, and he began to get that uneasy feeling again as he thought about Kotter. Every tine he had been around there had been trouble.

"I see that you have met my kids," Jim said, turning his attention back to their own little gathering.

Kate was sitting next to her Mom and a woman he recognized after a bit as Ron's schoolteacher from the year before. The kids had been playing in the hallway and stopped what they were doing as soon as they saw him.

"Yes, I have," said Tim, smiling as Jim sat down with the kids huddling close to him. "I must say that you have not been exaggerating in the least bit.

"What's going on?" he asked Kate, after Tim left to attend to some business and the kids got over their excitement at seeing him again.

"Nothing that I know of," she replied. "We just got here a few minutes before you did, and so far everyone had just been standing around talking.

"Do you remember Mrs. Mertz?" she said, identifying the woman sitting next to her Mom.

"Sure" he said, nodding at her introduction.

After saying hi to Midge, her Mom's old friend who was sitting across from them, Kate pointed out the strangers that were in CYS's little gathering. She denoted Mack and Dana as the ones who had been visiting Ron at her home. Kate indicated Judy Roman among the strangers, as the doctor that Jim felt had been brainwashing Naomie and Kristy.

Didi Hargrove came around the corner and after nodding at Kate, addressed him as sat there with Kristy on his lap.

"Hi, Mr. Hess—how are you doing?" she said, forcing her face muscles to reveal a slight smile.

"Fine," he said sarcastically, thinking it quite stupid of her asking such a question, considering the situation he was in.

The doors opened to the courtroom and someone came out, motioning for Tim and several others to come in. Neither he nor Kate, nor of the witnesses were asked to enter Jim assumed that it had to be some kind of a conference.

Ron who had been preoccupied playing with the pay telephones for the last few minutes, came over to join them. He stood between his Mom and Dad while the girls sat on Jim's knees.

Mariane paused for a second as she passed, glaring at Jim and giving him a contemptuous look as he sat there hugging Naomie and Kristy.

Jim stared back at her, withholding the urge to say something that would define the feelings he had in respect to the grief she had caused him.

He wondered as he and Kate followed Tim into the courtroom if she was married and had any children of her own.

All of a sudden, he felt like the walls were closing in on him. He glanced at Kotter, Didi Hargrove, Judy Roman, Mack, Dana, and Devlin, who had arrived while he was playing with his kids. The anxiety became overpowering as he began to feel like everyone was staring at him.

Taking the girls off his knees, he stood up. "Kate, I have got to get out of here for a few minutes," he said, trembling a little as he stood before her. "I will be down the hall if they come out before I come back."

He didn't know how long they were in there, losing track of time as he wandered down the hall, looking into the other rooms and pictures hanging on the wall. He did anything to take his mind off the meeting that was going on.

Tim appeared in the hallway as he was making his way back to the courtroom, motioning for him to join him. Together with Kate, the three of them went into a room that was unoccupied and Tim explained what was going on.

"It was worse than I thought," he exclaimed. "I had expected that they had something up their sleeve, but I didn't think they would have gone this far. CYS seems to have already come to a conclusion as to what they think the outcome of this hearing should be.

"Kate," he said, with a remorseful look on his face," When CYS arrived her today with their attorneys, they had every intention of removing the kids from your custody."

"And as for you," Tim said, addressing Jim before Kate had a chance to reply. "They had completely written you off. The possibility of you being granted visitation rights was not even on their agenda."

"GOD DAMN THESE PEOPLE!" Jim burst out in anger, befitting the oppressing news that was just handed him. "JUST WHO IN THE HELL DO THESE RIGHTEOUS BASTARDS THINK THEY ARE? HOW CAN THEY JUST GO ABOUT RUINING PEOPLES LIVES, AND SAY THAT THEY ARE DOING IT FOR THE WELFARE OF THE KIDS AND IN THE NAME OF JUSTICE?"

"Tim, they can't take my kids away from me, just like that, can they?" said Kate, in a trembling voice on the verge of hysteria.

"No, it hasn't come to that yet Kate" he said. "I have managed to forestall the Master from ruling on such extreme measures. We have come to terms on an agreement allowing you to keep custody of the kids, but there are some provisions that they have added that I need to go over with you two before I ask for your answer."

It was a half-empty storage room that they had slipped into for some privacy. There were boxes of files stacked along the wall, plus several empty desks, which they sat on while Tim explained the details.

Kate had breathed a sigh of relief when Tim mentioned the Master's decision for her to keep the kids. Now she sat almost emotionless as he went over the provisions that CYS had implemented into their agreement.

He began by conveying the issues that dealt with her and the kids. CYS was ordering that the kids be returned to all the programs that they had recommended for them, and that she was to continue to see her therapist, Didi Hargrove. Kate and the kids were also ordered to have psychiatric examinations.

Next, came the concession they had finally agreed to regarding Jim's rights as a parent.

Even with the DA's recommendation that the charges be dropped, Mariane and James still upheld their conviction that all three of the children had been molested. Along with the three attorneys appointed for his kids, they tried to get the Master to side with them and go along with their refusal to grant Jim his visitation rights.

Detective Kotter also put his two cents worth in, again stating that Jim had made a confession to him and upholding CYS's conviction that he had probably molested the rest of his kids as well.

After a heated discussion in which Tim repeatedly brought up Jim's past and the absence of any kind of a criminal record, it was recommended that he be required to go to counseling and be evaluated also.

"Tell them they can kiss my ass!" fumed Jim when Tim had finished. "I told that bitch Mariane before that I wasn't going to any counseling for child molesters, and I don't see why I need to have a evaluation to prove that I am mentally fit to be with my kids. There has never has been any proof that anything ever happened, and I don't see what gives them the right to recommend anything.

As for Kotter's statement, he added. "It seemed pretty obvious that he wasn't going to back down and just stand up there and tell the court that he made the whole thing up."

"But, Jim," Kate erupted in a surprised address to his apparent problem. "I don't think that CYS is leaving you any other choice. If you don't go along with them, they are never going to let you see your kids."

"Look Tim," Jim said, after pausing a few seconds to think it over. "I will agree to the evaluation, but I am not going to some meetings where people sit and discuss their what these idiots believe motivates me to perform deviate acts with children."

"I think that I can get them to go along with that," Tim said, getting up from a folding chair that he had managed to find earlier. "Now if we agree to everything else" he finished with glancing at the both of them. "I will go back in there and get this thing over with."

As they went back out into the hall, a woman came up to Kate that was a stranger to the both of them and addressed her. It was another surprising move that had apparently been arranged by CYS earlier without their knowledge.

"I am here to take your children," she said, bringing sudden panic to the both of them.

"What the hell is going on?" declared Jim in instant retaliation as he instinctively moved toward his children. "We were just told that Kate was allowed to keep custody."

"I am sorry," the woman said, apologizing for the way she spoke. "Maybe I should explain myself. We felt that since the children would not be required to testify, they would be in the way. I am here to take them down to the courthouse square building to one of our offices where they can be attended to. Her mother can pick them up later."

That is more like it, thought Jim, as he knelt down to say good-by to his kids before the woman took off with them.

"You be good," he said, giving the three of them a hug and not wanting to let go as he thought about how long it might be before he would see them again.

With the kids gone, a sudden silence overcame the hallway. Noone seemed to have anything to say, and they all just sat nervously awaiting any word.

The waiting was getting to Jim and he was just about to get up and go for another walk when Tim came out of the courtroom and motioned for him and Kate to come inside.

In relation to other courtrooms, this one was quite small. There was a long table surrounded by chairs in front of the judge's bench where the attorneys conducted their business. Aside from that, the only seating was several short rows of folding seats. Considering the nature of the matters that were attended to, the capacity of not more then thirty did seem quite adequate.

Lieutenant Kotter, the only other bystander in the courtroom that wasn't personally involved in the decision making beside themselves, sat stone-faced at the end of one of the rows of seats.

Jim glanced at him briefly as he sat down, wondering what he was thinking now that his scheme to put him away with his alleged confession had backfired.

He wasn't sure why they had called him and Kate into the courtroom. Since the attorneys had gone over everything that was required of him, Jim decided the only reason they were there was to tell them "Yes, they understood." Aside from that, they were asked nothing.

Jim couldn't get over the cold calculated way that CYS and the system attended to the highly emotional matters at hand. There was no empathy in their voices as they prescribed the programs that the children were required to attend. The evaluations ordered were due to their speculation and suspicion, and he and Kate were referred to as case numbers instead of human beings.

They gathered briefly at the end of the hall after they left the courtroom, while Tim explained a little more about the evaluations. Kate and the kids evaluations would be taken care of by CYS, but Jim would be required to make all the necessary arrangements for his on his own.

Devlin had joined them shortly after the hearing, which was all the more puzzling to Jim and heightened the doubt about Kate that had persisted for the last several weeks.

Jim tried to talk to her several times as they stood in the hallway, but she avoided any conversation with him, talking to Devlin and her mom instead.

He told her that he would call her later, and left her with her mom and Devlin as he walked out with Tim.

"Did you know that Kate has been seeing Didi Hargrove for the last couple of weeks?" Tim said, startling him as they reached the bottom of the courthouse steps.

"Dammit, I should have known by the way she has been acting that she was talking to someone," Jim exclaimed, after letting it sink in for a few seconds.

"Now, do you see why I had to settle this the way I did, instead of putting anyone on the witness stand?" Tim paused to explain.

"Yes, I see what you mean. If she has been seeing her therapist, there is no telling who else she has been talking to."

"God, Tim" he said, as a very bleak picture began to come into view. "I hate to think that you were right and after all I have been through, I might still lose her and my kids.

"I can understand how you feel, Jim," he said trying to comfort him. "I can see that you still care a great deal for her and I am not suggesting that you give up hope. You should hear from the DA in the next couple of weeks, and once the charges are officially dropped it might be a little easier attending to the other matters."

Tim had to get back to the office, so he told him that he would keep in touch as they parted on the street corner and headed their separate ways.

CHAPTER TWENTY FIVE

There were so many confusing thoughts whirling around in his head that Jim decided to stop where he could be alone for a while and think things out before heading home.

He recalled from the very beginning how Devlin appeared to stick to Kate like glue. She was on the phone with him every day, and nothing said or done in their household seemed to escape his ears.

It was also difficult to forget that Devlin was one of the ones that persuaded Kate to have him arrested, and after their little conference outside the courtroom he couldn't help but become wary that something strange was going on.

It was with the way she was acting about their relationship the last few weeks that began to bother him the most. He couldn't help seeing the gradual change in her that seemed to suggest that she was returning to the same pattern as when this all began.

Jane had not been there long when he arrived home. He came up the stairs to the kitchen to find her sitting at the table waiting to tell him some news.

"What the hell was that all about?" said Jim, referring to the three-way conversation they were involved in when he left them in the hallway at the courthouse.

"It seems that Devlin has had a change of heart," she replied. "Now that Kate has recalled her flashbacks, he tends to believe that she is telling the truth and was mistaken about her accusation against you."

"Christ, Mom—how stupid does he think we are? After all this time he decides to become a turncoat, and expects us to believe that he is on our side. I don't trust him, and I never will."

"I couldn't agree with you more, Jim. When this all began, she talked to him every day and never made a move without checking with him first.

"There is something else, Jim," she said, hanging her head, as if reluctant to reveal some kind of bad news. "I think she is playing you. She is my daughter and I love her, but I can't stand by knowing what she is doing and not say anything."

"That's all right, Mom," he said, trying to assure her that he understood. "I have had suspicions for some time that something out of the ordinary was going on."

Later when he called her from work and asked her what Devlin had to say, Kate answered in short choppy sentences, sounding very reluctant to give him a straightforward answer.

"Nothing," she replied. "We just talked about Ron."

They were only on the phone a few minutes, when she became uneasy and exclaimed that she had to get going so she could get the kids ready for bed.

The following week was pretty much the same. Their conversations on the phone were short and she avoided discussing anything about their plans for the future. Several times when he talked to the kids, he could even sense by the tone in their voices that something peculiar was going on. Their relationship that had been re-emerging over the last four months seemed to be fading.

He desperately wanted to believe that CYS could be held accountable for their recent and strange behavior. He was certain that they had regained their control over her and his kids, but still had a wrenching gut feeling that there was more to it then that.

About a week and a half after the hearing, the DA, as expected, contacted him. It was a little bit confusing at first when the DA asked for Naomie Hess. When Jane answered the phone, she explained to the DA that Naomie was her four-year-old granddaughter and lived with her mother. Exclaiming that it was her father that lived at this number, she handed the phone to Jim to continue the explanation. As Jim listened to the DA go over the remaining procedure required to have the charges dismissed, he still couldn't get over the fact of the DA calling to speak to Naomie. It seemed odd that after all this time he would not have knowledge enough of his case to know that Naomie was only four years old.

After receiving the good news that in a few days the ordeal of the last year would be over, he called Kate to tell her what the DA had said.

She did not seem at all surprised, which led Jim to believe that she must have already known what was in progress. It was her lack of emotion that bothered him, though, as he told her that in few days it would be all over and they could get on with their lives.

"Jim, she said when he finished, her next words hitting him like a slap in the face. "I think that it would be best if we didn't see each other for a while."

He had almost expected it after the way she had been acting the last few weeks. Deep inside, he had always felt it would happen; still, to hear her say it in her own words was something that he could never prepare himself for.

"Why, Kate? Why, for God's sake, after all we have been through?"

"I just don't think that it is going to work," she said, her voice still lacking what he felt was adequate emotion.

"Kate, please don't do this!" he pleaded. "What about the plans we have made? You can't turn your back on everything after we have come this far."

"What plans?" she blurted out suddenly. "What the hell kind of a future are we destined to have, with CYS breathing down our necks? How are we supposed to have any kind of a relationship when you are not even allowed to see your kids?

"Jim, I just can't go through with the hide-and-seek games we have been playing with the kids anymore. I think that we would both be better off if we waited until this visitation thing is all settled before we start making any plans."

Her sister Mary had told him that only an evil person could do what she had done. All the members of her family shared the opinion that she was still being manipulated by CYS. Even his own attorney seemed to feel that she couldn't be trusted.

In spite of all the opposition, he had still hung on to the belief that they could work things out and get back together again.

"Kate," he said as the thought of her admitted affair almost three years ago came to mind, "Is there someone else?"

It would all make sense if there was, he thought. Her unwillingness to talk about anything pertaining to their relationship; the suspicious conversations with his kids where he felt like she was telling them just what to say.

"Where the hell did you get that idea?" she snapped as if he had discovered something he shouldn't know. "I don't know who the hell told you that, but that is not the reason why I don't want you coming by the house any more. I just don't want to get in any more trouble with CYS."

He thought about the many times he had been lied to as he listened to her words. No matter how hard he tried, he couldn't stop the despairing feeling that began to overcome him. It was almost certain from the way she was acting, that someone else besides CYS had entered the picture.

"All right," he said, his feelings sinking to a new low as he suddenly began to feel very distant. "If that is the way you want it, but I would at least like to be able to call and talk to my kids."

What he had feared the most had happened. For whatever reason he still wasn't sure, but the message was clear: she wanted to end their relationship and didn't want to see him anymore.

With her having no objections to his simple request, and leaving little else to be said, they ended their conversation.

It was a chilly, damp day around the first of December when he walked up the steps and into the Warrington County courthouse. He was here to end the ordeal that had devastated the last year of his life and left scars that would remain with him forever.

Several minutes later, after signing a few papers and paying the required legal fees, he walked out the front door a free man.

He turned as he reached the bottom of the courthouse steps and looked up at the giant pillars adorning the halls of justice.

Almost a year ago, it looked certain that he would be facing a jury in one of those courtrooms. Somehow through a sudden twist of fate, the real truth was revealed and partial justice was served.

The court at least had concluded that there was reasonable suspicion to believe that there had been no crime committed.

Still, the fact remained that he was denied all visitation rights to see his children. CYS had taken it upon themselves to continue with their own prosecution, in spite of the decision of the criminal court.

He zipped up his jacket as he began to think about what he was going to do now, and headed down the street toward his car.

It was evident that CYS had gotten to her. His anger began to turn to rage, as he thought about how they were prying upon her helplessness. They knew how to get to her: they had done it once before and now they were doing it again. As long as they could keep him away from her, she remained under their control. Moreover, their latest play of threatening to remove their children from her care if she did not remain with their slated programs was their absolute assurance.

He had been through a lot and from the looks of things it was still far from over. No matter how bleak things seemed, he couldn't give up. He had been talking to his kids and he was still talking to her. As long as they were able to talk, there was hope.

It was hope, he thought as he started his car and pulled out in front of a vehicle that had stopped to take his vacant parking space. *Hope was what had kept him going for the last year.*